PIRATE VISHNU

"Forget about Indiana Jones. Jaya Jones is swinging into action, using both her mind and wits to solve a mystery...Readers will be ensnared by this entertaining tale. Four stars."

— *RT Book Reviews*

"Move over Vicky Bliss and Joan Wilder, historian Jaya Jones is here to stay! Mysterious maps, legendary pirates, and hidden treasure—Jaya's latest quest is a whirlwind of adventure."

— Chantelle Aimée Osman of The Sirens of Suspense

"I applaud author Gigi Pandian for unearthing the forgotten history of India's first immigrants to the United States and serving it up with plenty of suspense, humor and bhangra beats. If you are searching for a spicy new amateur sleuth series, this is the one."

—Sujata Massey,
Author of *The Sleeping Dictionary* and the Rei Shimura Mysteries

"Globe-trotting historian Jaya Jones is off on another treasure hunt...*Pirate Vishnu* is fast-paced and fascinating as Jaya's investigation leads her this time to India and back to her own family's secrets."

—Susan C. Shea, Author of the Dani O'Rourke mysteries

ARTIFACT

"Pandian's new series may well captivate a generation of readers, combining the suspenseful, mysterious and romantic. Four stars."

— *RT Book Reviews*

"If Indiana Jones had a sister, it would definitely be historian Jaya Jones."

— *Suspense Magazine*

PIRATE VISHNU

**The Jaya Jones Treasure Hunt Mystery Series
by Gigi Pandian**

<u>Novels</u>

ARTIFACT (#1)
PIRATE VISHNU (#2)

<u>Novellas</u>

FOOL'S GOLD (prequel to ARTIFACT)
(in OTHER PEOPLE'S BAGGAGE)

PIRATE VISHNU

A JAYA JONES TREASURE HUNT MYSTERY

GIGI PANDIAN

HENERY PRESS

PIRATE VISHNU
A Jaya Jones Treasure Hunt Mystery
Part of the Henery Press Mystery Collection

First Edition
Trade paperback edition | February 2014

Henery Press
www.henerypress.com

Copyright © 2013 by Gigi Pandian
Cover art by Fayette Terlouw

This is a work of fiction. Any references to historical events, real people, or real locales are used fictitiously. Other names, characters, places, and incidents are the product of the author's imagination, and any resemblance to actual events or locales or persons, living or dead, is entirely coincidental.

ISBN-13: 978-1-938383-97-7

Printed in the United States of America

For my father

ACKNOWLEDGMENTS

Writing a book is a solitary pursuit, but also one that couldn't be done without the help of many people. I sat down with the idea for this book years ago and spent countless hours writing it, but it was a team of amazing people who made this book what it is. To all the wonderful people in my life: thank you!

My early readers, who I can always count on to tell me the truth about what's working and what's not: Brian Selfon, Diane Vallere, Rachael Herron, Lisa Hughey, Lynn Coddingdon, Nancy Adams, Ramona deFelice Long. This book wouldn't have come together without each of you.

My writing pals, who follow the golden rule of chatting for 20 minutes and then getting down to work: Emberly Nesbitt, Sophie Littlefield, Juliet Blackwell, Mysti Berry, Martha White, Adrienne Miller, Michelle Gonzales. I would never have gotten to "The End" without you.

My publishing team: My incredible editor, Kendel Flaum, and the whole Henery Press team, for building something great with new authors. My agent, Jill Marsal, for believing in me for years without ever giving up.

My father, for inspiring this story and helping me get the history right. My mother, for always telling me I could do anything. And James, for not only putting up with the trials of living with a writer, but being the most supportive guy imaginable.

PART I

THE ILLUSION

CHAPTER 1

The first time Anand Paravar died, he was fifteen years old.

The year was 1895. Typhoid fever swept through the south of India. The sickness wended its way through the Kingdom of Travancore. It swept across its beaches of multicolored sand, through the banyan trees, and along the winding streets of the villages. The monsoon season brought uncharacteristically strong rain to the southern tip of India that year—and along with it the disease.

Anand didn't notice the rhythmic crashing of rain against the roof as his consciousness slipped away. A warm light enveloped the boy, pulling him toward its central glow. The aches of his thin body began to fade. A rough hand tugged his shoulder. Pulling him back.

Vishwan watched from the doorway as his older brother gasped. Their mother let out a strangled sob and held her boy close as he heaved violently back to life.

The next time Anand Paravar died, he was not so fortunate.

It was a decade later. 1906. Anand had left home in search of adventure. He often attributed his daring nature to that near-death experience during a formative time in his life. He wasn't content to follow his destiny and remain within a few miles of his birth as a boat builder with the rest of the Tamil Paravar caste. At the age of sixteen, he became involved with the fledgling movement for Indian independence. At eighteen, he left home for the trading port of Kochi. At twenty, fleeing prosecution for his revolutionary activities, he left India and used his skills constructing and fixing boats to make his way to the Middle East, Europe—and then America.

He was in San Francisco the day the Great Earthquake of 1906 struck. He tried to save the life of his friend Li. Neither of them made it out alive.

At least...that's the way the family legend of Uncle Anand goes. The story has been recounted by my family many times over three generations. And it's what I'd always believed—until the knock on my office door that windy August afternoon.

"Jaya Jones?" the stranger in my doorway asked, his eyes darting between me and the placard on my door in the history department.

"Can I help you?" I asked, closing my laptop and looking up at him. There had been a bit of press around the treasure I'd recently uncovered in the Highlands of Scotland, so I assumed he was a reporter. Most of the media attention had died down after a few days, so I thought it was safe to come to the office to get some work done on a research paper I'd meant to finish months before. I'd been at my office for most of the day, adding the finishing touches.

"Jaya *Anand* Jones?" he repeated.

A full head of salt and pepper hair flanked a distinguished face, and his features reminded me of someone from the northeast of India—European but with hints of China or South Asia. His tailored gray suit and the firm set of his jaw told me this was a man used to getting what he wanted.

"Are you a reporter?" I asked.

"No," he said, stepping into the office. "Steven Healy." The cadence of his voice made me wonder if he expected me to know the name.

I stood up to take his extended hand. His handshake was strong and curt, like the rest of his appearance. He was close to a foot taller than me, which isn't uncommon since without shoes I'm a hair under five feet tall.

"Your great-grandfather's name was Vishwan," he continued. "Is that right?"

Of all the questions I thought someone standing in the door of my university office might ask, that wasn't one of them.

"I can see that it was," he said. "Thirty years of reading the expressions of jurors and one can see the subtle changes in faces."

"You're a judge?"

"Attorney."

"Who wants to know about my Indian great-grandfather?"

"It's a bit sensitive," he said. "May I?" He indicated the open door, moving to close it before I could respond.

I don't like situations being taken out of my control, but I admit I was curious. My great-grandfather Vishwan and his brother Anand were the only two members of my family my mother had ever talked about.

I tossed an empty paper coffee cup into the trashcan and offered him the seat in front of my desk. He sat down, but perched on the edge of the seat and leaned forward. "What do you know about Anand Selvam Paravar?"

"Does your law firm deal with estates?" I asked, an idea dawning on me for the reason of his visit. "You have his belongings?" I knew almost nothing about most of my family, but the story of my great-granduncle Anand's heroic life was told to me as a bedtime story when I was a child, so I knew it well—including the pieces of his story that were missing. The diary my great-grandfather knew his brother kept had never been recovered.

Steven's eyebrows drew together. Was he surprised I'd guessed the reason for his visit? Or was he confused because he had no idea what I was talking about?

"My family never received any of Anand's possessions after he was killed in the Great San Francisco Earthquake," I continued. "They assumed everything was destroyed in the fire, or at least the aftermath was so hectic here that there was no way to identify peoples' belongings. But from the look on your face, I'm guessing that's not why you're here."

"I'm here on a *personal* matter," he said. He paused and watched me for another moment before continuing. "My grandmother left me a trunk of personal items when she died years ago. I didn't think much of it when I was a young man, and I forgot about it for many years. It was only when I retired recently that I took time to look carefully at what was inside." He shook his head. "I didn't believe it when I first saw it—"

"Saw what?" I asked.

"The information she left me," he said, not able to keep the excitement out of his voice. "It leads to a treasure from the days following the California Gold Rush."

"Ah." I leaned back in my chair, letting the squeak of its metal coils fill the room. Ever since news of the treasure I discovered hit the papers, I'd been expecting something like this.

There are two common stereotypes about historians. There are the people whose eyes glaze over as soon as you mention history, feeling sorry for the historian's boring existence holed up in the library. Then there are people like Steven Healy. They imagine the life of a historian is constant adventure, full of secret passageways and hidden fortunes. Both impressions are wrong. I love my job, but aside from my recent Scottish adventure, my research doesn't generally involve anything more heart-pounding than too many cups of coffee.

"I'm not that kind of historian," I said. "You have the wrong person. The treasure in Scotland wasn't something I sought out—"

"I don't have the wrong person," Steven cut in, his eyes locked on mine. "I'm not here because of that, although reading about you in the paper is how I found you. A relation of Anand Paravar who knows how to do historical research. It's perfect."

"What does this have to do with Anand? And hang on—how did you find out I'm related to him in the first place?"

My last name is Jones, courtesy of my American father. Paravar is a caste name, different from a surname as Western societies use them. Depending on the local custom, the initials of someone's father could be added before their given name, or the name of a village. Or if a family converted to Christianity, they might take a surname from the newcomers, as was the case when many Paravars were converted to Catholicism by the Portuguese. It makes it complicated to follow lineage. Traditional naming systems still exist to some extent, but by the time of my mother's generation it had begun to fade. It doesn't make it easy for us historians.

"Research," Steven said. "It's amazing how much time one has once one has retired." His lips formed a sad smile. "That's why I need to search for this treasure. It's a family treasure. Hunting for it would give me great satisfaction."

"The hunt isn't all it's cracked up to be," I said, remembering the freezing nights along the windy cliffs of the Highlands of Scotland earlier that summer.

"That's easy for you to say," he said, bitterness creeping into his voice. "You have your whole life ahead of you. I, on the other hand, need something meaningful to do with my time." He broke off, visibly upset.

I wondered why he had retired. He looked like he was in good health, and it seemed like he missed his job.

"I found you," he continued, "when one of the reporters covering your exploits did some research into your family history, since your connection to India helped solve the mystery in Scotland. It wasn't difficult from there. Now, may I ask what you know of Anand?"

"What does he have to do with your family treasure?"

"In my career in the courtroom," Steven said, "I learned to piece together seemingly irrelevant facts that together paint a full picture. I need some additional facts from you before I can explain more."

"I don't know what I could possibly tell you about Anand that could help," I said.

"I've identified a lost family treasure," Steven said, "but I don't have quite enough information to find it."

"What is *it?*" The longer I talked to Steven Healy, the less I felt I knew.

"Tell me what you know of Anand," he said instead of answering my question.

There was something commanding about Steven Healy's presence. I couldn't quite believe I was having this conversation, yet I found myself wanting to answer the question. He must have been a good courtroom lawyer. His body language created a feeling of familiarity, even though I'd never before laid eyes on him.

"He's my namesake," I said, "as I'm sure you figured out from my middle name. But I never knew him. He died long before I was born—long before even my mother was born—as a hero in the Great San Francisco Earthquake of 1906. He was killed trying to save one of his friends, but they both died."

"Is that all you know of him?"

"He was a grand figure who lived life to the fullest. That's how my great-grandfather always spoke of him to my mom. He was supposedly a wanted man for his support of Indian independence, which was revolutionary at the time because it advocated for freedom from both the British and the local kings. Since the ideas about Indian nationalism and independence weren't widespread until the First World War, when Mahatma Gandhi became a leader of the independence movement, I always wondered if the story was embellished because of the fact that Anand died tragically and heroically at the age of twenty-five in that famous earthquake. My great-grandfather was still a boy at the time Anand died. He was greatly affected by his brother's death."

"He saved the letters from his brother?" Steven leaned forward.

"Letters?"

"I know Anand wrote to his brother back in India."

"How can his letters be relevant to your family treasure?" I asked.

"You haven't read the letters?"

"Not personally. My mother's father shared them with her.

They'd have noticed if he mentioned a treasure. Anand barely had enough money to send some of it home, but that's it. He fixed boats and ships in San Francisco before the earthquake."

"So you really don't know."

"Know what?" I asked. My patience was growing thin.

"Anand Paravar," he said slowly, his eyes locked on mine, "didn't die a hero in the Great Quake of 1906."

I took a moment before responding, thinking through the stories my mother had told me while we walked along the beaches of Goa, past the colorful fishing boats like the ones the Paravars had built for generations. "Everything my family heard—"

"Was wrong," Steven cut in.

"How could you possibly know that?"

"Because this," he said, pausing as he pushed a yellowed piece of paper across the desk, "is the treasure map that led to his death."

CHAPTER 2

The map Steven Healy pushed toward me was a hand-drawn sketch of San Francisco. A sheet of plastic protected the faded paper. The edges were uneven and the ink was faded, but the central area with the drawing was intact and legible.

The city of San Francisco is only seven miles in each direction, so it's a compact enough area that the artist had been able to illustrate landmarks in the small drawing. The landscape and buildings depicted in the sketch were simple but clear, telling me the map had been drawn by someone familiar with the city but not an artist. The area surrounding the city oriented the city in its bay, with the Marin land mass to the north and several islands and Alameda County to the east.

The discoloration and uneven edges suggested the map was as old as Steven had claimed. I felt a small thrill as I studied it, a common reaction when I see a true piece of history in front of me. History often feels more real to me than the present. You can understand things about the past that the present hides from you.

The map included a few sites that were easy to recognize: the Ferry Building on the east side of the city, a shipyard on the southeast coastline near Potrero Hill, and the Cliff House on the northwest coast near Lands End. The land masses to the north and east were drawn close to scale, making them easy to recognize. In the center of the map were a few buildings that didn't look familiar.

The landmarks placed the creation of the map after the Gold

Rush, once San Francisco had grown into a real city. But this wasn't a map drawn by your average prospector. Using the same fountain pen that had drawn the map, someone had written notes next to several of the locations. Not in English. The map's text was written in the Indian language of Tamil. Uncle Anand, like all the Indian side of my family, was Tamilian.

I didn't speak much Tamil or have the ability to read the script. Since my father is American, I didn't practice speaking any Indian languages at home once we moved to the United States after my mother's death. Though I don't read the language, it has a distinctive rounded script that made it easy to recognize.

Someone else had already translated the Tamil into English. Across the top, *My Cities* was written. Close to the eastern coast, another path had been drawn, with the words *Path of the Old Coast*. On that path were sketches of two buildings with names that weren't familiar: *MP Craft Emporium* and *The Anchored Enchantress*. A store and a brothel, perhaps? Not an image of one's uncle one wants to imagine. I moved on. Under the building labeled *MP Craft Emporium,* in the downtown area of the city, the word *Lost* had been written. Along the water near the Cliff House at Lands End in the west was the word *Found*.

Most interesting of all, and what must have been the reason for Steven Healy's visit, was what was drawn next to the word *Found*: a large X stood out on the map.

X marks the spot.

Fantasy or not, my heart beat a little bit faster as I saw that *X* on the faded map.

"This is what your grandmother left you to find the family treasure?" I asked, my mind racing as I spoke. "A map in *Tamil*? And who made these English translations?"

"They were there when I found the map," he answered quickly. Too quickly...

"You aren't telling me everything," I said.

"There's a lot to tell," he replied. "With Anand's letters, it will make more sense."

"Why don't you try me?"

"Well," Steven said with a gentle shake of his head, "since you insist... I was merely trying to spare your feelings."

"Spare my feelings about *what*?" This conversation was getting stranger by the minute.

"Your great-granduncle," he said, "was a thief who stole a treasure from my family."

"Hold on—"

"I'm sorry," Steven said. "But Anand wasn't what you thought he was. He was a thief."

"Even if Anand drew this map—"

"He did. And it got him killed."

I opened my mouth but Steven cut me off again.

"I promise I'll explain everything," he said, picking up the aged paper and handing it to me. "I can tell you want to have a closer look." He was right. I wanted to know more. With the map in my hands, I spotted something I hadn't noticed before. Certain parts of the map had been drawn with a steadier hand than others. Since Anand was a ship builder and often traveled by boat, could this have been drawn while he was at sea?

"This *X* mark on the map hasn't led you to your treasure?" I asked.

"Unfortunately not."

"The map isn't signed," I pointed out.

"No, but—"

"I agree it's suggestive," I said. "This writing is Tamil, and there weren't many Tamils in San Francisco a hundred years ago. But it's not smart to leap to the conclusion—"

"My grandmother Maybelle knew him," Steven said. "The map was among her possessions that she left me."

There was so much missing from what I knew about the heroic uncle who had made such an impression on my mother through her grandfather's stories. I knew so little about the Indian side of my family, period. And here was a possible connection sitting across from me in my office. But could I believe what he told me?

"How did she know Anand?" I asked.

"He was friends with my grandfather."

"Your grandfather was Indian as well?" I again noticed the hint of Asian features in his appearance.

"No. But he was an immigrant, too. They looked out for each other."

I nodded, understanding the connection between fellow travelers in a foreign land. "Your grandmother is the one who told you Anand had stolen this treasure—from her and your grandfather? And that he'd been killed over it?"

Steven hesitated. "There's much to tell, but also much to learn. If you'll help me, I'll tell you everything."

I considered my options before speaking. I couldn't figure out what he was up to. Did he think I'd steal this secret treasure for myself, as he believed Anand had done?

"My great-grandfather Vishwan received a letter shortly after the earthquake," I said. "The letter told him Anand had been killed along with a friend he'd been trying to save. That's a more solid fact than an unsigned map. I know it's tempting to believe this old drawing is a treasure map, but—"

"That's what your family was told so they wouldn't go after the treasure," Steven said. "It was a lie."

I stared across my desk at Steven. Could any of this be true?

"Supposing there's some truth in what you're telling me," I said. "I still don't understand exactly what you're asking of me."

"The letters," Steven Healy said. "I need the letters Anand wrote to your great-grandfather."

"He didn't mention a treasure to his brother."

"You said you hadn't read the letters."

"It's the kind of thing my family would have mentioned."

"Not," he said, "if they didn't know what they were looking for."

"What should they have been looking for?"

Steven folded his hands in his lap with forced calmness. "I need those letters."

"I don't have them."

"But you can get them."

Surely my family would have known about this mysterious treasure if there had been anything in Anand's letters to Vishwan.

"There are a lot of letters over a lot of years," I said.

"1906," he said without hesitation. "It would be a letter from 1905 or 1906. Help me find those letters, and I can explain more."

I opened my mouth to object, but Steven cut me off. "Think over my offer."

I glanced at the map. Did I really want to get involved? I was in no mood for entering another search for a treasure, even if Uncle Anand was involved. But I knew I wouldn't be able to focus on anything else if I didn't at least look into it. Briefly. An hour or so of my time couldn't hurt.

"I'll need this," I said, picking up the map.

Steven hesitated, but he recovered quickly. He wanted me to cooperate. And I was sure he'd made copies already.

"Of course," he said, a false smile on his lips. "And you'll look into those letters."

"I will," I said, glancing at the clock on my computer monitor. Damn. Had that much time really gone by? I was going to be late.

Steven nodded and picked up his briefcase. But instead of standing up, he opened the case on his lap and removed a receipt book. He scribbled some words, then ripped out the top copy and handed it to me.

"Confirmation that you're borrowing the map," he said, snapping the briefcase shut and standing up. "I'll come back at the same time tomorrow. I trust that will be enough time to make initial inquiries."

I slipped the receipt into my messenger bag along with my laptop and research notes, then walked Steven Healy to the door. I watched him disappear down the hallway before locking my office door behind me. My hands fumbled with the key as I processed all the information I'd learned in the last half hour.

Murder. Treasure maps. Missing letters.

Was any of this real? The only thing I knew for sure was that Steven Healy wasn't the only one who could withhold information. I already knew exactly where the letters were.

CHAPTER 3

I rushed down the stairwell. I could have taken the elevator, but I think better when doing something methodical, like walking down several flights of stairs.

The letters Anand had written to his brother weren't in my possession. Nor were they with my family. The letters had been donated to a university library in south India.

The turn of the previous century wasn't a time when many Indians emigrated to the United States, especially the West Coast. I studied the British East India Company—traders who went *to* India, not the people who left. But Anand's letters were of historical significance to historians with different research interests from mine. The University of Travancore, which was renamed the University of Kerala after Indian kingdoms became consolidated states, jumped at the chance to keep the letters in their archives. I wasn't sure if they'd been digitized, but I could find out later tonight. India is twelve-and-a-half hours ahead of California, so I knew I could get in touch with someone at the University of Kerala when I got home that night.

As the echoes of my steps bounced off the walls of the empty stairwell, the feeling nagged at me that there was something very calculated about what Steven Healy had told me. I knew he was withholding information, but *why*?

If there was truly something to find in those letters, surely I'd be able to see it myself when I found them. And who was I kidding—it was entirely possible this phantom treasure didn't exist. Steven said himself that the X on Anand's map hadn't led him to a treasure. Uncle Anand had died tragically in the Great Earthquake of 1906. Period. Steven Healy was simply a man who was used to billing eighty hours a week as a lawyer and was now bored in his retirement. He made up a treasure when he came across an old map in his grandmother's belongings.

That was the simplest explanation. But was it the right one?

I took slow, deep breaths as I stepped out of the building and walked to the parking lot, trying to calm myself and make up my mind about what to do. I knew what I wanted to do. And it was a bad idea for multiple reasons.

I was aching to see Lane. We met earlier that summer when I needed help researching a piece of centuries-old jewelry from India. He turned out to be much more than a colleague who helped me solve the puzzle of a missing treasure and catch a murderer. I'd fallen for the guy.

We hadn't seen each other since returning from Scotland. I'd been busy dealing with returning part of the treasure I'd hidden in a safe-deposit box and trying to find out what would happen to the treasure. I'd learned more than I ever wanted to know about government bureaucracy and diplomacy between Britain and India. But that's not what had stopped me from seeing Lane. Though the media attention hadn't been overwhelming, it was much more than Lane felt comfortable with. He didn't want to be associated with the treasure at all, so he'd left Scotland before the authorities got involved. It was already too late. The locals knew about him. They were happy to talk in front of the television cameras. One of the people on the archaeological dig had shared a photo they'd taken with their cell phone—a photo of Lane on the dig.

Lane hadn't counted on that.

Before he was Lane Peters, art history PhD student who'd returned to graduate school in his thirties, he'd been something far different. Someone who didn't want to be found.

Lane was worried enough that he didn't want to have any connection with me until the media attention was gone. I understood—up to a point. Lane and I had become much more than friends over a short, intense period of time. Without him around, I already felt like a piece of my life was missing.

I told myself this puzzling treasure map was enough of a reason to go back on my word and see him, but I knew it was just an excuse. Lane's background was in art history and antiquities, not deciphering treasure maps. But I needed to talk to someone about Steven Healy's strange visit, and Lane was who I wanted to see.

I reached my car, but stopped before getting inside. I couldn't decide where to go. If I went to see Lane now, I'd be breaking my promise and I'd also risk being late.

Neither argument was winning me over.

Taking out my phone, I called Lane. It went straight to voicemail. Great. I threw my messenger bag into the passenger seat of my roadster and headed toward the Bay Bridge to see him.

I doubted Sanjay would be upset if I didn't arrive on time at the Tandoori Palace. It was Raj, the manager of the restaurant, who'd kill me if I was late.

Sanjay and I played musical sets of sitar and tabla two nights a week at the restaurant. Me on the tabla drums, Sanjay on the sitar. It's not a real job for either of us. I was a professor of history—I had been for a year now—and Sanjay was a professional magician. Not your average profession, sure, but he was *good*. As The Hindi Houdini, he sells out shows at a winery theater up in the Napa Valley that books him for the spring and summer tourist seasons. He liked the rhyme of "Hindi Houdini" better than the more accurate "Hindu Houdini," and the title has served him well. He's become something of a weekend getaway enticement to supplement the entertainment of wine tasting.

Sanjay was meticulous on stage. I'd never guessed the secrets of his big tricks, and God knows I'd seen them often enough. Playing sitar was how he unwound. It served the same purpose for him that the tabla did for me.

Unfortunately, Sanjay was one of the world's most mediocre sitar players. But he loved it, and he was the one who got us this gig. Raj had always booked professional musicians to play during busy Friday and Saturday nights, so he liked the idea of having additional weeknight entertainment without the stiff bill. Raj was a smart man; my microphone was the only one with the volume turned up. The rhythmic drumming of the tabla stands on its own, so diners enjoying Chef Juan's tandoori oven specialties on a Wednesday or Thursday night were serenaded by tabla ragas with the faint sounds of a sitar in the background.

Raj would be livid if I wasn't there when Sanjay began to play. I told myself he would be equally unhappy if I was so distracted that I screwed up the music. Besides, if traffic wasn't too bad, I'd still have time to make it to Berkeley and back before I was due at the restaurant.

Any illusion I had about being on time faded as I approached the bridge. It was the start of evening rush hour, and traffic was crawling. How did people commute like this every day? I lived and worked in San Francisco, so the most difficult part of my commute was parking.

Traffic started to flow once lanes had merged onto the bridge, and it didn't take long to get to Berkeley.

Lane's apartment was a freestanding in-law unit behind a cute bungalow. Small magnolia trees led the way to the unit. I rang the doorbell and followed up with a knock on the door. No answer.

I peeked in the front window through an opening in the curtains. I hadn't been to his apartment before, since we'd agreed not to see each other yet, but from the glimpse I caught of the living room, I immediately felt at home. Though the unit was tiny, Lane had made it his own. A bronze-colored reading light was positioned next to an Eames chair. A stack of books was piled high on an antique trunk that served as a coffee table. From where I stood, I couldn't see if there was any other furniture on the other side of the room. The sliver of wall I could see was covered in framed reproductions of South Asian paintings. I could see why he was an art historian. He had a great eye. I didn't know enough about art to recognize any of the pieces, but each one was stunning.

The bark of a dog from a nearby house startled me and reminded me I was prying. As I walked back to my car, I felt closer to Lane than ever. He was exactly the man I thought he was. And it made sense that he wasn't at home. It was late afternoon, so he could still be on campus, hopefully in his graduate student office.

There's not great parking in downtown Berkeley, but once you've lived here a while, you learn the tricks, such as which main drags have nearby residential side streets with just enough space between their driveways for a small car. I squeezed into a spot on a street lined with student apartments.

I felt my palms grow sweaty as I walked through the building on my way to Lane's office. His door was slightly ajar, and it opened wider as I knocked.

It had only been a little over a week since I'd seen him, and it felt simultaneously like it had been ages and that I'd never left his side.

Lane looked the same as he had that last time I'd seen him. Dark blond, wavy hair falling over his face, tortoiseshell glasses hiding his prominent features, which I had learned was a purposeful decision made not for style but to hide his appearance. His tall figure was dressed casually in jeans and an untucked dress shirt. The sight of him still made my stomach do a little lurch. All right. A big lurch.

When our eyes met, I could tell he felt the same. His eyes lit up and his lips formed a smile as he spotted me. But the expression only lasted a second. It was quickly replaced with something I couldn't gauge. It was as if he'd put on a mask.

"You shouldn't have come," he said. "We agreed—"

"I know there were a few news stories," I said, stepping into the cramped office, "but I haven't had any reporters contact me in days."

Lane's fingers tensed around a book he was holding. I noticed, then, that he was putting books into a box on his desk.

"Cleaning up," he said, setting the book into the box. He was always good at reading my expression. "You shouldn't have come."

"I'll hide under the desk if the paparazzi catch up to me," I joked. Lane didn't laugh. He didn't make a move from where he stood behind his desk either. I hadn't exactly expected him to rush around the desk and sweep me up in his arms. Okay, maybe I thought it was a possibility.

"Jones," he said, unable to hide the tenderness in his voice when he called me that. "We need to talk."

"That's why I'm here," I said, wondering how the simple use of a name could affect me so much. "I've missed you, and I—"

"That's what we need to talk about."

"Do you want to come to dinner at the restaurant tonight?" I asked. "While I drive, I can tell you about the crazy thing that happened to me."

Lane's shoulders tensed. "Is everything all right?"

"What's the matter with you?"

"You're okay?" he asked. His eyes searched mine, full of concern.

"Of course I'm okay. Why wouldn't I be?"

"You said something crazy had happened."

I pulled the Tamil treasure map from my bag and held it up for him to see. "An amateur treasure hunter found me."

Instead of relaxing, Lane's body tensed even more. His jaw was set so firmly that I wouldn't have been surprised if it snapped. "Who?" he asked.

This wasn't at all how I thought the conversation would go. And why had he asked like he might already know the answer?

"Steven Healy," I said. "A retired lawyer. He came to see me this afternoon. Said he found this in his grandmother's possessions that she left him. He said—"

"Oh," Lane said, his shoulders relaxing. "Then it wasn't... Never mind."

"What's going on with you, Lane? I thought you'd want to know—"

"You thought wrong."

I stared at him, confusion replaced by anger. "I get it that the media attention we got wasn't the best—"

"When we were in Scotland," Lane said, "it wasn't real life. Now that I'm back, I've realized that."

"Life is always complicated," I said, trying not to shout. "If you're trying to break up with me, that's a pretty lame excuse."

Lane glared at me but didn't speak for a few moments. Finally he shook his head and looked away. "You don't understand."

"Then why don't you explain it to me?"

Lane crossed his arms and looked up to the low ceiling of the cramped office. "I'm really busy," he said. "I'm sorry you thought things would work out differently." He looked down from the ceiling, but busied himself with the box in front of him, refusing to look at me.

Only when it became clear I wasn't leaving did he meet my gaze. A flash of tenderness crossed his face, but he shook it off so quickly that I thought I had imagined it.

"I'm sorry, Jaya," he said, while my head spun with confusion at the disjuncture between his actions and his words. "We're done."

CHAPTER 4

I made my way back to my car, blinking back tears and hating myself for letting them form in the first place. I paused at a street corner off Telegraph Avenue, trying to remember where I'd parked.

"You okay?" asked a gaunt homeless man sitting on the sidewalk. He held a cardboard sign asking for spare change in exchange for art. Half a dozen beautiful postcard-size line drawings of Berkeley street scenes were spread out next to him.

"Only if you can tell me that everything that happened today has been a dream," I said, "and I'm about to wake up."

"I hear ya, sister. That's been my day every day for the last six years."

I took one of his drawings of Berkeley's Sproul Plaza and bought him a sandwich from a nearby café before returning to my car. I fumbled with my keys as I tried to open the door of my roadster, dropping them in the gutter. Once I managed to get the door open, I sat in the driver's seat before starting the car. My hands shook on the steering wheel. I hated that Lane had that much of an effect on me. I hated that *anyone* had that much of an effect on me.

My stomach rumbled. I should have gotten myself a bag of chips at the café. I'd be fed at the restaurant, but I had no idea how long it would take me to get there. I needed to pull myself together for the drive back to San Francisco. I squeezed the steering wheel. It was as good a stand-in for Lane's neck as I was going to get.

My hands had stopped shaking, but I was still angry and unfocused. I had planned on looking up someone to contact at the University of Kerala that evening, but I couldn't imagine being in shape to send a coherent introductory email any time that night, so I did the next best thing. I pulled out my phone to text my friend Tamarind, a librarian at my university's library.

Tamarind Ortega was amazing. She helped me with a research project shortly after I started my teaching job the previous year, and became one of my few good friends. She'd be able to maneuver the University of Kerala's website and find a librarian to contact about Anand's letters. I sent her a text message asking if she could help, then immediately followed up with a second message explaining why I needed to get started that night.

There was nothing else to do. I was as calm as I was going to get. I started the car and headed to the Tandoori Palace.

I wasn't as late as I feared I might be. By the time I pulled into a parking spot a block away from the restaurant, I was only five minutes late for our first scheduled set. I hoisted my tabla case out of the trunk and hurried down Lincoln, the road that runs along the south side of Golden Gate Park. Taking my phone out to make sure the sound was off, I saw that Tamarind had already texted me back: *I'm on it!*

"Jaya!" Raj called out as I stepped through the back entrance. "You like to give an old man a heart attack!" He mopped his bald head with a handkerchief, even though there wasn't a drop of sweat anywhere on his head.

Sanjay stepped up behind Raj, putting one hand on the restaurateur's shoulder and flipping his bowler hat onto his head with the other. I swear that hat was his security blanket. A security blanket he could pull a rabbit out of. Sanjay shunned the traditional magician's top hat, but I never saw him without his bowler.

"I told him I could cover for you," Sanjay said, "but he was worried."

Raj gave me a conspiratorial grin. "You are so small, Jaya. I hate to think of you at an unknown location after dark."

He thought nothing of the sort. Both Raj and Sanjay knew I could take care of myself. In one of my father's rare moments of clarity, once he saw I wasn't going to make it to five feet tall, he insisted on enrolling me in every martial arts class he could find.

"What's the matter?" Sanjay asked, offering me his elbow. He knew better than to offer to carry my tabla case.

"Nothing," I said with a shake of my head. I wasn't ready to talk about everything that had happened that day.

I left my shoes at the edge of the small stage. Tucking my feet under me on the carpeted stage floor, I focused my attention on the two goatskin drums that make up the tabla. I ran my fingertips around the rim of the taut material as Sanjay got situated with his sitar. In spite of his graceful movements as a magician, the long-necked sitar was an unwieldy instrument in his hands.

I immersed myself in the music. If I didn't force myself to focus, I'd be playing as badly as Sanjay, and driving myself crazy thinking about Steven Healy, Uncle Anand, and Lane Peters. Fortunately, focusing completely on what I'm doing was something I excelled at. It doesn't always make for the most balanced life, but it's great for situations like this. For the next half hour, I was lost in the music, not lost in my life.

After we finished our first set, I turned off our mics, took a deep breath, and turned to Sanjay. "We have to talk."

Sanjay frowned as I led him toward the room in back of the kitchen. I wasn't sure why. It's not like we were dating or anything. And his ego certainly would never allow him to think he'd played a less than stellar set.

For the first time that evening I didn't feel completely miserable. Confused, yes. But no longer completely lost. One of the great things about being able to focus so completely is that it lets your subconscious have time to go to work. I was ready to talk to someone. My best friend was in front of me. Sanjay could help me think through what was going on.

"I've got a magic trick for you," I said. "How is it possible that a boat builder born in India in the late 1800s drew a treasure map of San Francisco with clues written in Tamil, and nobody has managed to decipher the map in over a hundred years?"

Okay, I wasn't ready to talk about Lane yet. But Sanjay could help me with the riddle of Uncle Anand and his map.

Sanjay paused to seriously consider the question. "That's not a very good riddle, Jaya," he said. "Tamil writing can easily be translated."

"It was."

Sanjay stared at me. "We're talking about a real guy and a real map?"

"My great-granduncle Anand," I said. "My mom's grandfather's brother."

"I thought you didn't know anything about your mom's family."

"I didn't know much until an amateur treasure hunter came to see me today," I said.

The head chef, Juan, poked his head into the break room and handed us a plate of steaming samosas. "Extra-extra spicy," he said with a big smile.

"You're a lifesaver." I accepted the plate and took a large bite of fried potato goodness. He wasn't kidding about the level of spice. My tongue and lips burned as I chewed. It was heavenly.

Someone called for Juan and he rushed back to the kitchen, leaving the door open. I offered a samosa to Sanjay, knowing he'd decline. Though he refuses to admit it, Sanjay hates spicy food. He shook his head and hopped up on the counter next to the staff lockers.

"A real treasure map?" he said. "That's why you looked so upset when you arrived tonight?"

I had too much nervous energy to sit down. Standing in front of Sanjay with my plate of spicy samosas, I went over the details of Steven Healy's visit. As I did so, I replayed the key facts in my mind, trying to make sense of them. Steven's grandparents knowing Uncle Anand, his story about how he found the treasure map in his grandmother's possessions, and his theory that Anand's letters would shed light on how to find his missing family treasure. Sanjay's eyes stayed transfixed on mine as I told the story, and he interrupted only to take the empty plate. He said it looked like I was going to drop it due to my enthusiastic gestures.

"He told me," I concluded, "that Uncle Anand stole this treasure from his family."

"Wow," Sanjay said. "That story is really—"

I didn't get to hear what Sanjay thought. He broke off at the sound of someone quietly clearing their throat.

"Grace," he said, hopping down from the counter. "What are you doing here?"

Sanjay's magician's assistant stood in the doorway of the break room, a look of distress on her face.

"Your phone was turned off," Grace said to Sanjay. Her voice was barely above a whisper, and her thin shoulders were slumped in a way that suggested she was trying to make herself invisible.

That was normal for Grace. She was painfully shy. You'd think a stage magician's assistant wouldn't be a good job for her, but it suited her perfectly. The stage allowed her to become a completely different person. Multiple reviews of their show had called her fearless. While Grace's tentative words and body language didn't surprise me, there was something else going on. Something was off. Grace clutched her purse in her hands so tightly that her knuckles were white.

"I knew you'd be on break around now," she continued, pulling her eyes from the floor to look up at Sanjay. "I needed to talk to you."

"What's going on?" Sanjay asked.

"Sorry to interrupt," she whispered, looking back to the floor.

"Don't worry," Sanjay said, squeezing her shoulder. "What's the matter?"

Grace came to life at his touch. Her thin body straightened up and her eyes widened as she looked up at Sanjay. I suspected she was in love with her boss, but Sanjay was clueless.

"There was a death in my family," she said.

"I'm so sorry," I said at the same time Sanjay murmured something similar. I knew that Grace had a large extended family, many of whom had come to the U.S. from Thailand after having trouble with corrupt authorities. From the pained look on her face, this was someone she must have known well.

"I need to go out of town for the funeral," she said.

"Of course," Sanjay said. "You didn't need to come here to tell me that."

"The thing is," she said, "the funeral is the same day as that benefit show we agreed to do."

"Don't worry," Sanjay said without missing a beat. "Jaya can cover for you."

"I can do *what*?" I said. Grace and I were about the same size, but there was no way I could do the contortions Grace did as Sanjay's assistant. She'd been a gymnast before being sidelined by an injury as a teenager. There was no way I could come close to replicating what she did.

Sanjay shot me a sharp look. "I think Grace's family emergency is kind of important."

"Of course," I said. "I didn't mean Grace shouldn't go. But I'm sure there's someone else who can cover—"

Grace's gaze darted between me and Sanjay. "Jaya can't cover for me!"

Even though I didn't think I could cover for her, I was surprised she felt the same way. Sanjay kept telling me how Grace idolized me, but apparently he'd been mistaken.

"We'll skip the levitation," Sanjay said. "It's not a problem. We weren't planning on doing a full show anyway, since it's not our full setup from the Napa theater."

"But—" Grace and I protested at the same time.

"Children!" Raj cried, popping his head into the break room. "You have no sense of time tonight." He tapped his wristwatch. "The diners are waiting."

* * *

"That set nearly killed me," Sanjay said when we were done with our second set of the evening. Grace had gone home to pack, and Sanjay and I were back in the break room.

"No kidding," I agreed.

During our set we played a raga that made me think of northern India, and by association, my thoughts had returned to Lane. Earlier that summer, his research on northern Indian art had been instrumental in piecing together the history of an Indian artifact with a mysterious history.

"You have to show me that treasure map," Sanjay said.

"First you have to tell me why on earth you thought you could volunteer me to be your magician's assistant."

"You're the same size as Grace."

"Why does that matter? I can't do the contortions she does."

"I'm used to working with someone her size," Sanjay said, "and I planned these acts around having an assistant."

"But—"

"It's a great cause, Jaya. A benefit for a San Francisco homeless shelter." On his phone, he pulled up the website with details about the benefit and handed it to me so I could read about it.

"You know why it's important," Sanjay said.

I did know. Sanjay had dropped out of law school to become a magician. His parents hadn't been pleased. For the two years it took him to establish himself, Sanjay lived in a fleabag motel. A lot of his neighbors from that time never made it out of there. Because he knew what it was like to live so close to homelessness, he was exceedingly generous and also didn't have any guilt about enjoying life's luxuries.

I scrolled through the information, but I wasn't retaining anything I read.

"Isn't there a magician's guild or something you can go to for emergencies like this?" I asked.

"I trust you," Sanjay said.

He spun his bowler hat in his hands as he spoke, then flipped it back onto his head and met my gaze. "I trust you with my secrets." His almost-too-large dark brown eyes had won over many an admirer. But I know the true Sanjay, the one with the maturity of an eight-year-old boy.

"No need to be so dramatic."

Sanjay fiddled with the collar of his shirt. A nervous habit from the days when he was starting out as a magician, he told me once. He never did it on stage anymore, but I'd seen him tugging at his starched white collar a few times.

"There's nobody else," he said.

"You mean besides Grace."

"I made her sign a confidentiality agreement when she came to work for me."

"Seriously?"

"I told you there's no one else."

My resolve started to waver. Time to change the subject.

I was about to get the map out to show Sanjay when Raj walked in. He was there to retrieve us for our next music set. He ushered us out of the break room onto the little stage, muttering about how there was something in the stars that made us forget all sense of time that day.

By the time we finished our final set of the evening, the kitchen was winding down for the night. Juan and his staff turned on the TV in the kitchen.

"The suspense is killing me," Sanjay said, but I barely heard him. On the TV screen in front of me was a photograph of Steven Healy.

I pushed my way past the kitchen crew and turned up the volume on the set to hear above the rain that had started to fall outside. The rain sounded like a tin drum as it hit the kitchen vents.

"What are you doing?" Sanjay asked.

"That's him." I swallowed hard. "The man in the photograph on TV. That's the man who came to see me today."

A fair-haired reporter with carefully styled hair stood in front of an upscale San Francisco Victorian house, holding an oversized black umbrella in one hand and a microphone in the other.

"Steven Healy was found dead in his home this evening," the reporter said. "His death is an apparent homicide."

CHAPTER 5

Kingdom of Travancore, South India, 1900

Five years after Anand Paravar nearly died of typhoid, he made the decision to leave Travancore to travel the world. He had been working in Kochi for two years where he met supporters of the controversial Indian independence movement. He realized he had been too vocal in support of their ideas, for he heard the maharaja was not pleased with the work he was doing. Though he was not afraid, as he was told he should be, Anand nevertheless thought it a prudent time to follow his heart and see more of the world.

Anand had seen glimpses of life beyond the Kingdoms of Travancore and Kochi -- and he wanted more. Although the British did not technically control the southern kingdoms, which were princely states under the control of local rajas, the foreign influence could be felt. Men left their villages to work in the tea plantations. Children learned English. Strange-looking women with golden hair wore clothing puffed out from their lower bodies. Light-skinned men in military uniforms told stories of dangerous sea voyages. There was a strange and fascinating world to see -- and it could be seen by traveling across the ocean.

Before he could depart, Anand almost changed his mind about leaving. On this day, he was returning to his village of Kolachal, in southern Travancore, from Kochi. The rains fell more heavily that day, or so it seemed to Anand. He was going to share his plans with his mother and little brother.

Anand's white tunic clung to his thin body as the rain soaked the fabric through to his skin.

The monsoons had always struck the kingdom of Travancore twice each year. During the hot season, the waters swelled and the people resigned themselves to being as thoroughly soaked as if they had fallen directly into the ocean.

The kingdom wouldn't be nearly as prosperous without the rains, Anand knew, but still he wasn't happy about it as he extracted his feet from the muddy road.

He had been away in Kochi building and fixing boats, as his Paravar caste had always done. Throughout the coastal southern kingdoms, the easiest way to travel was by boat. Foreign traders came by large ships in the Arabian Sea and local men traveled through the backwater lakes and canals. There was enough work for him near Kolachal, but he'd grown restless. His friend Faruk Marikayaer, from the Muslim caste of merchants and boat builders, invited him to work with him in Kochi. A rough season of high winds had left the port underserved by skilled workers.

The men in Kochi had not been like the men in Travancore. Muslims from the north and Chinese from the east worked alongside the Hindus and Christians. Anand had learned to speak some Arabic and improved his Hindi, but Chinese remained a mystery.

Almost a mile from his home in Kolachal, Anand stopped to adjust the sodden bag he carried over his shoulder.

As he did so, he spotted his little brother Vishwan. Vishwan was too far away to call out to, so Anand turned off the main road to get closer. Vishwan wore no sandals on his feet, and ran quickly through a cluster of coconut trees in spite of his lungi being tangled by the rain. A coconut fell on the ground a few meters away from him.

Anand looked up at the coconut tree. The rain was light, almost done for the day. It wasn't falling hard enough to dislodge coconuts.

"*Anna!*" the little boy shouted upon seeing Anand, using the affectionate term to hail his big brother.

"What are you doing, *thambi*?"

Another coconut fell to the ground, this time accompanied by the familiar screech of a monkey.

"I'm helping Mother gather food," Vishwan said proudly. "I sold our sick chicken at the market, and bought Mother spices. I wanted to bring some fruit to her, but the tree was too high and too wet to climb. I did not wish to hurt myself, so I did as you said."

The rain had finally stopped falling. Vishwan wiped his face with his shirt, which was as wet as his skin.

Anand saw a small rhesus monkey jumping up and down at the top of the coconut tree. Vishwan knelt down to pick up the two coconuts from the muddy path.

"What do you mean you did as I said?" Anand asked.

"I followed your wisdom, *anna*. I saw the monkey go up the tree, where I could not go, so I threw rocks at him until he wanted to throw things back at me. He had no rocks up in the tree, so he needed to use coconuts. You told me the story with betel nuts, but I thought coconuts would be the same, no?"

Anand nearly fell to the ground as his body shook with laughter.

"That was a children's story, *thambi*! To make you go to sleep. I never threw rocks at a monkey in my life. And I never met a monkey who threw them at me."

Vishwan's large eyes grew wide. "But..." He looked up at the tall tree.

"How long have you been attempting this?" Anand asked.

"I tried since the month you left for Kochi."

"All these months?"

"You weren't home to help me, *anna*. I thought I must be doing something incorrectly."

Anand tried to stop laughing. "You finally found a monkey smart enough and angry enough to make your persistence pay off."

Vishwan's lower lip quivered for a short moment, as if he might cry. But as only a child can do, a second later a wide smile replaced the sadness.

"I did better than you!" Vishwan cried out.

He gripped the coconuts firmly in his hands and ran toward the house.

Anand watched his little brother run through the tall grass. He knew he was destined to travel the world, but how could he leave Vishwan on his own?

CHAPTER 6

The cold rains of San Francisco are nothing like the humid rains of south India I remembered from my childhood. I shivered as I walked the three blocks from my car to my apartment. In San Francisco an umbrella is a must even when it's a clear blue sky when leaving the house. But I hated to give up the space in my messenger bag. Between my laptop, photocopies of documents from the library, magnifying glass to study original documents, music player, phone, notebook, and pencils, who has room for an umbrella?

I left my tabla case at the restaurant, since I'd be playing another set the next night, so at least my drums would be dry. I, on the other hand, had hair plastered to the sides of my face. Water droplets pooled at the ends of my hair before falling onto my neck.

The treasure map was safely in its plastic sleeve inside my messenger bag. But at the moment I didn't care about the map. I wasn't sure how much of my shivering was caused by the rain versus the knowledge that a man I met a few hours before had been murdered.

The timing of Steven Healy's murder could have been a coincidence, couldn't it? I knew nothing about him and his life. For all I knew, he could have been a loathsome guy who a lot of people wanted to kill. Maybe something in his legal career had caught up with him. Was I supposed to call the police? What could I tell them?

I was so distracted by my thoughts that I nearly walked past my house. I had to back up a few steps to get to the side gate. I lived on the upper floor of an old Victorian house in the Haight Ashbury neighborhood of the city. My landlady Nadia Lubov had converted the spacious attic into an apartment with its own entrance, accessed by a set of stairs at the side of the house. My wet shoes squeaked with each step as I climbed the stairs.

The four-foot-square landing at my doorway was empty. I must have beaten Sanjay back. Not surprising. He drove like one of the timid bunny rabbits he could pull out of a hat.

I had agreed to meet Sanjay at my apartment. He said I shouldn't be alone. But that's not why I agreed. I'm good at being alone. But I think better with someone to bounce ideas off of, and there was a hell of a lot that I needed to figure out. Just because I didn't understand what was going on with Lane, didn't mean I would stare at my walls feeling sorry for myself.

Sanjay was a better person to help me, anyway. With no romantic entanglement, there wouldn't be any distractions. And I trusted Sanjay completely. He was like the little brother I never had. My older brother Mahilan had always been more like a father to me than a brother. At least much more like a father than our dad, who self-medicated his problems away. Mahilan had told me he wasn't always like that, but I was too young when our mom died to remember much.

My mom died so long ago that I didn't actively miss her. Yet sometimes I felt her presence. I wished I could have asked her more about Anand. As a child, I hadn't realized that I would want to know more, or that her time with me would be cut short.

I knew that Anand had made an impression on my mom's grandfather, Vishwan. Through Vishwan, Anand had touched many lives. My mother gave me the middle name of Anand, which means "happiness" in Sanskrit. My first name, Jaya, means "victory," a testament to what she was able to achieve by marrying a man of her own choosing, because of the uncle who had come before her and made his own choices.

But what if nothing we knew about him was true? Even if I wanted to learn the truth, my last link to the past was now dead. All I had was the map.

Where was Sanjay, anyway? I was in no mood to be left with my own thoughts.

I changed out of my wet clothes, slipping into a pair of black leggings and trading my black turtleneck for a fuzzy black sweater. I wrapped a towel around my wet head just before Sanjay knocked on the door.

"You didn't have an umbrella?" he said, looking at the towel. "You should have told me. I would have given you mine."

"People survived for thousands of years before the invention of the umbrella."

"You really need to move to a building with parking," he said, closing his sprawling umbrella and wiping his feet before stepping inside. He removed his bowler hat and twirled it in his hand.

"Do you want anything to eat?" I asked, remembering that he hadn't eaten at the restaurant.

"You actually have food in your house? That would be a first."

"Probably not." I opened the fridge. "Definitely not. Unless you want to eat that half-full jar of spicy mango pickle. But I can offer you the finest coffee this side of Golden Gate Park."

"You don't have any milk," Sanjay said, peering over my shoulder into the fridge.

"Lightweight."

"Some of us like our stomach linings intact. I don't think that type of cheese is supposed to be fuzzy. Can I put that in the trash?"

I closed the fridge and turned to face Sanjay. "I can't believe he's dead."

"I know," Sanjay said. "That's a really odd coincidence."

"We should put on the news to see if they've said anything else."

"I was listening to the radio on the way over here," Sanjay said. "They're now saying how he was killed—someone bludgeoned him to death."

My knees felt weak. "What the hell is going on?"

"I'll make the coffee," Sanjay said. He tossed his hat so it landed squarely on the coat hook next to the door. I leaned against the counter and watched Sanjay struggle with the stovetop pressurized contraption.

"That's not an answer."

"Are you going to call the police?" Sanjay asked.

"And tell them *what* exactly? That he told me one of my ancestors was murdered because of some mysterious treasure over a century ago? Maybe he was a horrible guy and someone completely unrelated to the treasure killed him."

"Are you going to give the map back to his family?" Sanjay asked.

"God, I hadn't thought of that. I suppose I should."

"Don't do it," Sanjay said. "He gave it to you. Besides, it's probably rightfully yours."

"He loaned it to me," I reminded Sanjay. "He even gave me a receipt. I think a receipt from a lawyer is a little bit better provenance than my saying a distant relative may have drawn it to hide his illegal treasure."

"Point taken," Sanjay said. "It's too late to do anything tonight, anyway."

"Maybe I should go to the police," I said. "What do you think?"

"I think you should show me this thing that may have caused all this trouble."

The Italian coffeemaker hissed. Sanjay poured us two cups of strong black coffee as I retrieved the map from my bag.

I hung the map on a corkboard on the wall across from the couch, careful to pin the protective sleeve so I wouldn't damage the map. I placed it between copies of a detailed map of British India from the 1940s and a set of black-and-white photos of unnamed Indian Sepoy soldiers. I liked to tack up photocopied pages of research to help me organize my thoughts. To the casual observer, my apartment might have looked like a disaster area, but I knew the purpose of each of the papers strewn about my furniture and across the floor. It was easier to spread out at home than in my office since colleagues and students came by my office on a regular basis. Fewer people visited my apartment, so I could mostly avoid comments about my organizational habits. I could gather my thoughts together at home, then get work done at the office.

"Whatever this map leads to," I said, "nobody has found it in over a century."

Sanjay handed me a mug of coffee and we stood in front of the map in silence. I breathed in the strong scent of the coffee. As the warmth from the ceramic mug began to warm me up, I wondered what Uncle Anand had thought of San Francisco after growing up in India's tropical south. The map of San Francisco didn't look exactly as it did today, but a lot had changed in a hundred years, especially after the earthquake that destroyed so much of the city. As I'd noticed before, there wasn't much text, and I only recognized some of the locations. I looked again at the English translation at the very top. *My Cities*. Shouldn't it have been *My City* instead?

"You weren't kidding," Sanjay said. "A real treasure map with an X that marks the spot." He pointed to the script next to the English translations. "That's Tamil?"

I nodded. "Quite possibly written by Uncle Anand."

"You can read it?"

"Of course not."

"Jaya, you really are the worst Indian ever."

"You're just begging for a pickle-eating contest," I joked, but I was all too aware that my words came out as stiff and serious as I felt.

It's a conversation we had all the time. I smothered imported hotter-than-hot Indian pickle on a lot of things I eat, unlike Sanjay, who was born in California and grew up eating organic foods from Silicon Valley farmers' markets and food festivals. In spite of my affinity for any food that would make most grown men cry, Sanjay was right that I had some serious gaps in my cultural knowledge. Sanjay was the one with a more ingrained sense of Indian culture. I only lived in India until I was seven years old. My father was an

American hippie who had gone to India to find himself and met my mother. But after she died, he thought it would be easier to raise my brother and me back in America. I grew up with the aging flower children of Berkeley, not within an Indian community.

"I don't think that jar of mango pickle in your fridge is sanitary," Sanjay said.

"Coward."

Sanjay cleared his throat. "I guess we should get back to this map. Are these good translations?"

Sanjay was Punjabi, and his parents were from north India, whereas my family was from the south. The languages of the different regions were nothing alike, and the only thing Sanjay and I had in common in this case was that neither one of us were equipped to read the Tamil writing.

So much can be lost in translation. It's one of the hazards for a historian when reading non-primary accounts. Luckily for my own specialty, the British East India Company, most accounts and records were kept in English.

"I'll have a linguist check it out," I said.

"Meaning you decided to keep it," Sanjay said.

I glared at Sanjay before retrieving my phone. I snapped two photos of the map. "There," I said. "Now I can give the map back. Happy?"

"If Anand Paravar was as clever as your mom led you to believe," Sanjay said, "maybe he put invisible ink on the map."

I glared at Sanjay again.

"Don't shoot the messenger, Jaya."

I groaned and sat down on the couch. I couldn't resist the historical lure of the map. As soon as Steven Healy came to me, there was little chance of my turning back. And now...

"*Lost* and *found*," Sanjay read aloud from the map. "*Path of the Old Coast*. I've never heard of the *MP Craft Emporium* or *The Anchored Enchantress*. Sounds like a video game. And what do you suppose this drawing to the north of Lands End is? Looks kind of like wobbly triangles."

"Wobbly triangles?"

A loud pounding at the door startled us both. Sanjay was good at masking his reactions, since he's a performer, but I saw his shoulders tense.

"It's Nadia," I said, getting up to answer the door. "That's the way she knocks."

My landlady wore a black one-piece jumpsuit that looked straight out of 1968. She hated colorful clothing, just like me. It might be one of the reasons we got along so well. A hint of musky perfume hovered around her.

"You did not come for your mail today," she said. I didn't think my apartment was legally supposed to exist, so all of my mail was delivered to the main mailbox at Nadia's door. "I hear voices upstairs, so I know you are home and awake."

I ushered her inside from the rain as she pushed a handful of mail into my hands. Rain drops glistened on her white-streaked blonde hair. I wasn't sure how old Nadia was, and she wouldn't tell me even after we'd become friends. I knew she'd come to San Francisco from Russia as a young woman in the 1960s and fallen in love with the city. My apartment used to be the space where she grew pot plants for medical marijuana patients.

"Sorry if we woke you, Nadia," I said. My wall clock, an antique from a thrift store in London that worked most of the time, showed it was well after eleven p.m.

"Of course not, Jaya. You know I never sleep until well after midnight. I was finishing dinner."

"You eat dinner at 11 p.m.?" Sanjay said.

Nadia's blue eyes narrowed as she noticed Sanjay. She told me once that she disliked all magicians. I'm sure there's a story there, which I might ask her about when I had a full evening to spare.

"A good meal is a civilized way to end the day, no?" Her eyes caught sight of the map on the wall. "What is that?" She walked across the room until she stood a few feet in front of the map.

"Just a map I picked up for my research," I said casually, catching Sanjay's eye and giving a shake of my head while Nadia's back was turned. For all of the benefits of having a free-spirited landlady who couldn't care less that I tack, nail, and duct-tape my latest research projects to my walls, the downside was she had a nosy streak. It's how she knew Sanjay in the first place.

"I did not think you studied local history," Nadia said. "Why is this on your wall?"

"It's—" Sanjay began.

I "accidentally" stepped on his foot.

"We can't figure out what these are," I said as Sanjay swore. I pointed to the wobbly triangle hash marks above Lands End.

"Oh, that's easy," Nadia said.

"You know what those are?"

"Of course," Nadia said. "What I cannot understand is why on earth they are *here*."

CHAPTER 7

"You study history, Jaya," Nadia said, sighing. "Young people are not educated as they once were."

Sanjay cleared his throat.

"Chinese fishing nets," Nadia said, shooting a sharp glance at Sanjay. "This drawing is of Chinese fishing nets. The large nets that scoop into the ocean for fish. You are too young to have seen many of them, even on your travels. The technology has been replaced."

Sanjay and I glanced at each other. Chinese fishing nets. Nadia was right. That's exactly what they were. Huge contraptions with spider-like arms that controlled the nets below.

The Paravar caste of south India was a fishing and boat builder caste. The Chinese had come to the west coast of India centuries ago, bringing with them their tall fishing nets and interacting with the Indians who worked along the water. For centuries, the easiest way to get around the coastal regions of southwestern India was by boat, giving lots of work to the Paravars.

As a skilled boat builder who once worked in Kochi, Anand would have been familiar with the nets. But why had he drawn these fishing nets in San Francisco?

"This is not right," Nadia said, the wrinkles surrounding her lips accentuated by her consternation.

Nadia pulled the map off the corkboard. She took it out of its protective plastic, and held it in her hands to peer more closely at the markings. She shook her head before setting it down on the coffee table.

"The map is a hundred years old," I said. "Wasn't there a big Chinese population in San Francisco at the time?"

"There have never been fishing nets set up like that at Lands End," Nadia said. "I hope you did not pay much for the map. The person who drew it was not true to San Francisco history."

"It looks pretty accurate everywhere else," Sanjay said.

Nadia's eyes narrowed as she looked at Sanjay.

He gulped. "Would you like some coffee, Nadia?"

"You made it?"

He nodded.

"No. I should be getting back." She gave one last look at the mysterious map she'd left resting on the coffee table, then slipped out the door.

"What did I ever to do her?" Sanjay asked. He sighed and absentmindedly set his mug down on the coffee table. "And how the hell does she know what fishing nets were set up in San Francisco a hundred years ago. What is she, a vampire?"

"Before I lose all sense of reality, it's time for you to head home, too."

Sanjay hesitated before speaking. "You're not going to do anything after I'm gone, are you?"

"I'm going to get some sleep."

"You're not going to check out these spots on the map?"

Sanjay knew me well.

"It's the middle of the night," I said.

"That's not an answer."

"I'm not going to leave the house tonight," I promised.

"You don't seem yourself," Sanjay said. "Are you sure you're all right? Do you want me to come by in the morning?"

"I've got a date in the morning."

"A date?"

"I'm meeting Tamarind at the library."

"Oh, not a *date* date."

"She's helping me with some archival research. Before I return the map to the police or Steven's family tomorrow, I thought I'd take it to the library—Sanjay!" I broke off as I stared at the coffee table. I jumped up and lifted Sanjay's mug from where he'd set it down. "You set your coffee down on the map!"

"It's Nadia's fault," Sanjay grumbled, taking the mug back. "She flusters me. I didn't realize what I was doing. Why did she take it off the wall anyway?"

I slipped the map back into its plastic covering. It only had a small ring from the mug. No harm done.

"Definitely time to call it a night," I said.

After I finally got Sanjay out the door, I opened my computer. An email from Tamarind told me she'd found a good contact at the University of Kerala and that she should have more information by morning. With that taken care of, it was time for an internet search. I confirmed that Steven Healy was a lawyer, like he told me. But that's where the truth ended. He hadn't retired.

He'd been disbarred.

I clicked on one of the articles, and then another. Last year, prominent San Francisco attorney Steven Healy had been disbarred for falsifying documents against the opposing side in a court case— he even punched the guy at one point—and his law firm, Healy & Healy, went under as a result. Steven was ruined, and his son Connor hadn't returned to law.

Steven Healy wasn't merely bored in retirement. *He was a desperate man.*

There had been a scandal that played out on the television news. Connor's wife Christine was incredibly photogenic, and the television news had covered the story more than the print media. I might have read about it in passing, but I hadn't remembered it well enough to recognize Steven when he came to see me. Perhaps that's why I'd had a sense that he looked vaguely familiar. I could have spent hours reading news stories from the previous year, but it wouldn't have answered any more of my questions. I turned back to the map.

I looked up the two names on the map I didn't recognize: *MP Craft Emporium* and the *The Anchored Enchantress*. I couldn't find any references to either one having existed in San Francisco, so I tried the search from a different angle. I found an old map of San Francisco from 1900 that was detailed enough to show some locations. The map I found online wasn't comprehensive, but it was a start. The location of the two buildings placed them in San Francisco's notorious Barbary Coast neighborhood, known for establishments such as saloons, dance halls, and gambling dens that sprang up when the Gold Rush began in 1849. Again, neither name was listed. I made a note to ask Tamarind about them at the library the next day.

I'm a good historian because in addition to knowing a hell of a lot about my subject of British India, I'm good at putting together the puzzle pieces of history. Being good at academic research also means knowing where to go to find out what you need. In spite of what movies might have you believe, an individual can't be an expert at everything. As a librarian, Tamarind knows how to find things that a Google search would never reveal. And I knew exactly who would be a good person to do a translation. The problem was I wasn't sure if he'd help.

Naveen Krishnan was a fellow assistant professor of history at my university. Naveen and I were both hired last year as part of an expansion in the South Asian Studies program in the History Department. But with budget cuts looming, it was likely only one of us would get tenure. I really should have been putting the finishing touches on the research paper I needed to get published, not examining a treasure map. But having a brilliant linguist down the hall from me was too good an opportunity to pass up. I hoped he'd be willing to put our academic rivalry aside to help me with this personal matter.

I sent an email to Naveen to see if he was available to translate the Tamil on the map. There had to be more to those words.

It was a strange feeling, having something of Anand's after he'd been a grand, ghostly figure for all these years. *What were your secrets, Anand Paravar?* Because of Steven's death, would I ever know? Were both Anand's and Steven's deaths due to this map and the treasure it led to? A map that I now had in my possession. I shivered at the thought. I pulled a throw blanket from the back of the couch around me and looked methodically at the map. *Shipyards, Chinese fishing nets, unknown buildings that existed a century ago....*

The X on the map must have had a hypnotic effect, because the next thing I knew, I was lying on the couch with light streaming onto my face and a loud knock on the door jolting me awake.

I flailed around for a moment before realizing I was lying on the couch. Standing up, I knocked my shin on the edge of the coffee table. I wasn't so great at life before coffee.

"Jaya?" a male voice called out from behind the door, followed by another knock.

"Sanjay?"

"Of course it's me. Who else sounds like me?"

I reached the door and opened it. Sanjay stood in the doorway wearing casual clothes and his bowler hat, holding two paper cups of coffee.

"Why are you here so early?" I asked, accepting a coffee.

"It's almost nine," Sanjay said, stepping around me to enter the apartment. "Were you still in bed?"

"No," I said, running a hand through my messy hair as I shut the door. A benefit of wearing a lot of black clothes is that nobody notices if you're wearing the same clothes as the day before.

"You weren't answering your phone," Sanjay said, frowning.

"I must have slept through it," I said, yawning. I was a sound sleeper. When I needed to get up, I set multiple alarms.

"Do me a favor," Sanjay said. "The next time someone you know is murdered, leave your phone on its loudest setting."

"Why are you so jumpy this morning?"

"Because of what I heard this morning," Sanjay said.

"Whatever is going on, Jaya—be careful. You shouldn't follow the clues on the map—ever. It's too dangerous. You need to forget about this whole thing."

"What are you talking about?" My sleep-weariness was gone, replaced by the alertness that comes with anxiety. "What's happened?"

"Your lawyer friend. He was lying to you."

"Oh, that," I said, sitting back down and taking a sip of sugary caffeine. "I know."

"You do? I thought you were still asleep just now."

"I Googled him last night."

"Wait," Sanjay said slowly. "What are you talking about? It was only the morning news that had interviewed his friends."

"Why would the media need friends of his to report that he was disbarred?" I asked.

"He was disbarred?"

"That's not what you're talking about?"

Sanjay shook his head, his eyebrows drawn together in confusion. "I'm talking about the treasure."

"Someone told the press what the treasure is?"

"Unfortunately not," Sanjay said. "But Steven was bragging about having made a discovery of *great historical significance.* He wouldn't tell anyone what it was, but it sure as hell wasn't some little family treasure."

"None of this makes sense," I said. "How did an Indian boat builder end up with a treasure of historic significance?"

"That," Sanjay said, "is a much tougher riddle than the one you brought me last night."

"What's going on?"

"I don't know," Sanjay said, "but it's not good."

"No," I said. "It certainly isn't."

CHAPTER 8

The middle of the Atlantic Ocean, 1902

For close to two years, Anand wandered through Arabia and Europe, stopping in coastal cities where there was work building or fixing ships. Traveling westward, he wrote Vishwan a letter every week.

But there were some things he couldn't tell his little brother.

The English he had learned in school from the British served him well. He had taken to the subject, which had helped him much more than rudimentary Hindi in Kochi. Anand knew he was lucky that languages came easily to him. In Constantinople, he used his Arabic. In Calais, he became better at French. In Frankfurt, German.

He left Morocco for the north after a team of pirates wrecked a frigate he was repairing and the company employing him went bankrupt.

He left Frankfurt after an incident with the wife of a duke. She had not told Anand who she was; he never would have betrayed the hospitality of the man for whom he was working.

English came most easily to him but England was far from his favorite country. The men he worked with in Portsmouth did not know the meaning of being civilized. Unlike their ship-building brethren in India, these men on the docks of England had no education, often speaking English with less facility than Anand himself. Most of them thought nothing of going days without washing, and subsisted on potatoes and ale. Yet in spite of all this, they considered themselves superior to Anand.

Anand had heard of America. The further west he traveled, and the more coastal cities he visited, the more he heard about the wonders of this young country of America.

Though he missed his home of Travancore, he knew it was safest for him to stay away for a short time longer. Besides, there was still much more of the world to see. Ever since that day years ago when he had died of typhoid and been given another chance at life, he knew he was meant to see the world. Maybe even change it. There would be time for him to return to Travancore. When he did, it would be interesting to see how the land and people had changed.

When Anand stayed in a city for a long enough time to receive mail, his brother was able to write to him to tell him what was happening at home. Vishwan read the Tamil newspaper *Swadesamitran* and the English newspaper *Madras Standard*, and wrote to Anand of the growing movement toward independence. Such movements to break away from British rule and elect their own leaders had existed for years, but this time was different. The British were wary and the local kings were afraid.

Anand thought of the Heart of India, the giant elephant statue crafted in a Kochi workshop years before by a Muslim friend. It was brought to the water's edge of the coastal town of Thoothukudi, in southeastern India, where it was safe from interference from maharajas who opposed its message. There in the symbolic city of Thoothukudi, which had replaced Korkai as the Pearl Emporium from ancient times, the Heart of India was free to be seen by all. Men from many religions and castes had contributed their labor in creating the statue. Anand's Paravar caste had given the Paravar pearl held in the elephant's trunk. Yes, there would be time to return home and to see the statue again.

Anand booked passage on a large passenger ship which would take many days to sail from England to New York. The passengers from over a dozen countries told stories of boundless opportunities about which they could not possibly know, yet their faces were filled with such hope that it was impossible not to believe them.

Anand could tell America would be different.

CHAPTER 9

I walked to my large kitchen window and looked out at the tree branches swaying in the wind in Nadia's yard. The rain of the previous night had cleared, replaced by a thick belt of fog.

San Francisco was unlike anywhere I had lived before. I had lived in the city a year now, and though I grew up right across the bay in Berkeley, the energy of San Francisco was different. The people, the environment, even the weather. The people were both younger and older in the city—young people finding themselves who didn't yet want to settle down, and older free spirits like Nadia who had been there for decades. The numerous hills of the city helped shape the personalities of dozens of individual neighborhoods, and also controlled where the clouds settle.

"If you're okay," Sanjay said, "I should get going." He was absentmindedly spreading out the deck of cards between his hands. The cards seemed to float in midair, as if by magic.

"Why wouldn't I be okay?" I asked. But Sanjay knew me too well. He'd know I was lying if he got a good look at me. I quickly turned away and looked back out the window, thoughts of a dead Steven Healy flitting through my mind.

"If you're sure," Sanjay said. "I'll be setting up at the theater today, but you don't need to come by until tomorrow." He squeezed my shoulder on his way out.

Now that I was fully awake from Sanjay's visit, I finished my coffee while I checked my phone for email and voicemail messages. In addition to several missed voicemail messages from Sanjay and a missed call from my dad, Naveen had emailed me about meeting to translate the map. The map that had possibly gotten a man killed...

I pulled on yoga pants. I had never done yoga in my life—Sanjay would remind me that I was a terrible Indian—but I liked the stretchy gray cotton pants for running. I usually ran three miles, but that morning I ran at least five. Between the beats of the bhangra music on my headphones and the cacophony of raucous thoughts in my head, I must have needed the release. Confusing thoughts about murdered men and murderous thoughts about ex-boyfriends were drowned out by the loud beats on my headphones and by the furious beating of my heart as I kept up an intense pace through Golden Gate Park.

Bhangra was the perfect music to listen to while running. The traditional Punjabi folk music melded with British fusion in the 1980s, thanks to all the Indians emigrating to the UK, and created an even more danceable beat that was also fantastic for fast running.

The music lulled me into both an energized and meditative state. It allowed me to think clearly. To see clearly. Steven Healy had been lying about the treasure he was after. I still didn't know what it was, why he lied to me, or even if that was what had gotten him killed. I needed to give the map to the police. If they thought it was evidence, they could keep it. If it wasn't, they could return it to the family. It was the right thing to do. But Steven had brought me a problem to solve that had a more personal connection than one of the many puzzles of history.

After my run, my mind was clearer than it had been since Steven Healy had walked into my office. Life had taken some things out of my control, but that didn't mean I was helpless. I was going to get closure about Uncle Anand, and I was going to get closure with something in my own life. I showered and grabbed a bagel and coffee at the Coffee to the People café on the way to my car. Tamarind would be expecting me at the library soon, but I had unfinished business with Lane.

I blasted bhangra beats in my roadster as I drove across the Bay Bridge, letting the loud music mask my nerves. The traffic cooperated better than I expected, but it was only so it could set me up for a bigger disappointment.

The curtains of Lane's in-law unit on the sleepy Berkeley side street were drawn back. Standing on the outside looking in, I could see much more than I had before.

The apartment was empty.

Not merely empty of people, but empty of *everything*. No furniture in the living room. No pots, pans, or dishes in the adjoining kitchen. Nothing hung on the walls. The only proof that someone had lived there recently were indentations on the carpet where the chair and coffee-table trunk had stood, and numerous tiny holes on the wall where artwork had been mounted.

I didn't trust myself to believe my own eyes. After standing stupidly on the grass in front of the windows for a few long minutes, I got back in my car and sat there for a few minutes more. I started the engine, then turned it back off. I got out and walked back to the apartment.

It was still empty.

What was going on? I slammed the door of my roadster and drove to the Berkeley campus.

The parking space I found ten minutes later wasn't remotely legal, but I didn't care. My messenger bag bounced against my hip as I ran to reach Lane's office. The door was ajar when I reached it.

Standing in the doorway of his tiny office, I didn't believe what I saw. I looked at the number on the door, just to be sure. It was his office, all right. And it had been cleared out. There was no evidence left that Lane Peters had ever been there.

That's what he'd been doing when I came by the night before. He hadn't been organizing his office. He'd been packing.

I felt numb as I walked to the main office of the Art History Department to ask about Lane.

Lane, the guy I'd fallen for—hard—earlier that summer.

Lane, the bastard who'd made it clear he wanted nothing more to do with me but wouldn't tell me why.

Lane, the ex-jewel thief who I'd shown a treasure map to the night before...

He couldn't be involved... Could he?

I found the department secretary at her desk and asked her about Lane's empty office.

"I'm sorry," she said. "He's on leave."

"It's Lane Peters I'm asking about," I repeated.

"Yes, that's right."

"That's not possible."

"I'm quite sure of it," she said. "Lane Peters has taken a leave of absence. He's gone."

CHAPTER 10

It was almost noon before I met Tamarind at the main desk in the university library. Her short hair was dyed electric blue this week. She looked rather patriotic with her dark red lipstick set against her fair complexion with only a hint of olive. The thick silver loop through the center of her nose added flare to the presentation. She was more than a head taller than me, and about twice as wide. I know they say big-boned is a euphemism, but in Tamarind's case it was true.

"I expected you earlier," she said. "You sounded like this stuff was urgent."

"It is," I grumbled.

"What's the matter?" she asked.

"Nothing," I said, instead of what I was really thinking. I had thought my life was finally coming together, but I'd lied to myself. I had no idea what was going on in *any* aspect of my life. "I was following up on another lead."

"You went to *another* librarian?"

"I wouldn't dream of it. Sometimes there's work that can't be done at a library."

"I'm told this is true, but I've yet to see it with my own eyes. You look like hell, by the way. Did you get any sleep last night?"

"Yeah, just not in my bed."

Tamarind's bright red lips parted and her eyebrows shot up. "Spill."

"That's not what I meant," I added quickly, laughing in spite of my sour mood. "I fell asleep on my couch while doing research."

"Whatever you say. Anyway, I got through to someone at the University of Kerala who works with the university's archives. The guy emailed me that the archivist we need to talk to is named Joseph Abraham. What's up with that? They hired an Anglo guy rather than a local?"

"I'm sure he's an Indian guy," I said. "There's a big Christian population in south India, and Joseph Abraham is a common name."

"Huh," Tamarind said. "Well, whoever he is, he's not big on email. He wrote back a brief note to ask me to call him. Buzz kill."

"So you didn't find out anything about the content of the letters?"

"I didn't say *that.*"

Tamarind smiled, which she does more than you'd think for someone who believes herself to be a tough punk.

"Thanks for helping with this," I said. It was impossible to stay in a bad mood around Tamarind.

"Anything for my favorite professor."

"So you *did* find something about a missing treasure?"

"And do your job for you? Ha! Actually, I totally would have if Joseph had any information up front. *But,*" Tamarind added, "he said there was something *interesting* to discuss. I figure that's why he asked me to call him. *Tres interessant.*"

"Did you call him?"

"I didn't think the library would appreciate the phone bill. Besides, I thought you'd want to do the honors."

Tamarind gave me the number, and I dialed the international number from my cell phone. Because of the time difference, it was now the middle of the night in India. As I expected, the call went to an answering machine. I left a brief message.

"How are you going to read the letters once Joseph finds them for you," Tamarind asked. "Won't they be in Tamil?"

"Thanks to those lovely British," I said, "Anand wrote home in English."

"Sucks to be colonized. Did they have to use English?"

"They weren't forced to give up their language at home," I said. "It's just that a lot of education in India at the time was in English. So even though Anand and Vishwan would have spoken Tamil to each other at home, they would have been better at writing in English than in Tamil."

"Creepy," Tamarind said.

"Convenient for research, though," I added.

"You sure you're okay?" she asked. "You look really pale. Come on, let's go to the courtyard out back. It's time for my break. I made us sandwiches this morning so we could have a working lunch."

We stepped out into the small, shady courtyard enclosed by the library. Two students were smoking in one corner, but otherwise the concrete courtyard was empty.

"I don't think so," Tamarind said calmly, yet forcefully, in their direction.

The students immediately stubbed out their cigarettes. They hurried past the "No Smoking" sign and back into the library.

"You'd think they'd learn they can't get away with anything on my watch," she said to me with an overdramatic sigh. "Kids these days."

Tamarind had only finished her library science degree a few years before and wasn't much older than the "kids" she'd chastised, but in addition to being one of the most brilliant people I'd ever met, her physical presence was an asset at an urban university. Rumor had it that during her interview, she got up to help the security guard deal with a drunken and belligerent man who'd wandered into the library. She possessed the helpful combination of looking big and frightening while at the same time having a genuine desire to help people. She was able to get people to trust her and open up to her. For the few who didn't, her physical presence was threatening enough to remove the problem.

"You want a cigarette?" she asked me, pulling a pack from one of the many pockets of her zipper-covered black pants.

"Seriously?"

"What? I'm an authority figure. I can make my own rules."

"I'd rather eat." I sat down on the closest bench. "I'm starving."

"Suit yourself." She put the box of cigarettes back into her bag.

"You remembered to give me extra pickles," I said, opening the whole wheat sandwich.

"Who else eats pickles on their peanut butter and jelly sandwiches?" Tamarind said. "Like I'm ever going to forget that. I swear I'd think you were pregnant if you weighed more than a toothpick. Or if I'd ever seen you with a guy besides that hot puppy dog who follows you around while you ignore him."

"You mean Sanjay? I really don't think—"

"You saying he's not hot?"

"Maybe in the traditional sense."

"As in the traditional, oh-my-God-my-thighs-are-on-fire sense."

"Um, no. He's like my brother."

Tamarind rolled her eyes. "Suit yourself. But I don't see how you can resist fantasizing about running your fingers through that thick black hair of his. He has it perfectly styled without *looking* like it's been styled, you know?" She sighed wistfully. "Now tell me about this treasure or I'll take away your pickle-flavored PB & J. You seriously have a real-life treasure map?"

When I'd texted Tamarind the previous night, before Steven was murdered, this whole thing seemed more like a fun, if strange, adventure about a long-dead ancestor. The same sentiment was now evident on Tamarind's face. I hated to bring someone else into this mess, knowing what it had now become. But since I had told her about the map, she was already involved. I lifted the map from my messenger bag and placed it on the bench between us.

"Shut. Up." Tamarind stared at the plastic-covered map without touching it. "This is old. Like, you have the *real thing*. How did you make this discovery without me knowing about it?"

"I didn't find this through my research. There was a man who gave this to me—"

Tamarind's dark eyebrows shot up in interest.

"Not a guy *like that*. He's my dad's age—and he's dead."

Tamarind sat in stunned silence, her face turning a shade paler. "A *ghost* guy came to see you?" she whispered.

"Worse than that."

"You mean he looked all gross and rotted, like how his body would really look buried in the ground, not like our idealized images of ghosts? God, I always wondered—"

"Tamarind—"

"I mean, I always *thought* movies idealized death. Ghosts are always so ethereal and dressed in white and—"

Sometimes I had to remind myself of Tamarind's brilliance. She'd come through many times this year, finding obscure references for me that I'd never have found without her. But she was also a twenty-five-year-old punk who refused to walk under ladders—which can be rather inconvenient at a library that stacks the books twice as tall as me and has ladders in most sections.

"I'm not," I said firmly, "talking about a ghost."

"You're not?"

"I'm talking about murder."

Tamarind's pale face turned a shade paler. She inched to the far edge of the bench. "I'm going to sit quietly over here with my hands in my lap while you tell me *what the hell* you're talking about."

Now that I had the floor, I didn't quite know where to start. Since Steven Healy had lied to me, what did I know was true?

"The man who came to see me last night," I began, "Steven Healy, the guy I mentioned in my text. He said he was a retired lawyer who'd found evidence that a great-granduncle of mine—Uncle Anand, whose letters I asked you to look into last night—had stolen a treasure from his family and hidden it in San Francisco before being murdered in 1906."

"Shut. Up." Tamarind stared at me.

"But Steven Healy lied to me," I said. "It wasn't some family treasure, but something of historical significance."

"Which is...?"

"I don't know," I said. "But whatever the inconsistencies in what he told me, he had this treasure map with Tamil writing that may have been drawn by Uncle Anand."

"A map that leads to a treasure," Tamarind said.

I nodded. "But he was murdered shortly after he came to see me and gave me this map. It was on the news."

"What happened to him?"

"He was bludgeoned to death."

Tamarind winced. "Not a nice way to go. You think he was killed because of this treasure map? The map that's sitting here?"

"I have no idea. I just know he's dead."

"This is *awesome*," she said.

"Didn't you hear what I just said?"

"Well, it's not awesome that he's dead. But everybody dies. And this means it's a real treasure map. You couldn't have asked for better proof. But really, I'm not going to lose sleep over some lawyer capitalist pig being killed after living a long life."

"He wasn't—"

"Jaya, you have a *treasure map* from a *dead man*. You don't have the luxury of being generous. You need to start figuring out exactly who this man was—and what else he was hiding."

CHAPTER 11

"You should write a memoir once you find the treasure," Tamarind said. She even had a straight face as she said it. "And this time, I'm in."

"There is no *in*."

"Who do you think would play me in the movie?" Tamarind asked. "I don't think there are many actresses who could pull it off. Hollywood actresses don't have decent bone structure like mine. Aishwarya Rai would play you, of course. She looks half-white to me, no matter what those Miss Universe judges said."

"She can't do an American accent," I said. "Wait. Stop. I can't believe I'm having this conversation. I'm not writing a memoir. I don't know what I'm doing, but whatever it is, it's not that. I need to figure out what's going on. There's a missing treasure, incomplete information, inconsistent facts, an unsubstantiated accusation against Uncle Anand, and I've ended up with a Tamil treasure map."

"Very nicely summed up. You've got the professorial thing perfected, Jaya."

"Glad you approve," I said, taking a bite out of my peanut butter, jelly, and pickle sandwich.

"And I'm glad you're not so broken up about dear old Steven that you can't eat."

"My starving to death won't do anyone any good," I said, but at the same time I set down the sandwich. Even though I'd dealt with a murderer earlier that summer, it wasn't any easier this time. Death could be tragic. But murder was deeply unsettling.

"What did he tell you about this map?" Tamarind asked, staring at the faded piece of paper.

"Sorry, what?" I willed myself to focus.

"The map," Tamarind said. "What exactly did he tell you?"

"Nothing," I said. "He let it speak for itself. He said he'd tell me more when I saw him next."

"And then he..."

"Exactly. He was killed, so I don't know what he was going to tell me."

"He wanted those letters," Tamarind murmured. "He thought they'd tell him something."

"He thought I'd know where to find them. And he was right."

We ate our sandwiches in silence for a few minutes while looking at the map. A solitary student wandered into the courtyard and sat down in the far corner from us. Tamarind scowled in his direction as he opened his laptop, but the guy wasn't looking our way.

"Why did he need those letters if he had this treasure map?" Tamarind asked in a whisper.

"Well, it's not the most straightforward of treasure maps," I admitted.

"But the X mark—"

"It doesn't lead to a treasure," I said. "At least not one Steven Healy could find with just the map." I shook my head. "There was something he wasn't telling me about how he knew it was Anand Paravar who drew this map. I should have pressed for more information, but I had no idea I'd never see him again."

"But you know you can believe him about the map," Tamarind said.

"Why? He lied to me about his motives for finding the treasure—he even lied about the treasure itself."

"But," Tamarind said, "he believed Anand's letters were the key to cracking the map. So he believed it was Anand's map."

"I've been thinking about something else," I said. "Why would Anand have needed to draw a treasure map in the first place?"

"Um, because he was a thief who needed to show where he hid his treasure. Mwa-ha-ha."

"That's the thing," I said. "I don't think he did it."

Tamarind sighed dramatically, pouting her bright red lips. "Sticking up for the clan is all well and good, Jaya, but don't let it cloud your professional judgment."

"If you'd heard the way my mom talked about him, you'd find it hard to believe, too. He was this amazing figure to her grandfather. He was involved in a revolutionary group working for Indian independence. He left home in 1900 to see the world—supposedly a wanted man for his involvement in the cause—and sent money home while he was at it."

"Sounds like a thief to me."

"Even if I disregard all the family lore, *the dates don't fit.* He left home in 1900 and arrived in San Francisco a couple of years later. He was still living here in 1906—nowhere near India. There weren't flights to pop over to the other side of the world in those days. He wrote his brother a letter every week. And he didn't leave San Francisco once he got here."

"Okay," Tamarind said. "I'll admit that's some pretty good evidence. *If* it's true."

"I need to start with the dates," I said. "If this treasure is a big enough deal to get someone killed over a hundred years later, there has to be a record of it. Does the library have turn-of-the-century newspaper archives?"

"Not ours," Tamarind said. "But the San Francisco library's history center has digitized all the local papers, so if you've got a library card you can view the PDFs online. You can use one of the computer stations to check it out while I fondle the treasure map."

"I'll be back to check out the newspaper archives in a little bit," I said. "First I'm going to see Naveen."

"Why would anyone want to do that?"

"He's the best person to ask about Tamil writing and translations."

"I suppose so," Tamarind said. "See you later—if you survive, that is."

"He's not *that* bad."

"It's your funeral," Tamarind said, shaking her blue-haired head. "I'm going to have that cigarette now."

"What about him?" I motioned to the student wearing headphones and typing away at his laptop.

"He's not going to narc on me if he knows what's good for him."

I left Tamarind to her cigarette and walked across the quad to Naveen Krishnan's office. I shared Tamarind's feelings and wished I didn't need to ask for his help, but he was the best person to see.

Many kids with parents from two different regions of India speak English at home because it's the common language between parents. Naveen had an ear for languages, and in addition to the two languages his parents spoke, he also knew how to speak and read three other Indian languages that I knew of. Tamil was one of them. My brother Mahilan and I attended an English-language school back in Goa, so there was no need for us to formally learn other languages. We learned some Hindi and Marathi through school and being out in the community, but when we relocated to Berkeley after my mother's death, I didn't see another written Indian language until college.

Naveen and I had always been cordial with each other, but I was under no illusion that we were friends. Though we're in the same department, we approached history differently. He focused on linguistic cultural histories, and I delved into the movements of the European colonizing forces in India. We were both well-equipped to teach basic undergraduate world history and Indian history courses, so we both expected only one of us to get tenure. If this had been a normal project, I wouldn't have asked for his help.

Within minutes I stood in Naveen's doorway. His office was nothing like mine. Perfectly trimmed miniature bonsai trees in pristine white pots were aligned along the window sill. Every book and journal had its place in the metallic bookshelves. How could anyone think in such precise order? History was messy.

The office matched the man. Naveen was a few years younger than me, having started college at eighteen and finished his PhD in only four years. I finished my advanced degree in five years, but I didn't begin college until I was twenty, four years after I'd finished high school at sixteen. Though Naveen was young, he dressed more formally than any of the other history professors. I don't think I'd ever seen him without a three-piece suit, and he was usually drinking tea—and never out of a paper cup. His thick black hair was cut in a short, professional style that reminded me of the 1950s. Naveen wore a light brown flannel suit today. It was a warm day, so the jacket hung on a coat rack, but he wore the matching vest over his dress shirt. A mug of tea rested at his elbow.

"So nice to see you, Jaya," he said. "I wasn't sure if I'd see you again. It sounded like you were too busy chasing Scottish legends to bother with real academic research."

"Good to see you, too," I said, forcing myself to remain civil.

"It's too bad you can't do your own translations," Naveen said. "You're lucky I have a little extra time right now to help you with your work. The dean asked me to lead a symposium, so I'm going to be quite busy. I won't be able to bail you out in the future."

"This isn't for my work," I said. The dean had asked a second-year assistant professor to lead a symposium? I knew Naveen would want me to ask more about it, so I didn't.

"No?"

"I can do my own research perfectly well," I said. "This is a personal project."

"Have a seat," he said, frowning and taking a sip of his tea. "What was it you wanted me to translate?"

I painted a smile on my face and sat down.

"A Tamil treasure map."

Tea sloshed over the side of Naveen's mug, falling onto the uncluttered surface of the desk. He pushed his chair back to avoid spilling tea all over his pristine suit.

"A *treasure* map?" he asked, using a tissue from a white box that matched the bonsai plants to wipe up every drop of the spill. "Surely you're joking."

"I'm not." I spread the map across the desk.

Naveen stared at me for a moment before pulling a magnifying glass out of his desk drawer to study the map more carefully. For the next several minutes, he didn't speak.

"Where did you get this?" he asked.

"Long story," I said. "Can you translate it or not?"

"You may have noticed," he said, "it's already been translated."

"I can see that. But I don't know if the person who translated it was as skilled a linguist as you."

Naveen rested his elbows on the desk and gave me a thin-lipped smile. I didn't really want to get into the story of the map, so I hoped appealing to his ego would do the trick.

"The translations are good," he said.

"You're sure?" I'd been hoping the previous translator had missed something.

"You sound disappointed," he said, the slight smile on his face growing stronger.

"None of the writing refers to Chinese fishing nets?" I asked.

"Why would it say anything like that?"

I pointed to the illustration.

Naveen smirked at me. "Do you need a refresher course in California history? I'm sure one of our colleagues would let you sit in on their undergraduate class."

I ignored the insult. "What about the top of the map. Why is it *My Cities* instead of *My City*? I know Tamil is a complex language, so maybe—"

"I know when something is plural," Naveen snapped. He narrowed his eyes and looked back at the map. "This is formal Tamil, but there's no mistake."

"What about these things that look like place names. *MP Craft Emporium* and *The Anchored Enchantress*. I looked them up and they don't exist."

"This thing probably isn't even real. Who draws a treasure map?"

"You're probably right," I said.

"I usually am."

I stood up. "Thanks for the help, Naveen."

I knew a dead end when I ran into one. I didn't believe the map itself was a dead end, but Naveen had done all he could to help. There was something beyond the language that I was missing with the map.

Disappointed that a second opinion about the map's translation hadn't gotten me any further, I trudged across campus to meet Tamarind back at the library.

"The translations are a dead end," I told her, then found an open computer station near the main information desk where Tamarind was working that afternoon. I logged into the San Francisco Public Library's database and found the historic newspaper archive. Searches for Anand Selvam Paravar and Anand Paravar had zero search results in the newspaper. Steven Healy told me Anand stole a treasure around 1906. Even if the Great Earthquake hadn't killed him as I'd believed, he was killed sometime around then, so I focused on scanning newspapers that ran before April of that year.

Without knowing what I was looking for, I methodically skimmed headlines, starting at the beginning of 1906. The first hour went pretty well. I didn't find anything, but I liked getting into the groove of research. I let myself smile at a few entertaining headlines, but stayed focused on my task.

The second hour was the tough one. I was no longer under any illusion that this would be a quick search. But when there's a murdered man in the back of your mind and you don't know what's going on, it's tough to tell yourself that you can take a break.

A figure caught my attention, distracting me from the scanned newspapers. Startled, I saw Naveen heading straight for me. Not a pleasant sight. I'd had enough of him for one day.

"There you are," he said. "I don't know why you can't do research in your office like a sane person."

Tamarind cleared her throat from her nearby desk and shot Naveen a dirty look.

"You're not doing Jaya any favors," Naveen said to Tamarind before turning to me. "You don't win a prize for being a good team player."

"Since when is this a competition?" Tamarind said. "Oh wait. I forgot. For men with small—"

"What did you want to see me about?" I cut in.

"Yes, well..." He was still looking expectantly at Tamarind. "Well, Jaya seemed so *desperate* for my help, I felt the least I could do was spend a few minutes longer to double-check my initial reaction to some translations she brought me."

"I know about the map, Krishnan," Tamarind said.

"Shh!" A library patron glared at us.

"Honey," Tamarind said, raising her voice, "this is the main hall of a research library."

"Yes, well," Naveen said, lowering his voice, "I consulted a reference book on formal Tamil, and I was right. You seemed to doubt me, Jaya, so I wanted to let you know I was, in fact, correct."

"Thanks," I said.

"Yeah, thanks, Naveen," Tamarind added. "I'm sure Jaya will be forever grateful."

He didn't seem to catch the sarcasm in Tamarind's voice. He smiled and left.

"That guy," Tamarind said, watching Naveen walk out the library doors, "would be really delicious if he wasn't such a creep."

I turned back to the computer, trying to forget about Naveen and his symposium.

I'd made it to March of 1906. I had just pulled up a new page before Naveen arrived.

A black-and-white sketch in the scanned newspaper sparked a sense of recognition. I'd seen the man in the illustration before, hadn't I? But where?

My heart skipped a beat as I read the headline above the image: *Pirate Vishnu Terrorizes San Francisco Bay.*

I knew why the man a witness had sketched looked familiar. I'd seen him in my mom's family photographs. Pirate Vishnu was Uncle Anand.

CHAPTER 12

United States, 1903

After eight days at sea, the ship brought the group of strangers to the metropolis of the promised land that would become the new home to many of the weary travelers.

The men of New York were hard workers, which Anand respected. The weather, however, was intolerable. He did not need to see the sun every day, or feel the thirty-degree-centigrade warmth from home. But he felt as if he would surely freeze to death during the night in his boarding house that first winter. As soon as the snow was cleared, he took the railroad out west. That was how six months later he found himself in the most interesting city he'd ever encountered.

San Francisco was a new city. Before 1850, it had fewer than 1,000 residents. He heard the region used to be part of Mexico, but he didn't see much evidence of that from the men he worked with on the docks.

It was easy for him to find work at the Potrero Hill Shipyard. They were eager to employ skilled laborers who knew their way around the underlying structure of boats -- unlike the sailors who could fasten a knot and sail a ship but knew not how the vessel was put together, or the unskilled laborers who could lift heavy equipment but not do much else.

It was weeks before he realized they were paying him far less than the men with European origins he worked next to each day.

When he realized the injustice, Anand's jaw clenched and the muscles in his arms prepared for battle. He nearly started a bloody fight that day -- but stopped himself. He knew he was a boat builder, not a warrior. And this non-warrior Paravar was earning far more money than anywhere else he'd ever worked. It was more than enough to send some home to his family, stay in a warm boarding house, and save for his next adventure. Instead of fighting and being dismissed, he decided to let go of his anger by exploring an area of town he'd recently learned of: The Barbary Coast.

As night fell, he followed the muffled sounds of music and laughter. He didn't mind that there were few street signs in the city. Men newly arrived from Europe shook their heads in confusion, but like the Kingdoms of Travancore and Kochi, San Francisco was an organic city that made sense without explanation.

He followed the sounds onto a street lit with electric lights. An open door beckoned.

"You don't want to go in there, my friend," said a voice from the shadows.

The voice startled Anand. From the hidden shadows of an alley, a young Chinese man stepped forward. Unlike the other Chinese men Anand had seen, this one wore his hair short. He also spoke flawless, unaccented English.

"Why is that, my friend?" Anand asked.

The young Chinese man took a long drag on a short cigarette before throwing the last of it onto the street.

"If you're looking for a drink after a hard day's work, you'll be safer a block over."

"Why are you here, then?" Anand asked the stranger.

"I'm not going inside."

Anand turned up his collar as a cold wind picked up. He'd been hoping California would be warmer, but at least it didn't snow.

"You like freezing on the street?" Anand asked. "I've heard of some of the strange desires of the people in this part of town. You are a masochist, perhaps?"

The Oriental man laughed. "Let's get out of here. I'll show you a better place. Looks like rain. That's no good for talking to tourists when they exit the saloon."

Anand reached for his pocket, making sure this man hadn't picked it. The man laughed again.

"I'm not a pickpocket. I offer them--" He paused, and his voice changed when he spoke again. "I give good Chinatown tour. Secret streets, sir...Opium dens, sir."

Anand knew many Chinese traders in Kochi, and he recognized the accent. "Your Chinese accent is a little overdone," he commented.

"You think so?" The man was back to his American accent. "The tourists don't notice. My Western clothing puts them at ease enough that

they'll listen. But without the Chinese accent,
they don't think I'll know the best places to get
opium, or to get the thrill of seeing a real
opium den. Where are you from, my friend?"

"Not from anywhere that I need a tour of
Chinatown."

The man tipped his head before leading them
across the street. They cut behind a nightclub,
the sound of a woman's beautiful voice singing a
forlorn song escaping through the door.

"Welcome to the Barbary Coast," the Oriental
man said as they walked past. "I won't even
charge you for saving you from being run out of
that place. I'm Li." He pronounced it like the
western name Lee. He extended his hand. "Li
Fong."

"Anand."

"Only one name?"

Anand had met enough foreigners to know that
much of the world had family names that came from
their father. Anand's caste name of Paravar
served that purpose for identification once he
left home, along with using his father's name
Selvam as a middle name. But he had never
understood the need for more than one name.

"Don't worry," Li said, misinterpreting
Anand's hesitation. "We're going somewhere the
police won't raid."

The rain broke as they walked through a low
door and under a grimy wooden sign proclaiming
the establishment to be The Siren's Anchor.

"This used to be a ship," Li explained as they
walked past a giant mast.

"Wouldn't it have been easier to build it as a
building?"

Li laughed. "Where we stand today, fifty years ago was the ocean."

"I am not as gullible as the tourists."

"Faye," Li called out to the woman standing behind the bar. "Tell my new friend here how The Siren's Anchor came into existence. This is Faye's place," he added to Anand.

Faye was not an easy woman to characterize. Her features resembled the darker skinned women in Arabia, though her skin was fairer. Her hair was dark red with a texture he'd seen on Nubian women. She wore less clothing than a respectable woman, yet she had an air of integrity about her.

"He knows the rules of the place?" Faye asked Li.

"Good liquor, no trouble," Li said.

"Any man -- or woman -- of any color is welcome," Faye added. "But no prostitution allowed, and no shanghaiing."

"None intended," Anand said. He had heard about shanghaiing, when sailors were physically knocked out or given a knock-out drug in their drink, then carried off to a ship in need of a crew. He had thought it was a thing of the distant past -- not going on in the new century.

"We're standing on the old coastline," Faye said. "Several hundred ships were abandoned right here in the late 1840s when everyone had gold fever."

Faye paused to pour two drinks for two men who raised their empty glasses, tucking their coins into a hidden spot behind the bar.

"They abandoned their ships to head for the gold fields. When the city filled in the cove in the '50s, the ships were used as part of the land fill. This was one of the bigger ships. Parts of it stayed above ground."

"You are far too young for this to have been your ship," Anand said with a grin.

"You brought me a charmer, Li," Faye said.

"I'm Anand."

"Anand," Faye repeated, hesitating over the pronunciation.

"The emphasis is on the first syllable," Anand said. "You can remember it because it starts strong, like me."

"Faye's father built this place," Li said.

"Negroes weren't permitted to be gold prospectors," Faye said. "Worked out better that way. Most of those men didn't find any gold and died of starvation or disease. Supplies were low, so men who started businesses during that time could charge any price they wanted. My father built this place, and opened its doors to any man. Now it's mine, so any woman is welcome here, too."

Anand looked around the dark, well-kept saloon. A dozen men gathered around the bar and a few wooden tables, but there wasn't a woman in sight. If he hadn't known it was originally a ship, he would have assumed it was a regular building constructed to make sailors feel at home. A mirror behind the bar was made from portholes. A large anchor hung on the opposite wall, flanked by a fishing spear and a wooden ship's wheel.

"Now," Faye said, "what's your poison?"

CHAPTER 13

"Pirate Vishnu," I said, slapping down a printout of the page of the newspaper archive in front of Tamarind.

"Huh?" Tamarind stared into the distance beyond the glass front doors, distracted.

"You okay?" I asked, following her gaze. "You look distracted. You still hoping to catch a glimpse of Naveen?"

"There's some kid in a dark hoodie who's been lurking outside the doors since I've been back at my desk. He hasn't come inside, but that's a long time to be waiting for a study buddy. I thought I knew all the troublemakers, but he must be here just for summer session."

"I don't see him."

"You got off track?" Tamarind said, turning her attention back to me. "I know pirates are way cool, but you're usually more focused—"

"This," I said, pointing at the sketch, "is Uncle Anand."

"Shut. Up."

"This explains how he got his hands on the treasure," I said. "He was a pirate who stole it."

"Wow," Tamarind said. "Oh. My. Wow. Just *wow*."

"A ship that originated in India came to San Francisco, where their treasure was stolen by Pirate Vishnu, AKA Uncle Anand."

"The treasure originated in India," Tamarind repeated. "What do you think it was?"

"I'm trying to think what it could be that fits with that timing." I shook my head. "The ruling governance had changed from the British East India Company to the British Raj by then. There was a lot of wealth, but I don't know about anything that was being given to America. We weren't big players yet. Indian kings were giving gifts to Europeans, not Americans. And since the papers didn't report further details, I'm not sure how to narrow it down."

"You don't have to convince me," Tamarind said. "I know how big a country India is to research."

"It was both British trading wealth and also rich princely states that had treasures. That's why Anand was involved in the nationalist movement—sticking up for the little guy rather than colonizers or local royalty. My mom told me that he knew the men who created the symbolic Heart of India statue before it was swept out to sea during a bad monsoon season. India is a country full of treasures like that. You must have read about the treasure hoard discovered in the Sri Padmanabhaswamy temple in Trivandrum not too long ago. There's no shortage of possible treasures."

"I'm trying to think about how we can narrow it down," Tamarind said.

"I should have made him tell me what the treasure was before I would help him."

"You couldn't have known," Tamarind said. "Besides, I'm the one who's good at convincing people to tell things they don't want to tell." Her nose ring sparkled in the light as she smiled mischievously. "But hang on. This article doesn't say anything about a treasure. In fact, it says his crew attacked this ship and scared the crap out of them, but then they didn't steal anything."

"There were four more references to Pirate Vishnu in the paper," I said. "Three were just regurgitations of other articles and didn't say anything new. But one mentioned another ship that was attacked. During this attack, Pirate Vishnu and his crew took the ship."

Tamarind took the article printout from my hand, her bright red lips hanging open. "A crew member of the ship that was attacked reported a Negro man with a Chinese crew," she summarized, "but I'm guessing that's our guy."

"I doubt the sailor had seen many dark-skinned people from the south of India. And it's only a week later than the first article. The same reporter identified them as the same crew on the same ship."

"No deaths," Tamarind read. "They organized, attacked, and stole the entire ship, but they didn't kill anyone, or even maim anyone. It looks like that was much to the reporter's disappointment. His story is on the front page but below the fold." Tamarind frowned as she finished the article. "Even though they took the ship, there's still nothing reported about what the ship was carrying besides average trading supplies."

"I have an idea about that," I said. "What if he stole something that was *already stolen*?"

"Shut. Up."

"That would explain why it wasn't reported," I said. The facts were falling into place. I'd need more evidence to be sure, but I felt like I was finally onto something.

"You are *the man*, Jaya."

"Look at the facts here," I said. "On their first try, they attacked the wrong ship. That's why they didn't care at all about that ship and abandoned it."

"They were after something specific," Tamarind said.

"But what was it they stole?"

Tamarind grinned at me. "I have something to inspire you." She snuck behind her desk and reappeared a few seconds later. She handed me a sticker of a pirate flag—the skull and crossbones.

"I got this to put on my phone," she said. "But I think it's more appropriate for you to have today."

My stomach rumbled as I put the sticker in my back pocket.

"I need a snack break," I said.

"Not without me. You can't drop a pirate bombshell and not think it through without me. Let me get Sarah to cover for me."

I slung my messenger bag over my shoulder while Tamarind

went to talk to one of her colleagues. She came back a minute later with a sour expression on her face.

"I can't take another break yet," Tamarind said. "Sometimes I don't know how I ended up working for the Man." She scrunched up her face in silent protest.

"Back soon," I promised.

Walking out of the library, I headed down the few steps in the direction of my favorite campus coffee house. As I walked I noticed someone walking alongside me. A man with a black hooded sweatshirt took slow strides a few feet away. His hood was pulled over his head in spite of the warm day. His gait wavered, like he was nervous or high.

I hurried my pace, and the man fell back. I was just being paranoid because of everything that was going on. Even though it was summer, there were still people around campus. And this was San Francisco. Some of them were bound to be strange.

I relaxed. It was the wrong thing to do. As soon as I turned to look the other way, the man knocked into me. He slammed into my shoulder, knocking me to the ground.

"Hey!" I yelled, pain shooting up through my elbow and tail bone.

The man held out his arm. It wasn't an attempt to help me up. I felt a sharp tug across my body. He was after my bag.

I had my bag slung across my body, so although the sharp tug caught me off guard, my attacker didn't manage to pull the bag away.

Ready for his second attempt, I bent my knees from my prostrate position, planting my feet flat on the ground, and took firm hold of the strap of my bag. As he gave a second tug, my body lifted up along with the bag slung over my body. I pushed with my leg as he pulled, and we stood directly in front of each other. That's when I saw his face. Or rather, the lack thereof. A stocking was pulled over his head, obscuring his appearance.

Like most people, this man stood quite a bit taller than me. Between the pantyhose distorting his features and the bulky sweatshirt covering much of his body, that's about all I could tell.

Before I could cry out again, he gave another sharp yank to the strap of my bag, higher this time. It pulled across my back, yanking me sideways and knocking the breath out of me. The strap caught under my arm. He didn't loosen his grip.

None of the few people walking by on the far side of the quad seemed to be paying the slightest bit of attention to us. I was on my own. I spun on my heel to face away from the attempted thief. I lowered my center of gravity and heaved.

It's easier to throw someone over you than you'd imagine. As a small person, it's one of the most important things I've learned. The man tumbled over me with ease, landing on his back. He was even lighter than I'd imagined. My assailant groaned as he hit the concrete.

I didn't think, but acted on instinct from years of training. When you attend a self-defense or martial arts class where they send one big guy after another at you, you learn to react. But what they don't teach you is to think about your possessions along with your physical self. The man had kept hold of my bag as he twisted over me. As I flipped him over me, my bag went with him.

As soon as I realized what I'd done, I lunged forward. The man rolled away with my bag.

My right palm skidded across the concrete in my desperate forward grasp, leaving skin behind. I landed on my elbow. The mugger didn't look back. As pain throbbed in my hand and elbow, he jumped up and sprinted away.

All I could do was watch as he disappeared around the side of the building—and along with him, my laptop and Anand's map.

CHAPTER 14

I paced the hallway of the police station, silently cursing my lack of forethought. I *knew* that Steven had been killed over that treasure, and I had the map he believed led to the treasure. I'd had a false sense of security because I was at my university, a place I felt safe.

Though Steven's death happening right after he came to see me could have been a coincidence, another, completely separate act of violence related to this treasure couldn't be. I found it hard to believe the mugger had been after the academic research notes I'd pieced together for the paper I was working on—even though I have to say my theory about the organization of economic, political, and military factions was rather brilliant. And I never buy the latest phone or computer gadgets, yet the mugger had been hanging around the library waiting for me *specifically*. The only thing that made sense was that he was after the treasure map. What would he have done if I hadn't stupidly lost hold of the bag? I didn't want to think about it.

Even though the mugging had to be about the map, the attacker had gotten something far more important to my normal life: my laptop. I'm good at backing up my files, but I'd been distracted from the moment Steven came to see me. Besides hitting "save" regularly, I couldn't remember if I'd backed up any of that full day's work on my cloud server. As soon as I was done at the police station, I could use my office desktop computer to check for my latest backup. I took a deep breath and hoped for the best.

Even if my research paper was safe, there was something I had no chance of recovering. I'd backed up the treasure map with a photo—but hadn't counted on my phone being stolen. I swore.

I wasn't sure which loss I was more upset about at that moment. My paper on the British East India Company and the Battle of Plassey was so close to being done. The paper had been accepted by a prestigious academic journal, but they'd requested revisions that they were waiting for. The last handwritten notes I'd taken were tucked into my bag as well. I knew I could recreate the work, but it would take time, which I didn't have. The editors were waiting, and the semester would be starting soon. I'd worked hard to get here, and I needed this paper to have a shot at tenure against Naveen. I couldn't afford to have my work set back.

I wasn't usually such a negative person, but I couldn't think of a single thing that was going right at the moment. First Lane, now all of this. My stomach rumbled again. I'd never gotten that snack, so now on top of everything else, I was starving. I hated being hungry.

While I waited to talk to someone, I came up with a silver lining, albeit a small one. I'd left my pirate discovery research at the library. Whoever now had the map didn't also have more information about Anand. As far as I knew, I was the only one who'd made the connection that Uncle Anand was Pirate Vishnu.

The police officer who took my statement gave me some antiseptic and gauze for the concrete scrape on the ball of my hand and elbow. He looked all of twenty-two years old, but was a nice guy.

"A *treasure map*?" he said. "*Really*? You want me to write that in the list of items stolen?"

I guess I had my answer about whether I should have gone to the police with what I knew about Steven Healy.

Since the mugger had also gotten my phone, the policeman let me use a phone at the station to cancel my credit cards, ATM card, and phone. I even got in a call to Tamarind at the library to tell her why I hadn't returned.

I kept my keys in my jeans pocket—otherwise they always find their way to the very bottom of my bag—so at least I had my car and house keys. My injured elbow stiffened as I fished my keys out of my pocket on the way to my car. The pain from my hand and elbow was fully kicking in now that my adrenaline had worn off. I'd broken my arm the previous year, and even though it healed cleanly, it made me nervous when I got an arm injury.

I knew I should have gone home, taken some painkillers, and put ice on my elbow. But there was no way I was going home yet.

On the ground floor of the history department building, I was too anxious to wait for the elevator. I ran past the group of faculty chatting in the hallway and bounded up the stairs, praying that I'd remembered to back up my files the previous afternoon. I did most of my work on my laptop, since I could bring it with me between home, office, and the library, so I rarely used the office computer provided by the university. But the desktop computer was networked, so I'd be able to see if I'd dropped my files into the remote backup after my day of work before Steven Healy had interrupted me.

I was only a little bit out of breath when I reached my floor. I burst through the stairwell door near my office. A petite woman around my age gave a start as I did so. She jumped up from where she was crouched in front of my office door. It looked like she'd been about to slip a folded piece of paper underneath it.

"Can I help you?" I asked. She looked familiar, but I couldn't place her. I didn't think I knew her, but...

"This is your office?" she asked. Her eyes were red and her eye makeup smeared.

"That's right."

"I needed to see you," she said. She clutched the folded note tightly in her hand. "I'm Christine Healy."

That's why I recognized her. She was Steven Healy's daughter-in-law. She looked nothing like the perfectly made-up woman photographed in the news the previous year. Her rich brown hair was pulled back into a messy pony tail, and she hadn't made any attempt to fix her running makeup.

"I tried calling first," she said, "but I couldn't reach you, and it's important I talk with you."

"I'm so sorry for your loss," I said. Why did Christine Healy need to see me? I hoped it wasn't to retrieve the map.

She acknowledged it with a small nod.

"I was going to return his map—" I began.

"No, no," Christine said, waving off the suggestion. "We don't care about that. You can keep his awful map. God knows it's brought us enough grief already."

"Well, about that—"

"It's my husband, Connor," she said, urgency in her polished voice. "He knows his father went to see you right before he was killed. There's something you need to understand about Connor. He's not a bad man. But he's... unstable."

"You think he killed his own father?" I asked. "Shouldn't you go to the police with this—"

"No, it's not that," she said, reaching out to grip my uninjured hand. "I worry about what he'll do if this miserable treasure becomes a story in the news. I'm trying to keep Connor away from the newspapers by keeping them out of the house, but he can read whatever he wants online..."

"What is it you wanted to see me about?" I asked, confused by her rambling. "If it's not about getting the map back—"

"Oh, I suppose it is about the map, in a way," Christine said, keeping a cold hand firmly grasped around mine. "I know you're a historian, good at looking into things like the map Steven brought to you. I only hope that whatever you do with the map, you won't make a big deal about it to those media vultures. We had some trouble with them in the past... I don't know if Connor could handle it if this attention carries on much longer."

"You don't have to worry about me going to the press," I said. "I was trying to tell you a moment ago—the map was stolen."

Christine gasped. She let go of my hand and took a few steps back. "What do you mean it was stolen? He just gave it to you."

I held up my bandaged hand. "I was mugged."

"Oh, no," Christine said. She stumbled backward until the hallway wall stopped her.

"Are you all right?" I asked.

"No. I mean yes." She shook her head and tried to smile as she forced a little laugh. "I'm on edge from everything that's happened to our family, that's all. I'm sorry to have bothered you."

Without a backward glance at me, Christine Healy ran down the hallway and out of sight.

What was that about? She was frightened, but of *what*?

I told myself my brain would be more functional when I was safely back at home with ice on my aching elbow.

Slipping into my office, I turned on my computer and tapped my foot anxiously. It wasn't a slow machine, but every second felt like minutes.

I groaned as I checked my files. I'd made my last backup two days before.

I closed my eyes and thought back to the knock on my door that had started this mess. I remembered that I'd closed my laptop after hitting "save," and then promptly forgotten all about my own work. I hadn't followed my usual routine since the moment Steven Healy walked through my door.

As I headed for home, my emotions turned from pity to anger. I swung by a cell phone store, but without a credit card they told me they couldn't give me a new phone. I could have gotten a prepaid one with a new number, but how would anyone reach me? I couldn't call them either, since I didn't know their phone numbers. That's what phones were for. I drove the rest of the way home and walked warily up the stairs to my apartment.

I wish I could have said I knew something was amiss as soon as I stepped through the door. But honestly, I was exhausted. I doubt I would have noticed if a pack of monkeys was raging a war in the corner of the apartment.

I kicked off my shoes and walked to the kitchen to get some ice for my elbow. The only thing I needed to do was clear my overstimulated mind of everything that was going on around me. Well, taking some painkillers and eating would have been nice, too, but both meant venturing back out into the world, which I was in no mood to do. It was only a little over an hour before I had to be at the Tandoori Palace. Juan would feed me something delicious to cheer me up. I opened the freezer door and let the cold air wash over me.

It wasn't until I heard the voice from only a few feet away that I realized I wasn't alone in my apartment.

CHAPTER 15

San Francisco, 1903

The scream sounded almost inhuman. But the voices laughing were very human.

"What was that?" Anand asked as he pulled his coat on outside the doors of The Siren's Anchor. In the month since Anand had met Li, the two had become good friends, frequently visiting the welcoming saloon.

"It's best not to concern yourself with other peoples' business," Li said.

Another scream sounded. It was definitely human. A child. Anand ran down the dark alley without thinking.

"What are you doing?" Li shouted behind him. He swore something in Chinese that Anand didn't understand, but Anand heard his footsteps following.

The Chinese boy couldn't have been more than twelve years old. He lay sprawled on the ground, leaning on his elbow as he tried to push himself up. Blood flowed from his mouth and nose. One of his arms fell at an unnatural angle.

Four grown men stood above the boy. One of them held a metal bar in his hand. They looked up as Anand's feet came to a stop on the gravelly back street. Li followed seconds later, bumping into Anand in the poor light.

The man with the metal bar squinted at Anand and Li. The other men looked to their leader. The boy on the ground whimpered.

"This doesn't concern you," the man said in a slow, measured voice, with the hint of an accent Anand did not recognize.

"He's only a boy," Anand said, thinking of his own brother, Vishwan.

"The boy is a thief. You and your chink friend have five seconds to turn around before you'll be very sorry."

"I am never sorry," Anand said. "I have already died, and here I am. I have no fear of death. But I am guessing you do. I am going to give you and your friends those five seconds to leave, or it is you who will be very sorry."

Li gasped, as did two of the leader's men. The mouth of the man with the metal bar hung open, but he didn't make a sound.

"One," Anand said. "Two."

The smallest of the four men ran away.

"Stop!" the leader shouted after him. He turned his gaze to Anand. "Nobody tells me what to do." He lifted the weapon over his head.

Anand pushed Li out of the way, and ran past the man to help the boy off the ground. But the other two men began to move. One of them grabbed Anand's arms while the other one punched him in the stomach. He knew pain was meaningless, but it still hurt like hell. He would have fallen to the ground had it not been for the man holding his arms.

Li tackled the man with the weapon, wrapping his arms around the man's mid-section from behind, but the man was twice his size. Li was but a minor annoyance as the man stepped toward Anand, dragging Li with him.

"This doesn't look like a fair fight," said a new voice. It was the voice of an Irishman. He stood on the other side of the alley. Anand looked up and caught a glimpse of the newcomer just as a punch hit the side of his face. Pain seared from his jaw. He tried to focus his vision.

"Jesus Christ," the leader said. "What the hell is this? A party?"

"Just evening the score," the newcomer said. He took what looked like a step backward, but Anand saw what he was doing. His foot connected with a pile of dirt. He kicked up the dirt into a cloud of dust. The Irishman ran forward through the distracting dust cloud.

A smile crossed Anand's face right before another punch landed on his jaw.

Anand woke up choking. The sound of rain beat down, but Anand didn't feel the rain on his body. He lay on a soft surface. Pain pulsed through his head and midsection. For a moment, he was fifteen years old again, unsure of his surroundings but sure he was close to death. But this time was different. His unconscious sleep had not shown him a peaceful light. Only darkness punctuated by the taste of dirt and blood.

Now he tasted whisky on his tongue.

"I told you it would work," an Irish voice said.

"Anand," Li said. "Can you hear us?"

"Nobody's dead," the Irishman said. "So you can open your eyes and stop faking it."

Anand opened his eyes to glare at the Irishman. His expression softened when he saw the badly swollen eye that dominated the man's face.

"This is Samuel," Li said. "He was a boxer in Ireland before catching a steamer out this way for the Alaska Gold Rush in '99."

"I thought that ended in '98," Anand said, pushing himself into an upright position. Until he spoke, he hadn't realized how parched he was. He wondered if his own face looked as bad as Samuel's.

"The news didn't reach me until I was already in San Francisco," Samuel said, handing Anand a half-empty bottle of whisky.

Anand took a drink to moisten his throat. Looking around, he saw he was in a boarding house room, but not his own.

"And now you patrol the streets of San Francisco doing good deeds?" Anand said.

"I like fair fights. This one was not."

"How long have I been unconscious?"

"Only an hour."

"Where are we?"

"My place," Samuel said. "It's right around the corner from the alley. Your friend helped me carry you here. Nothing is broken, so your friend didn't want to take you to a doctor."

Anand nodded. Pain shot through his jaw from the movement. He raised his hand to his face and felt a solid bump. But Samuel was right. Nothing appeared to be broken.

"What about the boy?" Anand asked.

"Ran off home," Li said. "He whispered something to you before he ran away, but I think you were already unconscious."

"Yes," Anand said, nodding more carefully this time.

"You saved his life, my friend," Li said. "Don't make a habit of it."

CHAPTER 16

"I thought you were dead," said the intruder in my apartment.

I whirled around.

"You ever hear of checking the messages on your phone?" he continued.

Sanjay sat on the couch with his cell phone in one hand and a splayed pack of cards in the other.

"People have been murdered around you," Sanjay continued. "It's not nice to leave me hanging like that."

"You know I hate it when you do that," I said. "Would it really be too much to ask that you don't break into my apartment whenever you feel like it?"

"I was worried. You didn't answer your phone or return my calls. What happened to your arm?" Sanjay's eyes focused on the gauze bandage wrapped around my palm.

"I was mugged earlier. That's why I don't have my phone."

Sanjay jumped up, spilling the deck of cards onto the floor. "That's why I scared you! Jaya, I'm so sor—"

"Forget it," I said. "I'm fine. And you didn't scare me. You just *disturbed* me." I turned away from Sanjay, grabbing a handful of ice and wrapping it in a kitchen towel.

"Please tell me this was a random mugging," Sanjay said, "that you were just in the wrong place at the wrong time."

"He got the map. Along with my phone that had the picture of the map."

Sanjay breathed deeply. "You aren't badly hurt?" he asked, watching me as I leaned against the kitchen counter and rested the ice on my elbow.

"Superficial."

"Good," he said. "Then I can still be pissed at you."

"For *what*?"

"You fought back, didn't you? Because you knew you'd lose your only copy of the map. That's why you got hurt."

"He got my laptop, too."

"You're going to get much more seriously hurt one of these days."

"Thanks, *dad*."

Sanjay's olive skin flushed. "This is serious."

"I know." The ice wasn't helping, so I tossed it into the sink and went to the kitchen junk drawer. I took out a map of San Francisco and opened it up on my small round dining table. I instinctively reached for my bag before remembering it was gone. Sanjay didn't speak and I rummaged through more drawers to find a red marker. I drew an X on the location that had been marked on the original hand-drawn map. I wrote *Lost* and *Found* where they had been marked before. I wouldn't have a chance to check the translations now. I circled the few buildings I remembered being drawn on Anand's map.

"What are you doing?" Sanjay asked.

"Isn't it obvious?"

"You can't be serious about recreating the map. *You're going after the treasure?* Weren't you listening when I told you earlier about the new information about Steven Healy? That's why you got mugged. This is dangerous. Not a retired man's hobby like we thought, but something big. Something that could get you killed."

"After what Tamarind and I discovered today, I definitely need to go back."

"They *know about you.*" His dark eyes creased down at the edges. "I don't want anything to happen to—wait. What did you say? You discovered something?"

"Yeah, it looks like it might be a treasure originally from India, and—"

"Never mind," Sanjay said, cutting me off. "I shouldn't have asked. I don't need to know. *You* don't need to know either. I don't want to encourage you about this thing and doing something stupid."

"When have I ever done anything stupid?"

"Do I need to remind you about what happened earlier this summer? You didn't tell me what was going on, and look at the mess you got yourself into."

"I don't have to tell you everything I do. You're not my dad. You're not even my boyfriend."

Sanjay turned bright red. "Of course not. I just meant—"

"I didn't do anything stupid there," I said, "and I'm not going to do anything stupid now."

"Right." Sanjay paused to pick up the deck of cards he'd spilled on the floor. "In that case, I suppose you should tell me what you found out at the library."

I still had the pirate flag sticker in my back pocket. I handed it to Sanjay.

"Tamil pirates?" he asked.

I stared at Sanjay. "How did you know?"

"It's just one of those things one picks up."

"About my Uncle Anand, the pirate?"

"What are you talking about?" Sanjay asked. "I was talking about this flag. You said you'd learned something about an Indian treasure and showed me this."

"So you don't know about Pirate Vishnu?"

"Who's Pirate Vishnu? I was talking about the Jolly Roger pirate flag."

"I thought the flag was English. Or at least European of some sort."

"Yeah, but one of the theories of where the *name* of the pirate flag came from is that it was named after the Tamil pirate Ali Raja. You know the English with their nicknames. They called him and his flag Ally Roger or something, which evolved into the Jolly Roger. You don't know this? Jaya, you really are the worst Indian ever."

"You know too much random Indian trivia."

"What does the pirate flag have to do with Anand?"

"Tamarind and I discovered why he would have needed to draw a treasure map—he was a pirate in the San Francisco Bay a hundred years ago."

"A real pirate who commandeered boats and made people walk the plank?"

"As far as the newspapers reported, he didn't make anyone walk the plank. But the year he attacked ships was the same year of Anand's letters home that Steven Healy was after."

"Listen," Sanjay said after scowling at his phone, "are you really all right?"

"I'm fine."

"Then I should go. I have to stop by the benefit theater before our music set tonight to check on something. But if you'd rather not be alone, you could come with me to get familiar with the stage."

"Why would I need to do that?"

"You agreed to be my assistant tomorrow."

"No, I didn't."

"Yes, you did. Jaya, it's just this once. Grace is gone. I can't do it alone."

"Can't you do card tricks like the one you were practicing?"

"Don't you want to help the orphans?"

"Orphans?"

"Well, it's not *only* orphans. It's a homeless benefit, like I told you. I'm sure many of them were formerly orphans. It's a good cause."

I felt my will caving. I was now ridiculously behind on my research paper, had to get a new computer and phone, needed to find out how my family history could have been so wrong, and on top of it all I had to be careful in case a murderer was after me. But how could I say no to such a request from my best friend?

"What do I have to do?" I asked.

Sanjay grinned. "Show up at the Folsom Street Theater at noon tomorrow and I'll show you. Bring some shoes that make less noise than your usual heels."

A flower appeared in his hand out of nowhere. He handed it to me and was out the door.

After closing the door and making sure it was firmly locked, I pulled at the petals on the flower. The flower wasn't plastic or silk, but was a real daisy. Sanjay was good. It reminded me of the first time we ever met.

It had been on the first day I moved to San Francisco a year before. I was moving into the apartment above Nadia's house. My clunky old car had been double-parked in front of the Victorian. It was before I inherited my roadster from my dad's friend. I'd been bouncing around for so long that I hadn't acquired any furniture, so all of my earthly possessions, aside from my books, fit in my car. I'd just carried a box of clothes inside. I walked back outside and found Sanjay sitting on the back bumper of my car.

Of course I didn't know his name at the time. What I saw was a fashionably dressed South Asian man with meticulously styled hair, somewhere around my age, holding a bowler hat in his hands.

"This your tabla?" he asked in a California accent.

My tabla drum case sat nestled lovingly between a duvet and a bag of sweaters.

"If you're the owner of a local live music venue, the answer is yes."

Sanjay smiled the broadest of smiles, revealing the whitest of white teeth. Out of nowhere, a bouquet of flowers popped into his hand.

"Almost as good," he said, handing me the flowers.

I sniffed two fragrant red roses and looked up at him in surprise. "These are real."

"But of course."

"How did you—?"

"A magician never reveals his secrets."

"One of the roses is a little squished." I prodded a limp red petal.

"Really?" He got up from the bumper of my car to inspect the petals more carefully. "Damn. I thought I'd solved that."

"You were telling me how you were going to give me a moonlighting job."

"I can't give you one myself, but I can get you one."

The next night I brought my Indian drums to the Tandoori Palace, and the rest is history.

A knock on my door startled me from the memory. I reached for the doorknob without looking through the peep hole, figuring Sanjay had forgotten something.

Instead, an unsmiling man with an unruly head of black hair stood in my doorway. Maybe Sanjay was right and I was in over my head. I was about to slam the door and hope for the best when the dark-haired man held up a badge in his hand.

"Inspector Valdez," he said. "Homicide."

I didn't know whether to be relieved or not.

"You Jaya Jones?"

"That's me."

"You want to tell us why a murder victim gave you a handwritten receipt for a valuable object hours before he was killed?"

CHAPTER 17

"You're talking about Steven Healy," I said to the detective standing in my doorway.

He nodded but didn't speak. Was he waiting for me to say something else? He watched me for a few seconds.

"May I come in?" he asked after I didn't continue.

I stepped aside.

Valdez took his time stepping inside. He walked slowly, looking around as he did so. Had I just given him permission to search my apartment by letting him in?

He could have been anywhere between forty and sixty. His tan face had the weathered look of either a long life or a hard one. His black hair showed only the faintest touches of gray. A close-cropped beard covered his face.

"What's your connection to Steven Healy?" he asked.

"I'm a history professor," I said. "He came to see me for help with some historical research. That's why he looked me up and left an old historical document with me, so I could conduct further research."

The inspector nodded but didn't speak.

To fill the awkward silence, I had the urge to keep talking. But I didn't.

"You know him for long?" he asked once it was clear I wasn't going to say anything else.

"I met him for the first time yesterday."

"I tried to reach you at your office," Valdez said, "as well as on your phone. You're a tough woman to find. This apartment of yours doesn't exist."

"My phone was stolen when I was mugged earlier today," I said, hoping television shows were right that homicide detectives didn't care about illegal apartment dwellings.

His face registered surprise.

"You didn't know I was mugged today?" I asked.

He frowned as he pulled a phone out of his scruffy jacket pocket and scrolled through his messages. His clothes and the stance of his body said to the world that he wasn't really trying. But his eyes told another story.

"Where was this?" he asked, looking up from the phone.

"Outside my university library," I said. "A few hours ago. Midafternoon today. The mugger stole the map Steven Healy gave to me yesterday."

"You gave a description of your attacker?"

"I couldn't see his face. He had a stocking over it."

"What else was stolen?"

"He also got my laptop and phone."

"The receipt we found said the map he loaned you was valuable."

"Maybe. I was helping him figure that out."

"You two were close?" Valdez asked. He scratched his beard and glanced around my apartment, seemingly uninterested in the conversation. I had a feeling he wanted me to think he wasn't nearly as sharp as his observations indicated.

"I told you, I only met him yesterday."

"Oh, right." He looked back at me. "You mentioned that."

"Look, Detective—"

"It's Inspector," Valdez said.

"He needed help with some historical research." I paused. I knew I should tell him everything and let the police take care of it, but I didn't know how to convince him that a treasure map from a century ago had the relevance to today that I knew it had.

"You were going to say something else," Valdez said.

"He thought," I said, "that the map led to a treasure. That's why someone must have stolen the map."

"A treasure? What kind of treasure?"

"He didn't tell me."

Valdez scratched his beard again. "Didn't that seem odd to you?"

"Of course it seemed *odd*," I said. "This whole thing is odd."

"What seems strangest to me," Valdez said, "is that a man who had lost everything would loan out something so valuable."

"I didn't know that about him when he came to see me."

"Why did he come to you?" Valdez asked. "I know, I know, you're a historian. I get it. But there are a lot of you guys around. Wouldn't he have gone to someone with more experience?"

"You mean someone older?" I said. "He thinks—thought—an ancestor of mine was the one who drew the map."

"His son and a good friend of his say this was something big he was looking into. Did he have a partner?"

"The mugger?"

"Or maybe you," Valdez suggested.

I stared at him. I suddenly felt my heart beating in my throat. "You don't think that I had anything to do with—"

"You say this mysterious treasure is what got Steven Healy killed, and that he just handed a valuable treasure map over to you. Seems awfully strange for someone he'd only met a few hours beforehand, wouldn't you say?"

"Not really." Was my voice shaking? But surely anyone who'd been accused of something would be nervous. "He couldn't find the treasure without help, and he thought I could help."

"Exactly. He needed a partner."

"But I just met him," I stammered. "Surely you can check phone records or something."

"This mugger," Valdez said, "he took your whole purse? Including your wallet, like any mugger would take?"

"Wait, now you *don't* think it's connected?"

"This can be a dangerous city. You're a petite young woman. Easy prey."

My muscles tensed. "I can take care of myself."

"I can tell. The way you hold yourself. I wouldn't want to mess with you."

Damn. He'd elicited the reaction he meant to.

"I'll bet you have no trouble hitting someone hard enough to do some real damage," Valdez continued. "As a strong woman who can take care of herself."

"That doesn't mean—"

"Where were you yesterday evening?"

"You mean, do I have an alibi?"

"Just getting all the facts together."

"I play music at the Tandoori Palace restaurant," I said. "I was there last night."

"No kidding." He smiled. "My daughter loves that place. You were there all evening after Steven Healy left your office?"

"Oh. I had an errand to run in Berkeley first."

"You care to elaborate?"

Aside from being suspected of murder, discussing my break-up was the worst thing I could think of telling a homicide inspector. I scribbled Lane's name and contact information on a piece of notepaper.

"I was with him," I said.

"Have a good evening, Miss Jones. I'll be in touch."

I wasn't arrested, but I didn't feel at all at ease after the inspector left.

There was no way I was going to take a nap now. A nervous tingling crept up the back of my neck. Should I have gone with Sanjay as he'd suggested? What if it hadn't been a police officer who'd been behind the door?

I reached for my phone to call Tamarind, but remembered I didn't have it anymore and wouldn't until my new credit card arrived. Without my phone or laptop, I was completely isolated from the world. What did people do before phones?

Not wanting to be alone in my apartment, I went downstairs to see if Nadia was around. She wasn't.

I admit I felt a bit ridiculous driving back and forth from the university so many times that day, but I didn't want to be alone at the house.

When I got to the library, I didn't see Tamarind's blue hair at the front desk, but I knew she wasn't due to get off work yet. I found her in the stacks.

"Jaya!" she whispered with more enthusiasm than I thought possible for a whisper. "You are *the man*. Did you really go all Kung Fu on a mugger?"

"Jiu jitsu, actually. But it didn't work. He got my bag."

"I'd have been there with you if it hadn't been for the authoritarian practices of this library," Tamarind grumbled. "I need to raise the issue at our next staff meeting."

"It happened so quickly, you wouldn't have been able to help anyway."

"Like hell—"

"Tamarind," I said, "I think it might have been the same guy who killed Steven Healy."

"Shut. Up."

"He got *the map*. He's after Anand's treasure."

"Did you tell the police about the connection?"

"I tried, but I don't think it worked. And what's up with calling themselves *inspectors* rather than detectives?"

"It's a San Francisco thing."

"The police think I might have something to do with it."

"No way! Because you're related to a pirate? That's totally *ancestor profiling* or something. What are you going to do?"

"Find Anand's treasure before the murderer does?" I said.

"Awesome. I'm in."

I hesitated. Having someone else back me up made the plan more real. Maybe it wasn't the best idea.

"What else can I do?" I said, trying to convince myself more than Tamarind. "Sit back and wait for the police to figure out they shouldn't be focusing on me and should be looking for someone else?"

"Hell no," Tamarind said. "How can I help?"

"The inspector seemed like a really smart guy. He got me to say things I hadn't meant to say. But he's not going to focus on a theft from a hundred years ago, and that's the key to this."

"Your personal librarian is at your service."

"There can't have been many men with the name Anand Paravar in San Francisco around 1900," I said. "We can look through records—"

"He was probably the only one," Tamarind interrupted. "But that won't help us. Jaya, do you realize that's the absolute worst time in San Francisco history to find records about the population? The earthquake and fire wiped out City Hall records. It was one of the great equalizers, letting people reinvent themselves—at least the people who survived. Otherwise I would already have looked."

"There has to be something we can find."

"There is." Tamarind paused. "I did some more digging for you this afternoon. I haven't had this much fun in months. Not since those scientist students found an obscure text about early airplanes and built their own for a fall semester final. You should have seen it—"

"Tamarind."

"Right. I'm babbling because I haven't been able to think of the best way to broach the subject. That's why I didn't come right out with it."

"What are you talking about?"

"You're in a different kind of danger than you think," Tamarind said slowly. "Before I tell you what I found, tell me one thing about your mugger. Then I'll know I'm right. Did you get a look at his face?"

"No, he had his face covered."

"I knew it!" Tamarind said. "I know who's after you."

* * *

With the information Tamarind gave me, I left for the Tandoori Palace. I hadn't yet figured out how I was going to play my set that night. The small and large drum that make up the tabla create the instrument's unique sounds when a musician drums their fingers in different spots while simultaneously running their palm across the drum surface. It's sort of like a DJ scratching an LP on a turntable. With my palm scratched up by my lunge after the mugger, I'd have to be creative that night.

I arrived fifteen minutes early, making Raj smile happily. Juan set a plate of samosas in front of me. "Not spicy tonight," he said, adding a large scoop of hot mustard sauce on the plate. He's a man of few words, but he knows the way to a woman's heart.

I was dipping the last of the fried samosas into the sauce when Sanjay arrived.

"*You* talk to *me* about cutting it close?" I said.

"The Folsom Street Theater isn't set up for the magic arts." He sighed and took off his hat. "The lighting hides nothing."

"You've got a coin stuck behind your ear."

Sanjay grumbled and tucked the coin into his pocket. "You see what they're driving me to? But never mind. Are you all right? No more muggings?"

"I'm better than all right. Tamarind may have solved part of our mystery. She kept searching through historical records. She found one of Anand's friends who he was photographed with in 1905. She thinks he might bridge the gap between past and present. You'll never guess what Anand's friend did for a living."

CHAPTER 18

San Francisco, 1904

The man with the badge didn't believe him.

"Let's try this again," he said, staring down at the handcuffed Anand. "How did the money to pay the workers go missing from the safe?"

"I don't know anything about missing money," Anand said.

"The other workers vouch for each other," the man with the badge said. "You calling them liars?"

Anand braced himself for being punched again. The pain of being hit repeatedly blurred together as the kicks and punches kept coming. It was only after he was close to unconsciousness that the man with the badge believed he hadn't stolen the money. He uncuffed Anand and helped him up. Unable to stand, Anand fell to the floor.

It was the second time he'd lost consciousness in San Francisco. The doctor said his leg had been broken in the beating and that Anand would have to stay off it for several weeks. That meant he wouldn't be able to work. He had a small amount of savings, but he sent much of it home. What would he do for money? No matter. He knew he would figure something out. He always did. It wasn't the lost wages that angered him. It wasn't his fellow workers that angered him at that moment either. It was the police who wouldn't believe he was innocent in spite of all the evidence to the contrary.

Li showed up at Anand's boarding house the next day with a crutch. It was six months after Anand, Li, and Samuel had saved the boy from being beaten. The three friends were now inseparable.

Samuel had been working with Li. Once the swelling around Samuel's eye and cheek went down, he shaved off his beard. The transformation revealed a handsome man with fair skin and strikingly sharp features. Almost exactly Anand's height -- a hair under six feet tall -- Samuel's frame held at least two stones more, all of it muscle. He struck the perfect balance between being gruff and charming, walking that fine line between a fellow you wanted to befriend and a man you were afraid of. It was exactly right for playing tour guide to tourists afraid of Orientals, but who wanted a look at the wild side of life in San Francisco without being shanghaied. Samuel neglected to tell the tourists that a shanghaiing hadn't been much of a problem in over a dozen years. He paid Li a cut of his earnings for taking the gullible visitors to the opium dens Li had shown him.

The smallest of the friends, Li stood only a few inches over five feet. From behind he was often mistaken for a child, for nobody would have thought a Chinese man would have cut off his queue of long hair worn in homage to the Chinese emperor.

The swath of bound hair was mandated by Chinese law, but having been born in California, Li felt no allegiance to the Chinese emperor. His parents settled in San Francisco after his father spent his youth building the transcontinental railroad. Instead of living in his parents' home until he was married -- and probably consigned to stay there even then -- Li moved out at sixteen, cutting off his hair the same day to ensure his father would not insist upon his return.

Anand had learned that Li nearly starved to death that first year on his own, shunned by the Chinese community. In spite of being judged the most intelligent pupil in his Chinese school, Li had few worldly skills at the time. That year taught him much.

To Li, the thought of living an obscure, subservient life was much worse than the thought of death. It was no surprise that he and Anand became fast friends.

Samuel was a different story. Anand remained skeptical of Samuel's motives at the beginning. Drawn from gold rush to gold rush -- or in the latest case, toying with the idea of heading to the Colorado Silver Rush -- Anand was never sure what Samuel was after. It wasn't simply money. Samuel was a hard worker, and could have been making much more money as a laborer instead of chasing belated mineral rushes or showing wide-eyed men to opium dens. It was almost as if Samuel needed to feel that he was getting away with something. He wasn't afraid of hard work, but an honest day's labor was not good enough.

But Samuel had other qualities. He had saved Anand that first night they met, and continued to come through. A few minutes after Li arrived with the crutch for Anand's leg, Samuel walked into the room with a bottle of whisky.

"This should get you through your nights until you're on your feet again," he said, setting the bottle down on the sole dresser in the room. Samuel was a generous friend. "In the meantime, let's get you out of here for tonight."

The two helped Anand down the stairs. It was much quicker than when Anand had gone up by himself.

"Where are we going?" Anand asked, trying to forget about the sharp pain pulsing through his leg.

"Where do you think?"

The sun was setting as they walked through the door of the Siren's Anchor. Anand caught sight of a figure that wasn't quite right. The small man stood at the counter, only it wasn't a man -- another look and he realized it was a woman dressed as a man. But why would a woman disguise herself to get into the Siren's Anchor? It was common knowledge women were welcome.

Li let out an angry burst of words in Chinese, directed at the disguised woman. He rushed over to her and grabbed her elbow.

"Mai!" Li said. He pronounced it like "May."

"Who is Mai?" the woman said in English, avoiding Li's gaze.

"You shouldn't be here, Mai," he said, switching to English.

So this was Li's little sister Mai. Anand had heard about her, but they'd never met. She must have spent hours putting on her disguise. She'd even spread a fine coating of dirt on the lower part of her face, mimicking a beard. It was a nice touch, Anand thought. But Li was right. At fifteen, Mai was too young to be in The Siren's Anchor, disguised as a man or not. He understood why she would want to come. She idolized her big brother, probably even more so after he defied his parents and left home.

"That," Samuel said at the top of his lungs, "is a bloody awful disguise, Mai, my belle. But you've got gumption, I'll give you that. Let me buy you a drink." He motioned to Faye to pour two shots.

The girl let out a string of expletives that would have been impolite almost anywhere else. "Am I so obvious?"

Samuel laughed. Anand wouldn't have liked to embarrass the girl so publicly, but he couldn't help smiling. Samuel was right. She certainly did have gumption.

"They allow ladies in here," Samuel said. "You didn't have to dress up."

"But someone might have recognized me," Mai said, shaking free of her brother's grasp and looking between Anand and Samuel. "You must be Anand. I've heard of you."

"And I of you," Anand said. "I'm honored to meet you."

Li remained silent throughout the exchange, but his face was red and turning darker by the moment.

"If Father finds out you're here--" Li began.

"Father won't let me do anything," she said. "The only reason I have already met your friend Samuel is because he saw us when you were walking with me. How do you expect me to live like that?"

In a swift movement, Li grabbed Mai by the elbow again. As he pulled her out of the establishment, he spoke Chinese in a hushed voice. She squirmed to break free of his hold, but his grip was stronger.

Samuel leaned back against the bar and laughed. Anand stood awkwardly with his crutch a few feet from all of them, no longer amused.

"She's not going to be drinking this shot," Samuel said to Anand. "But I bet you could use an extra one."

The two dozen patrons in the saloon watched the scuffle with only mild interest, going back to their own affairs as soon as the pair disappeared through the door.

Samuel helped Anand to an empty table before collecting their drinks. He wiped off the wooden surface with a towel before resting his elbows on the table. Anand had never seen his friend concern himself with the cleanliness of a bar table before. Now that he was paying attention, he noticed that his friend also wore an expensive, tailored suit under his coat.

"You've grown respectable in the weeks since I've seen you," he said.

"Respectable..." Samuel repeated. "Now that would be something." He swallowed his drink in one gulp. He motioned for Faye to pour him another. Normally she didn't come out from behind the bar to deliver drinks, but Samuel had a way about him.

"It's been a while since you paid off your credit, Samuel," she said. Yet she poured the drink with a smile before returning to her spot behind the counter.

"When Li said he hadn't seen you much recently," Anand said, "I thought you might have taken off for Colorado to try your hand at the silver mines."

He snorted. "You know I've got a bloody bad back."

Samuel said he had a bad back whenever it was convenient for him to say so. From what Anand had seen, Samuel was healthier than most men who worked as shipwrights.

"Prospecting was a bad idea in the first place," Samuel said. "My talents have been wasted all these years. Until now."

Faye scooped up his empty glass and set a new one in front of him.

"Cheers," Samuel said. "To our new life."

"Our new life?"

"Didn't I say? I need your help with one small part of my new occupation."

"Which is what?"

"You lived in New York before coming out west. You've heard of the spiritualists helping people connect with their departed loved ones?"

"I attended a performance once," Anand said. "A man locked himself in a cabinet and proceeded to make ridiculous noises. Two women in the audience fainted."

"Not very impressive, eh?"

"Made for an eventful evening to pass the time instead of shivering in my unheated room. But no, the man himself was unimpressive."

"They say there are men who truly possess the gift."

Anand appraised his friend. "This is why I have not seen you recently? You think you are one of them?"

"Of course not. But haven't you wondered why spiritualism is less popular on this side of the country? The needs of the people are the same."

"Perhaps the people here are more intelligent. They had the sense to leave snow-covered New York."

"Or perhaps," Samuel said, "they have been waiting for a void to be filled."

"You plan to fill it?"

"I have already begun."

CHAPTER 19

"A spiritualist, huh?" Sanjay said.

"Yeah, kinda like a magici—"

"*Nothing* like me," Sanjay cut me off. "A magician who sets out to deceive people is a con artist. I *entertain* people. They know they're being deceived."

"Hit on a touchy subject, did I?"

"This is the kind of misunderstanding that makes people like Nadia dismiss magicians."

"Tamarind thinks it's Anand's friend, the spiritualist, who's after me and who killed Steven Healy."

"Wouldn't he be at least 125 years old by now?"

"She thinks," I said, "that he's back from the grave."

"You're joking."

"The point is that *she's* not joking. Tamarind found 'Spiritualist Samuel' listed in the society pages in the newspaper right after the turn of the last century. He wasn't listed as a con artist, but as a true friend of wealthy San Francisco society, even the Lancaster family. Tamarind's theory is that he was the real thing, that he knew about his friend's treasure, and now he's back from the dead to reclaim it. She says I'm in danger from Samuel's ghost."

"*This* is the person who's been helping you with research?"

"She's brilliant. I'll grant she has some unique ideas, but she's one of the smartest people I've ever met."

Sanjay frowned. "How did she put him together with Anand?"

"It was written in the papers that 'Spiritualist Samuel' was known to appear with his Hindustani guru. There's a photograph of Samuel with an Indian man who looks a hell of a lot like Anand."

"Well, well," Sanjay said. "Anand certainly did get around."

"I don't think they're back from the dead, but this is another piece of the puzzle."

"Remember," Sanjay said, "you're not supposed to be working on this puzzle."

"I don't think I have a choice."

"What's that supposed to mean?"

"The police think I might have had something to do with Steven's death."

"*What*?" Sanjay gaped at me.

Raj stuck his head into the back room. "My wonderful entertainers, there is a table of lovely ladies asking about the entertainment."

Sanjay's face relaxed a little bit. His groupies were here tonight.

On our way out to our makeshift stage, Sanjay paused to kiss the hands of three women in their early twenties. The women blushed and giggled. I hoped I hadn't acted like that when I was that age. Sanjay flirted shamelessly for a few more moments as I took my shoes off and got myself situated at my tabla. I felt a twinge of jealousy as I watched them. What was the matter with me? It must have been because my own love life was a mess.

Raj left our sound set as usual, with my tabla mic turned up more than Sanjay's sitar mic. Sanjay's fans weren't there to hear skillful sitar playing.

I admit Sanjay has a certain charm—if you happened to like tall, dark, and handsome good looks mixed with the overinflated ego of a small child. Regardless of my frustrations with Sanjay, he and I had been through a lot together, and he had always come through. When he was performing a magic show at the Edinburgh Fringe Festival last year, he helped me solve a seemingly impossible theft that affected a friend of mine, even though it meant he had to follow me into a dangerous situation.

Sanjay's groupies were finishing their dinners as we completed our first set of the night. They invited him over to their table for a drink. Their invitation didn't extend to me.

On my way to the restaurant kitchen, I heard Sanjay inviting them to the homeless benefit show the next night. They *ooed* and *ahed*, as if their hearts were melting. Now he'd be Saint Sanjay to them in addition to being hunky Hindi Houdini.

Juan plied me with tandoori prawns. He said he'd accidentally made more of them than an order called for. I wondered if he did it on purpose so he'd have the excuse of feeding the extras to me. Even though I was 30, my small size tended to bring out the parental instincts in people.

Sanjay's groupies ordered a bottle of wine and stuck around for our next set. My hand and elbow ached so I stuck to simple beats, following Sanjay's lead rather than the usual other way around. I transported myself to another time and place during that straightforward set.

I thought Lane and I had shared a connection when we met earlier in the summer. I often made snap judgments about people, and generally that was a good thing. Nadia and I hit it off from the day we were introduced by an old friend of my dad's, and Sanjay felt like family within a month of meeting him. I was so sure I'd been right about Lane, too. I didn't know how I could have gotten it so wrong.

Was I that clueless?

I didn't feel like thinking anymore. When our last set was over, I slipped out without saying goodnight to Sanjay. He was engrossed with his entourage so I doubt he noticed.

The fog was thick outside the restaurant, blowing in from the Pacific Ocean and settling in the nearby hills that surround the Inner Sunset neighborhood. It was heavy tonight.

My eyes darted around as I walked quickly to my car. I'd parked on a small residential street as usual, away from the bustling main drag. I no longer had anything in my possession that anyone wanted, but would that keep me safe? It was not knowing what was going on that was killing me.

In my apartment, I hung the map I'd drawn from memory on the wall. I closed my eyes and tried to remember if there were any other details I had forgotten.

I fell asleep on the couch again that night, but jolted awake before sunrise. I must have been dreaming, because I woke up with my heart racing.

My neck was stiff and my hand and elbow still ached, but I needed a run to clear my thoughts. Even without headphones to listen to music, I ran hard.

As I ran, I remembered the dream I'd had that night. I had been both in India and in San Francisco at the same time, as dreams have the trick of doing. It was raining, but I didn't feel it. Lane was there, whispering to me. I felt his warm breath on my ear, but I heard no sound. When I turned my head to look at him, Sanjay was there in his place, pulling a monkey out of a top hat. He reached back inside to pull something else out. In the dream, I had a feeling I knew what he was going to pull out of the hat. It was something important. But as soon as I woke up, I couldn't remember what it was.

I had the nagging feeling that I was missing something I'd already seen. Was it an illusion, or was there truly something I'd seen that would lead me to that treasure and Steven's killer? I ran harder, but the thought was still a step ahead of me.

I turned to head home, keeping up my fast pace instead of slowing down like I usually do at the end of a run. I needed to check something out.

I took a quick shower and put fresh bandages on my hand and arm before slipping on my heels and heading out the door.

Since I hadn't found any evidence that the map's *MP Craft Emporium* or *The Anchored Enchantress* still existed, I was heading to the western edge of Lands End, where the X was drawn. The national park hugs the northwest edge of the city, looking over the Pacific Ocean to the west and the opening of the San Francisco Bay and the Golden Gate Bridge to the north. It's not a beach, but rather a series of cliffs that drop off sharply to the rocky waters below.

A strange sensation came over me as I reached my car. I glanced around, but didn't see anyone aside from a guy walking his dog and a woman in a suit talking on a cell phone. Neither one paid any attention to me. It must have been my nerves.

As I stepped into my car, I noticed which shoes I was wearing. I'd slipped on three-inch heels after my shower. Since I'm not quite five feet tall, I always automatically wear heels unless I'm going running. But I swore as I realized which heels I was wearing—the pair that Lane had given me in Scotland after I'd lost my shoes.

The X had been drawn over the water, right next to land. Did that mean the treasure was under the water? Or that it was buried right along the edge of the land? Either way, running shoes instead of heels wouldn't help me. There was a paved road and parking lot next to the Cliff House. I'd be fine.

The forest-like park wasn't a popular spot on the overcast day. The fog hung thick over the coastal waters. I saw only a handful of people as I made my way along the path to the lookout point above the water. I passed a sign saying: *CAUTION: Cliff surf area extremely dangerous. People have been swept out from the rocks and drowned.*

I continued on the path, pausing at a lookout point to read a large placard. It named the sunken shipwrecks that lay in the water beneath the cliffs. Most of the ships had their names commemorated, but one was an unnamed ship that must have been far enough off course that it could not be identified. I wondered if any of those ships had ever been attacked by pirates before finding their final resting place off the rocky coastline of San Francisco.

Waves lapped over jagged rocks below. Now *this* was a place where I could imagine a buried treasure. Except for the fact that the whole overlook area had been paved over by concrete. Any treasure here would have either been discovered long ago by workmen or buried deep beneath the concrete. Why had Steven been so sure the treasure hadn't been found?

I watched the crashing waves below, hypnotized by the rhythmic splashing of the surf. I closed my eyes for a moment, letting the cool morning air wash over me and breathe some sense into me. The waves splashed again. The tide was coming in. If I was going to get a closer look, it was now or never.

There were no railings along this wide path leading to the overlook. It wouldn't hurt to step off the path and take a closer look.

I paused for a moment, looking down at my three-inch heels for the second time that day. Perhaps I should have turned back after all. Then again, I'm skilled at walking in these shoes. It's a hell of a lot easier to get used to walking in heels than it is to ask strangers for help whenever you need to reach something at the store. And this side of Lands End wasn't nearly as steep or high as the north side. I stepped off the path.

The area surrounding the path was grassy, not rocky. My heels sank into the earth and kept me grounded as I walked down the steep hill leading to the rocks. The tide was rising quickly. The spray of the ocean tickled my face.

Where the land met rock, I thought of Anand's map. Wouldn't Anand have drawn a more specific location on the map than an X right next to the coast? Unless he'd drawn an X on the spot where he'd hidden the treasure as well. I sighed to myself. There was no X mark on any of the rocks in front of me.

As I began to turn around to head back to the path, the heel of my shoe caught in the earth again. I lost my balance. I pushed my heel into the earth to steady myself. It worked, but only for a second.

The earth gave way beneath me.

My heart pounded in my throat as my body began to slide toward the rocks below. I knew I should cry out, but my vocal chords refused to work. I threw my arms behind me, desperately hoping to grab hold of some weeds strong enough to hold me.

Instead of dirt or grass, my arm made contact with something else. A strong hand grabbed my wrist and pulled me back from the edge.

As I scrambled up and found my footing, the fingers around my arm held tight, not allowing me to fall. Before I turned around, I knew who was holding onto me. It wasn't a stranger pulling me back from the ledge.

It was Lane.

CHAPTER 20

"I wish," Lane said, "that you would at least wear proper shoes if you're going to insist on rooting around at the edge of a cliff."

He let go of my arm only once he was sure I was standing on stable ground, several feet from the edge. Several large pebbles were lodged in my shoes, but I didn't care.

"What are you doing here?" I asked. "You dump me, you clear out of your apartment, but *now* you're following me?"

"Inspector Valdez called me."

If I didn't know him, I'd have sworn his voice was calm. Even distant. But I knew him well. He was forcing himself to act the opposite of what he felt. He was full of some barely controlled emotion and was about to burst.

"Sorry he had to trouble you for an alibi," I snapped. "I know you don't want anything to do with me."

"You don't understand," Lane said. "You don't know what's happened."

"Then why don't you tell me?"

"Jaya, I..."

The fog swirled around us as he broke off. I kicked off my shoes to get rid of the pebbles that had lodged inside when I slipped, while I waited for him to say more. But he didn't go on.

"What?" I said. "What's so hard to say?"

"I was worried," he said, a look of deep sadness sweeping over his face, "that someone from my past had found you."

"What do you mean?"

"I hoped—I wanted so badly to have put my old life behind me."

"Oh my God," I said, starting to shiver in the cold fog. "You had something to do with this! That's why you acted strangely when I came to see you, and why you're leaving!"

I thought about the treasure we had found in Scotland. Lane had been alone with it for a short time before anyone else saw it. I hadn't wanted to think he'd taken any of the jewels. But I'd wondered. As he said, it was hard to leave an old life behind.

"That's not what I meant, Jones."

"You didn't used to be this cryptic," I said.

Though part of my brain told me I was being irrational, I felt completely safe as I stood at the edge of Lands End with Lane. I had no doubt that I could trust him completely with my life. I didn't believe he would harm me, or that he could have been the person who killed Steven. As for stealing a treasure? That was another story. Since Lane wasn't opening up to me, what was I supposed to think?

"The details don't matter," Lane said.

"They matter to me," I snapped.

"What's important is that you're better off without me—and you're better off forgetting about this treasure."

"This is me," I said. "You can cut out the chivalry."

Lane smiled, and for a moment it looked like he was going to lean forward to hug me or kiss me. But he didn't do either.

"When we got back from Scotland," he began, "I knew I wouldn't be able to work with my advisor anymore."

"I get that's why you're on leave. But moving out of your apartment so quickly?"

"My past caught up with me, Jones," Lane said. A pained expression passed over his face. "He found me."

"*Who* found you?"

Lane closed his eyes, as if the memory pained him. "He's not someone you'd want to know."

"You told me you never used violence when you stole things."

"I didn't lie to you about that," Lane said, his eyes snapping open. "Please don't think I would do that. But some of the people I associated with at the time didn't have the same code of conduct."

"He found you because of the picture Fiona took of you," I said. "She gave it to the press." I knew I hated that woman.

Lane nodded slowly, a look of resignation on his face.

"Are you in trouble?" I asked.

"I wasn't sure at first," Lane said. "One of my past associates wanted me to do something for him. I'm good at disappearing, though. I'm not worried about myself. It's you I'm concerned about. I thought he might have gone to you because of *me*. If that ever happened—" He broke off.

"You thought if he knew you were in a relationship with me that he could use it against you?"

"I couldn't live with myself if anything happened to you, Jones. Especially if it was because of me."

"But this map and murder have nothing to do with him."

"It looks that way," he said. "I got away before he could tell me what he wanted from me. But it's only a matter of time before—"

"So you're okay?" I asked. "You're not in danger from this guy right now?"

"I'm fine, but you—"

I cut him off by slapping him.

"What was that for?" he asked.

"If you have to ask, then you're a lot less intelligent than I gave you credit for."

"You're right," he said, rubbing his jaw. "I deserved that."

"You should have told me."

"I thought it would be easier for both of us," he said.

"You mean easier for *you*." I had the worst luck with men. Why did they do one thing when they felt another? "You could tell yourself you were making a sacrifice by breaking my—never mind. There are more important things to talk about. Like why you're following me."

"After Inspector Valdez talked to me, I got worried. I went to your house, and I saw a guy outside looking for you."

"A guy?"

"Indian guy in his late twenties."

"Oh, that's just Sanjay. You don't need to worry about him."

"Sanjay?" he asked.

"My best friend. The guy I called a few times while we were in Scotland. Nothing to worry about."

"He comes to see you early in the morning?" Lane asked. I thought I detected a hint of jealousy in his voice.

"I don't have a land line in my apartment," I said, "and with my cell phone stolen, people have to come see me—"

"Your phone was stolen?"

"I thought you talked to Inspector Valdez?"

"I did," Lane said, his face dark. "He called about your alibi for this murder. Not about your phone being stolen."

"He didn't tell you my bag was stolen, with the map inside?"

"No." His jaw tightened visibly. "He left that out. That's how you hurt your hand?"

"It is."

Lane swore. Vividly. He was losing control of his emotions, and I could tell he wasn't happy about it. When we'd been searching for the person we thought killed my ex-boyfriend Rupert, Lane had kept his cool in the most trying situations. He'd gotten involved at first because of the apocryphal treasure related to his South Asian art history research, but he stayed involved because of me.

"Treasure hunting is a dangerous business," he said. "What is it you've gotten yourself into?"

"If you're going to make a one-sided decision to stay out of my life, you don't have any business knowing." I felt awful fighting with Lane. But it was his fault.

He started to reply with something harsh, but the words caught in his throat. He broke off, but his eyes never left mine. A range of emotions crossed over his face before he finally spoke.

"You're right," he said.

"I am?"

Instead of answering, he walked a few paces away from me. He looked out at the ocean.

"You could help me—" I said.

"I don't have it in me to argue with you anymore," he said, a defeated man speaking to the wind, before turning to face me. "Seeing you... All I want to do is take you away with me."

"You do?" His words weren't what I had expected, but at the same time felt oddly natural.

"Can't you tell?" he asked.

"You could have told me."

"It wouldn't be fair to ask you to go with me," Lane said. "You have a life here."

"So do you."

"Not any more, Jones. Not anymore."

I tried to think of something to say to him, to make him see that he was wrong. But as much as I didn't want to admit it to either of us, I couldn't see how he was wrong.

"I told myself I wasn't going to see you again," he said. "But you forced my hand."

"By almost falling over the edge? I wouldn't have fallen too far, you know. I would have gotten a few scratches but been fine."

"I know," he said, smiling a sad smile and running a hand through his hair. "That's why I know you'll be fine without me."

With that, he turned to walk away. I reached down to slip my shoes back on. When I looked back up, he had already disappeared into the fog.

By the time I reached the theater to meet Sanjay, my stomach was growling loudly enough to rival the voices of the men shouting at each other on the stage, and I was almost angry enough to join them. At least I no longer looked disreputable, having stopped at home long enough to change.

I had no idea where he came from, but suddenly Sanjay was standing next to me.

"I hate it when you do that," I said. "What's going on here?" I indicated the men arguing on the stage.

"Problem with the lights."

"Have you eaten breakfast?" I asked.

"No," Sanjay said.

"Then let's go. But, just so you know, you're buying. I don't have my replacement credit card yet."

"Are you okay? You look like you've seen a ghost."

"I'm fine," I snapped. "Just fine."

We walked down the street to one of the numerous cafés lining the nether regions between SOMA and the Mission. While I ate a croissant and plenty of bacon, Sanjay drank coffee and listened to me go over the latest I'd learned. I don't know why, but I felt extremely awkward mentioning Lane, so I left him out of it.

"You went to the cliffs of Lands End?" Sanjay bellowed. "By yourself?"

"I know you just came from practicing on stage," I said, "but you can cut out the theatrics."

"I am *not* being overly dramatic," Sanjay said through his teeth. "This is a treasure that people have been killed over."

"Sanjay—"

"I'm not going to let anything happen to you, you know."

I rolled my eyes at the stilted dramatics.

"This isn't funny!"

"Sorry," I said. I'd never seen Sanjay like this before.

"If you're not going to back off, then I'm going to help you figure out what's going on."

"Really?"

"I've been thinking about it already," he said. "You said that there are locations on the map that don't exist—both the picture of the Chinese fishing nets, and the names of those locations in the center of the city."

"That's right."

"What if," Sanjay said, "it's *a code*." He sat back, looking very pleased with himself.

"Anand wasn't a *spy*."

He frowned. "You've got a better idea?"

"Sanjay!" I said. I said it louder than was strictly necessary, but I couldn't contain my excitement. I did have an idea. "Give me your phone."

"What for?" he asked, but handing me his phone all the same.

"Because you're brilliant."

"I know. But what does that have to do with this?"

"The map," I said. "I think you're onto something, but not in the way that you meant. Not with Anand being a spy, and not with a code in his letters—but something hidden in plain sight."

"You're losing me."

"Why would someone need to draw a treasure map?" I said.

"Um, because they had a treasure?" Sanjay looked at me as if I was going crazy.

"Because they were *hiding something*," I said. "Meaning they would also need to disguise the map in some way."

I clicked on a map of Kochi, on the northern edge of the old Kingdom of Travancore. I zoomed into Fort Kochi, the central land mass of the port city. It was a perfect fit. I held the screen to Sanjay.

"Why are you showing me an old map of San Francisco?" he said.

"This isn't San Francisco."

This was it, I could feel it.

"This," I said, "is Kochi. The famous spice trade city on the western coast of southern India."

"I know what Kochi is," Sanjay said. He grabbed the phone.

"Anand worked there after he left home as a teenager, before he came to America. He built and fixed boats there, just like he did in San Francisco."

"It's the same," he whispered. "They're the *exact same* shape and orientation. The peninsula with similar land masses to the north and the east. Even the same islands in between."

"And more than that," I said. "Chinese fishing nets line the north coast of Fort Kochi. *This* is what Anand was drawing. The connection he was making. Anand drew this map of Kochi, not San Francisco. Steven said Anand had written to his brother Vishwan about the treasure. He knew his little brother would recognize Kochi if he saw this map."

"That is one good trick," Sanjay said.

"Since Anand had lived in both port cities, he would have realized that their layouts were eerily similar. If his treasure map had fallen into the wrong hands in San Francisco, nobody would have guessed it was a map of a different city."

"And nobody did."

"That," I said, "is why nobody has found Anand's treasure in over a hundred years. They were looking on the wrong continent."

CHAPTER 21

"I can't believe I let someone steal that map!" I paced around the stage at the theater. I was so angry I'd nearly forgotten about my sore hand and elbow. "My memory of it is all screwed up because I'm remembering it as San Francisco. But since it's Kochi, then the locations take on a whole new meaning. The treasure is in India. The answers we need are in India, too. I need that damn map. "

"Let your subconscious work on it," Sanjay said.

I stopped pacing and looked at Sanjay standing under the spotlight.

"That's not like you."

"It is right now," he said. "If we're going to pull off this show, we need to get to work."

"But—"

"If you didn't have to practice, what would you even do?" Sanjay asked.

He had a point. "Fine," I said. "Let's practice."

Even though I wasn't badly hurt, Sanjay insisted we not do any of the physical acts.

"You remember the words and phrases I taught you for mind reading?" he asked.

"People didn't come here for that."

"You're not up for losing your head right now. It's a physical act, tough to get right while injured."

"You'd behead me if I got it wrong?"

"Of course not. But the audience would see the secret of the illusion if it goes wrong. That's almost as bad."

"Grace will be back before your next season starts up in Napa, right?"

"She better be," Sanjay grumbled distractedly as he rooted through a costume trunk. He smiled as he pulled a skimpy red and silver costume out of the trunk.

"You can't be serious," I said. The thought of wearing the shiny costume that had barely more material than a bathing suit was enough to make me forget about my discovery.

"You'll look great in it," Sanjay said. "We want the audience distracted by you. Remember distraction is what we need for the magic to work."

"At least there won't be anyone I know here tonight."

Sanjay cleared his throat. "I, uh, may have mentioned it to Nadia."

I groaned.

"I thought it would convince her not to hate me," Sanjay said. "She likes good causes."

We practiced all afternoon. Mind reading takes concentration, so I had to give it my full attention. Of course it wasn't *truly* mind reading. But it's an illusion that takes some practice.

I remembered most of the key words from when Sanjay had taught me the illusion before, but it took practice to seamlessly pick up on the signal words and give the correct response. My other tasks involved helping Sanjay with a Houdini-like escape, and setting and clearing items from the stage at planned times when he needed a distraction. And damn him, Sanjay managed to convince me to wear the silver costume. It was the best way to be distracting, since my sleight of hand skills were nonexistent.

Even though Sanjay was right that I needed all the practice I could get, I insisted on taking a short break to pick up my new credit card that was being overnighted to me. After getting caught up talking to Nadia, I barely had time to make it back to the theater. I really needed a new system of getting my mail.

The Folsom Street Theater was a quirky little theater in an up-and-coming neighborhood that hadn't yet taken off. The seats looked like originals—classic red velvet upholstered seats a bit smaller than seats made for today's audiences.

Two other acts were appearing on the bill. A comedic magician Sanjay knew, and a local singer-songwriter. The lineup didn't make much sense to me, but when you're a benefit I guess you use your contacts to get what you can.

"I told you that you'd look great in the costume," Sanjay said to me as he straightened his bow tie in the mirror backstage.

I peeked out at the audience, and sure enough, Nadia was there. I looked down at the skimpy costume. The red and silver sparkles would twinkle in the bright lights for the added distraction Sanjay wanted.

I was discombobulated more than nervous. I wasn't accustomed to wearing bright colors and I was only used to being the center of attention when teaching college students subjects I knew intimately. The invisible person tracking down bits of history in libraries all over the world? That was me. Not a colorful stage distraction. Nadia would never let me live it down.

Sanjay and I began with mind reading to warm up the audience. I stood on the stage blindfolded, while Sanjay went through the audience and held up personal items for them to see, but without speaking the name of the item. I identified a diamond engagement ring, a man's loafer, a gym membership card, and a child's doll.

For our concluding audience member, Sanjay gave me the cues to identify a cell phone with a picture of a married couple on the screen.

"I see a phone," I said. "A cell phone. And not only a phone." I acted as if I was concentrating, pressing my fingers into my temples like I imagined a psychic would. "I see an image on the phone. A happy couple."

"Sir," Sanjay said. "Can you tell the audience what you hold in your hand?"

"Yes," said a man's voice. "I'm holding a phone with a picture of a married couple who were once very happy until two days ago when the woman on stage killed my father."

CHAPTER 22

I pulled off my blindfold. My eyes watered in the adjustment from darkness to light as I stared into the bright spotlight pointed at Sanjay and a man standing in the aisle at the back of the theater.

The man standing next to Sanjay looked familiar, but I couldn't place him. He had black hair and Asian features but with piercing blue eyes that glared at me. The woman seated next to him tugged at his arm. His face softened as he turned to look at her. It was Christine Healy. That's when I realized why the man looked familiar. He was indeed his father's son.

Steven Healy's son carried himself with a different type of assurance than his father. This man wore an untucked dress shirt over skinny jeans, rather than a suit, and his short hair had been styled within an inch of its life with hair gel that shone in the spotlight.

I have to hand it to Sanjay, the consummate performer. He handled the situation better than I would have thought possible. He signaled the booth above the seats with an unobtrusive gesture, and the spotlight on the audience instantly cut out. Two new spotlights began to swirl around a spot on the stage several feet away from where I stood. Before I noticed that he'd moved, Sanjay appeared on the side of the stage with the spotlights, ushering the musical performer back on stage. His back to the audience, I saw him mouth "Thank you" to the musician before scooping me backstage.

* * *

Less than a minute later, we were in a dressing room with Steven's son and Christine. Following behind them, Nadia stepped into the room. She was never one to miss a party.

Christine held his arm, as if her gentle touch could hold him back. Nadia's eyes narrowed as she looked between us.

"I'm so sorry," Christine said. Unlike the last time I'd seen her outside my office, her face was perfectly made up. But circles under her eyes betrayed her fatigue.

Steven's son glared at me. Now that I was closer to him, I noticed paint stains on his fingers, and even a spot under his chin. I also smelled alcohol on his breath. I was suddenly very aware that I was wearing a ridiculous slinky magician's assistant costume. I grabbed a shawl from a costume rack and draped it over me.

"Forgive us," she continued. "This is my husband, Connor."

"Jaya Anand Jones," he said. I might have imagined it, but his glassy-eyed glare softened as he looked at me. "You're not what I expected. Dad said he was going to see a history professor. You know we're—"

"We're so sorry," Christine cut in.

"That wasn't what I was going to say," Connor said, shaking Christine's hand off his arm, his attention focused on me. "Did you kill him?"

"I'm so sorry for your loss," I said, "but I don't have any idea who could have killed him—"

"She doesn't look like she's lying," Connor said to his wife. "Is she lying? I thought I'd be able to tell if she was lying." Christine's cheeks flushed, and I wondered how often Connor was this drunk.

"How did you find me here?" I asked.

Nadia clicked her tongue. "They told me they were friends of yours. I thought I was helping by telling your friends where you would be."

"Connor wanted to see you," Christine said, "because we knew his father was working with you—"

"She wasn't working with him," Sanjay cut in.

"I never meant for us to disrupt your performance," Christine said quietly, her eyes focused on the floor.

"You were the last one who saw him that night," Connor said, his paint-stained finger pointing at me. "He gave you that map of his that he thought led to some mysterious treasure. You had to have been the one—"

"This is what the police are for," Nadia said. She spoke in a calming, maternal voice. "They already spoke with her."

"You know about that?" I asked.

"The inspector came to my front door first."

"But they didn't arrest her," Connor said. He stumbled forward toward me. "They should have—"

"One more step," Nadia said, her maternal voice replaced by one of pure ice, "and I will call the police."

"Good," Connor said. "The police should be working harder on my father's—"

A crack sounded from behind us. The greenroom door burst open. A small, dark-haired woman stepped into the room.

Sanjay's assistant Grace stepped toward us—a knife in her outstretched hand.

"Stop threatening Jaya!" she yelled.

Christine screamed as Connor gasped and Nadia dropped her phone. I didn't blame them. I'd never seen Grace like that before. At least not when she wasn't on stage.

Sanjay reached Grace quickly and took hold of her wrist.

He moved her hand so the knife hit his arm. Rather than cutting through the fabric, the blade retracted. Sanjay twisted her wrist a little more and the knife clattered to the ground.

"What the hell?" Connor said, stumbling backward.

"It's a fake knife," Sanjay said. He picked up the knife and demonstrated more slowly how the blade retracted into the hilt.

"The people in front said someone was threatening Jaya," Grace said softly to Sanjay. It sounded like she was back to her usual self.

I couldn't quite figure Grace out, with her combination of shyness and onstage gusto. She was dyslexic and had dropped out of high school, waitressing until she became Sanjay's magician's assistant. He'd noticed the way she held herself as a former gymnast and was impressed by how she mentally kept dozens of orders straight—an instrumental skill for a magician's assistant. Waitressing was one of the things I did during the four years I took between finishing high school at sixteen and starting college at twenty, so I knew what a difficult job it was. It was tougher than getting a PhD in many ways, but I suspected what I'd achieved through my education was why Sanjay imagined that Grace idolized me.

"We're alright, Grace," I said. "It's a misunderstanding."

"What are you doing here anyway?" Sanjay asked her.

"I drove all the way back here after the funeral to help," she said, her voice still barely above a whisper. "I didn't know if Jaya would be able to pull off the show—" She broke off and looked between us. "I wanted to help. But I guess you didn't need me."

Christine took Connor's hand again and pulled him to the door. "We should go."

"Wait," I said.

"Let them go," Sanjay said. "They should talk to the police. Not to you."

Christine led Connor away, passing a stagehand in the doorway.

"You going to go back on?" the stagehand asked.

Sanjay gave a curt nod. "Five minutes."

"You up for taking over for me?" I asked Grace.

Her slumped shoulders shot up. "If Sanjay needs me."

"He needs you," I said. "Believe me, he needs you."

I went to my campus office to use the computer to pull up a map of Kochi. On the full-size screen, I was even more certain of my conclusions. The two cities and their surrounding bodies of water and land masses were virtually identical. The treasure map was Kochi.

I knew about the historical significance of the port city, but I hadn't even given much thought to its modern geography.

The Portuguese, Dutch, and British all laid claim to the city at one point or another before India's independence in 1947. The Portuguese constructed a large fort there, which was later destroyed by the Dutch, but the piece of land that made up the center of the city was still known as Fort Kochi. The peninsula continued to be a strategic trading post with a cosmopolitan population.

I looked up the *MP Craft Emporium* and *The Anchored Enchantress*. Both had been a dead end in San Francisco, but not in India. I was onto something with the *MP Craft Emporium*. There was a whole section of town with craft shops, right where I remembered that building on the map. I couldn't find the exact name of the store, but a store from over a hundred years ago wouldn't have an internet presence. The location fit. This was what I was looking for.

I opened a new tab and looked up flights to south India. There were seats left on a flight to Trivandrum, via Hong Kong, out of SFO the next morning. I impulsively clicked "buy" with my new credit card before I could talk myself out of it. Since I was born in India and had a Person of Indian Origin card, I had a long-term visa. I could travel to India at any time.

Trivandrum was over a hundred miles from Kochi, but the University of Kerala was located in Trivandrum, so I could stop and see the archived letters first. Even without the treasure map, I hoped Steven was right that one of Anand's letters to his brother held the missing piece of the puzzle.

I was finishing filling in the last details to purchase the plane ticket when I was interrupted by someone at my door. Naveen leaned in the door frame and crossed his arms.

"I thought you'd like to hear the news," he said.

"News?"

"I've just signed the contract for a book deal for my work on the historical migration of languages across India."

I would scream if Naveen got tenure over me because of this lost paper. Not that I'd give Naveen the satisfaction of seeing that.

"Congratulations!" I said. "That's great."

"Oh."

"It's not great?" I asked in my most innocent voice.

"Well, yes," Naveen said stiffly. "It's quite an accomplishment. I wasn't sure if you'd see it that way. I know you're still struggling to publish a paper."

I'd co-authored several well-received papers during graduate school, and published a chapter of my dissertation as an article in a magazine that was more general interest than academic.

This latest paper was the first one I'd authored on my own that had been accepted into a prestigious academic journal. I hadn't shared the news with anyone yet, since they were waiting on my revisions.

"A book deal is a great accomplishment," I said. "Not all of us can be so prolific. Especially when on the verge of a major historical discovery."

Naveen frowned. "A discovery?"

"I wouldn't want to bore you with the details," I said. "I know you've got a book to write."

After Naveen left, I tried calling Joseph Abraham, the archivist at the University of Kerala, one more time before leaving campus. My call went to voicemail again. It was morning in India now, late enough that I was hoping the archivist would have been there. I left a message letting him know I'd be stopping by the following day.

The streets were relatively empty at the late hour. I turned up Talvin Singh's tabla beats on the stereo and drove my roadster as it was supposed to be driven.

Back at my apartment, I pulled a suitcase out of the top of my closet and began throwing clothes into it.

A knock sounded on my door. I was really going to have to go get a new phone so people would stop showing up unannounced. I opened the door.

"Miss Jones," Inspector Valdez said, "may I come in?"

Damn. I should have checked.

"It's late," I said.

"I know. I'm sorry, but with your phone stolen it was the only way to talk to you. Connor Healy stopped by the station tonight. I know he and his wife disrupted a magic show you were in tonight. I didn't realize you were a magician in addition to a professor and musician."

"I'm not," I said. "I was only helping a friend. What did Connor tell you? Is he the reason you're convinced I had something to do with Steven Healy's death?"

"He's got some interesting ideas."

"Maybe *he's* the one who did it," I suggested. "His wife thinks he's unstable."

"He's got an alibi."

"From what I can tell, his wife would say anything he wanted her to say."

"They didn't alibi each other," Valdez said. "They were both at an art show with dozens of witnesses."

"I know you talked to the people I was with, too."

Valdez nodded. "I checked out what you told me. Looks like you were on your own for quite a while that evening, stuck in some pretty bad traffic." The homicide inspector ran a hand through his wild black hair. I couldn't tell if he was smiling or stifling a yawn. "I'm not here to arrest you, you know."

"Why did you come?"

"Connor Healy isn't going to bother you anymore. But you aren't planning on going anywhere, are you?"

I shifted the angle of the door to block his view of my suitcase.

"My wallet was stolen, remember?"

I didn't add that my passport hadn't been in my wallet. It was probably best to not completely lie to the police when one was a suspect in a murder.

PART II

THE MONSOON

CHAPTER 23

The plane touched down in the middle of the night.

I was wide awake, my adrenaline pumping with nervous energy. Far away from the danger of a murderer and the confusion of a potential romantic entanglement, a hopeful feeling crept up in me. I wasn't sure I was ready to let myself feel optimistic about the prospect of tracking down the secrets of Uncle Anand and his treasure, but I couldn't quash my excitement.

Why had Uncle Anand been declared a pirate by the San Francisco press? What treasures did he steal from the San Francisco Bay? How did one of those treasures wind up hidden in Kochi? My fingers drummed against my knees as the plane taxied to our gate. I was so close to finding answers to those questions.

Even in the dead of night, the temperature in India could rival San Francisco's hottest day of summer. Stepping outside of the Trivandrum airport, I breathed in the humid air. Muggy, but not sticky. Hot, but not the kind of heat you feel right away, until it catches you off guard and hits you like a brick. There was something about the power of the monsoons that produced a quality in the air I had never felt anywhere outside of India.

Unlike a rainstorm back home in the U.S., monsoon rains are fickle. The rain crashes down full force, drenching everyone to the bone within minutes, then clears out as suddenly as it appeared. It had stopped raining when I emerged from the airport, but I could tell it was in the air.

Since India had been moving back to the traditional city names that existed before British rule, the city of Trivandrum was now called Thiruvananthapuram. The locals still called it Trivandrum; it's significantly faster to say.

Before India became a series of unified states, the city of Trivandrum was part of the princely Kingdom of Travancore. My great-grandfather and great-granduncle grew up thinking of themselves as from Travancore, not as citizens of India.

I caught a cab to my hotel. Three o'clock in the morning was one of the only times the roads weren't overflowing, so the trip didn't take long. It once took me two hours to get four miles across town in Bangalore. It would have been quicker to walk at the time, but then I wouldn't have had the protection of a metal vehicle, which came in handy on the dangerous roads.

After checking in, I checked my email in the hotel's business center. I sent off quick emails to Sanjay and Nadia to let them know where I was and that I'd arrived safely.

That left me time for a few hours of sleep before heading to the university.

I must have hit snooze on the hotel alarm clock without realizing I'd done so. My subconscious had an annoying habit of taking over when I was in need of sleep. The university staff would have arrived hours ago. I took the world's shortest shower and pulled on a white blouse and a skirt before jumping in an auto-rickshaw.

Auto-rickshaws, the small three-wheeled taxis that are ubiquitous in India, were the presence on the road that truly reminded me I was back in India. They shared the road with motorcycles, scooters, cars including Tatas, classic Ambassadors, imported Suzukis and Hyundais, police Jeeps, colorful hand-painted trucks, and bicycles ridden by braver souls than I.

India's big cities didn't only rival America's most crowded cities—they could drink them under the table. Like the better-known cities of Delhi, Calcutta, and Bangalore, Trivandrum's streets carried millions of people on roads that looked like they should carry two lanes of cars, but drivers squeezed five lanes of traffic into them.

I held my breath as we zigzagged through streets that lacked both street signs and lanes. I suppose you could technically say they had lanes, since there were lines painted on some of the larger streets, but I had yet to see a single driver stay inside one.

The words "sound horn" were painted on the back of most of the trucks, like I remembered. It was meant as a remedy for the chaos. Drivers were supposed to honk their horns if they planned to pass a truck, signaling the truck driver not to weave too erratically until the other vehicle had passed. With the number of people honking at a given time, I never understood how anyone knew if any particular honking was directed at them. But it seemed to work most of the time. The rickshaw driver and I made it to the university without dying or killing a single pedestrian.

I quickly realized that the university campus wasn't one central complex, but a series of buildings around the same central part of town. Even though street signs were rare in India, the driver found the section of the university I was after without too much difficulty.

I walked past the dark red wall that surrounded the section of the campus where the archivist worked. Like most things in India, what could simply have been a utilitarian fence was instead an ornate affair. A low concrete wall was painted red and topped with a decorative wrought-iron fence that raised the height of the wall while allowing people to see inside the campus. White pillars with painted red flowers stood at the entrances.

The signs on the campus were written in both English and Malayalam, so it was easy to find the building. I entered a hallway that I hoped would lead me to the archivist's office, but stopped in my tracks. For a second, I thought I saw a familiar face.

It wasn't possible. I must have been so tired that my mind was playing tricks on me. I could have sworn I saw Naveen Krishnan disappear around a corner.

I hurried ahead, following the man. When I turned down the hallway, I found several men walking and talking. None of them looked like Naveen.

I rubbed my hands over my eyes, feeling the effects of the long flights. My mind must have made a subconscious connection, making me think I saw Naveen because I was standing in a university hallway and saw an Indian guy with a similar build. I desperately needed some coffee to think straight, but I was so close to finding the man who had Anand's letters.

The sparse hallway lacked the bulletin boards I was used to at my own university. The concrete floor was clean, but the signs of age were apparent. New universities were springing up outside of urban areas across the country to keep up with the demand from the growing educated population, but this was one of the older institutions.

The door of the office I was seeking stood open. An elderly man with a well-kept mustache and wire-rimmed glasses stood beside a metal desk in a sparsely furnished office. A large crucifix adorned an otherwise barren wall.

"Ah!" The man said when he spotted me. "You must be the American professor. I'm sorry I missed your telephone calls."

"Nice to meet you, Mr. Abraham." I said.

"A pleasure, Professor Jaya." He used the standard Indian greeting of adding a title to someone's first name. He extended a thin hand. "Please, I am Joseph."

"Thank you for letting my colleague know you have the letters I'm after."

"Such an interesting project. I'm sorry we have not yet digitized these letters." He paused and adjusted his glasses, an unreadable expression on his face. The delicate frames matched his thin body. "May I offer you some tea before we retrieve the letters?"

A hot plate with a rusty pan filled with steaming water sat on a metal side table.

"Thank you," I said, relishing the thought of sugary caffeine.

Indians love their coffee and tea sweetened, so sugar was a

given. Water in India wasn't safe, even in big cities, so boiled drinks were common even in the hot climate. I was up-to-date on my vaccinations, but there were a lot of nasty waterborne diseases. When I was a kid, we boiled our drinking water and used precious space in our tiny fridge to keep it cool in glass jars.

Joseph mixed a cup of tea with even more sugar than I was expecting before picking up a rotary phone on his desk. I sipped the sweet liquid—heavenly—as I listened to him speak quickly in either Tamil or Malayalam to the person on the other end of the line. The languages were related so I couldn't easily tell them apart.

Even though I didn't understand the words, I could tell he was agitated. His voice rose, and he spoke more quickly. His mustache twitched from side to side.

He put the receiver down into the cradle of the phone.

"I'm so sorry," he said, "but the letters are gone."

CHAPTER 24

San Francisco, 1904

"I can help you find work while your leg heals," Samuel said to Anand.

"Working as a spiritualist with you?" Anand asked. "I think that is best left to you."

"Hear me out."

"My living in New York for some months hardly qualifies me to help with your deceptions."

"Deception is such a harsh word."

"Since when have we ever been polite around each other?"

"You're right," Samuel said, "I suppose not. I'll get right to the point then. I have a patron. Mrs. Lancaster."

"Should that name mean something to me?"

"She's from one of the wealthy families that helped build San Francisco. Don't you read the papers, Anand?"

"Not as carefully as you do, it seems. Some of us work for a living."

"Mrs. Lancaster is getting on in years," Samuel said, ignoring his friend's remark. "She has become interested in spiritualism from the Orient. At first, she wished to contact her mother, who had passed some years ago -- which was easy."

"For a man of your talents."

"Now that she has faith in me, she confided her interest in spiritualism from the Far East. She has quite a collection of artifacts from your homeland and also from China."

Anand broke into a smile. "You need more details of my kingdom's gods to impress the lady?"

Samuel looked down at his hands. "Not exactly...I may have mentioned to her my guru lived locally in San Francisco."

"Your guru?"

Samuel looked up and met Anand's eyes. "She wants to meet you."

"I can't believe you're making me wear this," Anand said a week later, adjusting his turban in the small mirror above Samuel's dresser. "I've never worn one of these in my life."

"Mrs. Lancaster will love it," Samuel said.

Anand grumbled under his breath in Tamil.

"Admit it," Samuel said. "You're having more fun than you have fixing ships."

"I'm only doing this because I have to let my leg heal for another few weeks before going back to work."

"It's not right how they treat you," Samuel said. "First paying you less even though you have more skills, and now blaming you for the theft."

Anand felt his face darken.

"A lot of things are not fair in this world. Such as a charming young man deceiving wealthy old women."

"I bring her more happiness than she's seen in years. And I'm not exactly forcing you to join me tonight."

"You would go regardless."

"Of course," Samuel said, nudging Anand aside to adjust his tie in the mirror. "But this brings a bigger payoff."

"I thought she was interested in China, too. Why didn't you ask Li to help?"

"He knows much less about China than you know about India. He can't even do a proper Chinese accent. Can you believe the tourists buy it? You, however, my dear Anand, are the real thing."

CHAPTER 25

My excitement from earlier that morning turned to fear. I was losing my hold on what was real. I was so sure I had temporarily escaped the present-day problem by eluding the person who was willing to kill for this treasure. Nobody else knew Anand's letters were there. Steven and his family didn't know which was why he had come to me. *How had the treasure-hunting killer followed me across the ocean?*

Joseph and I sat drinking strong coffee for ten rupees a cup at the India Coffee House on MG Road located in the basement of a concrete high rise. All the major cities in India seemed to have an MG Road, short for Mahatma Gandhi. I was buying. Ten rupees was approximately twenty-five cents, so it wasn't especially generous of me.

The India Coffee House wasn't one of the modern trendy coffee houses that had started springing up. The chain had been around since before I was born. The strong coffee and cheap food kept it in business despite the sparse decor. We sat in plastic chairs in the crowded café.

"I don't know what could have happened," Joseph said. "It does not make sense that the letters could be gone from the archive reading room. They should not have been removed!"

"Could they have been misplaced or misfiled after you first found them?" I knew it was unlikely, but I didn't want to believe Steven's killer was a step ahead of me.

Joseph shook his head. "The whole box is missing." He added something in a language I didn't understand. From the guttural sound in his throat I guessed he was cursing.

"It makes no sense," he continued. "We have never had a theft. And to think it happened under my supervision. You have my sincerest apologies, Professor Jaya."

"I'm sorry," I said. "This is my fault." I glanced anxiously around the bare-bones surroundings. I couldn't tell if it was the smell of sweaty bodies or the fact that my problems had followed me to India that made it difficult for me to breathe.

"Your fault?" Joseph said. "For asking for help of a colleague with research? No. I only wish I could have been more help. To think you came all this way—"

"There's more going on than a simple research project," I said.

"Your family history, I understand." Joseph looked dejectedly into his empty coffee cup.

"Let me order us more coffee," I said, hailing the waiter. I was stalling as I decided how much to tell Joseph. I didn't want to drag him into this mess, but it appeared that he was already involved. Because of me, he was the latest victim. But I didn't understand how someone had followed me across the ocean. What was I missing?

The waiter appeared at our table. I ordered fried cutlets to go with our coffee. I hadn't had breakfast, and it felt like dinner time to my stomach.

"I'm sorry for getting you into this," I said after the waiter had left. "I should tell you that the letters might provide information leading to a treasure. There's a lot at stake. That's why someone has stolen them."

"Yes, this is what Miss Tamarind indicated when she first contacted us. It is always exciting when our archives can provide such relevant information." He smiled and adjusted his thin glasses.

"There's something else you should know, too," I began slowly, "in case you come across the person who has taken the letters. The person might be dangerous. A man was murdered."

Joseph's coffee cup clattered to the table.

"Murdered?" he whispered, the color draining from his face.

"A man was murdered in San Francisco," I said. "He was the person who contacted me to find the letters."

"Murder," Joseph repeated over and over as he attended to the spilled coffee as best he could with the thin napkins on the table. He avoided my gaze as he repeatedly pushed drenched napkins across the table. Seeming to notice the futility, he stopped, but he didn't seem to know what to do once he ceased mopping up the mess. His thin hands flitted nervously from his glasses to his empty coffee cup.

"I'm sorry to have to tell you," I said, "but I thought you should know."

"Yes," he said slowly. He resumed absentmindedly wiping the spilt coffee on the table. It wasn't the kind of place where a doting waiter would appear to help. Joseph looked up, his large brown eyes meeting mine. "He was murdered over the letters? You are sure of this?"

"Unfortunately," I said, "I am."

The old archivist looked more frail than he had an hour ago as we walked out of the coffee house. He assured me he'd be fine, and I caught an auto-rickshaw back to my hotel.

In the hotel lobby, I walked past an Anglo man dressed in local attire. He sat alone, reading an English-language Indian newspaper. I could only see an obscured view of his head, and in spite of the fact that he wasn't wearing glasses, he reminded me very much of Lane Peters. I was about to kick myself for continuing to think about him, when the man turned his head.

It wasn't my imagination. It was Lane.

I don't remember walking over to him, but I found myself standing right in front of him. He smelled of aftershave and sandalwood. I felt a comforting familiarity in his presence, the force of which took me by surprise.

"For someone who says they want nothing to do with me," I said, "you've got a really strange way of showing it."

"I had to come," he said. He stood up and tossed the newspaper aside.

I felt my stomach do a little flip, only to be followed by a sinking feeling when I heard what he had to say next.

"I didn't want to," he said. "But Naveen Krishnan is in India. He killed Steven Healy. Now he's after the treasure."

CHAPTER 26

"You'd better start at the beginning," I said.

If Naveen was in India, did that mean it hadn't been my imagination at the university? Why couldn't I know people who didn't have their passports at the ready? Both Naveen and Lane did research in India, so of course they would have long-term visas.

"Not here," Lane said.

"Where, then?"

"My room is more private."

I nodded, not trusting myself to speak. There were a lot of things I might have wanted to do in a hotel room with Lane, but talking about a murderer wasn't one of them.

"You okay?" he asked, raising an eyebrow. He was far too observant for his own good.

"Fine," I said as he led the way. "Just fine. Um, what are you wearing?"

"I thought that would be obvious." He couldn't help smiling.

He was wearing a white dress shirt and a white lungi cloth that looked like a long skirt. With his fair coloring he would never pass as an Indian He was dressed more like an American in India for enlightenment, like what my father had done over thirty years ago. As part of his past life as a thief, Lane was good at disguising himself. He wasn't hiding his identity in his current disguise, but he was blending in as a certain type of person.

Lane unlocked the door of his hotel room. As soon as he closed it behind us, he tilted my head up and kissed me. It wasn't a casual kiss to say hello. He brought his mouth down on mine with such force that he pushed me against the wall.

I didn't resist the kiss. I pulled him closer to me, and he responded in kind. His lips were urgent and his breath spicy.

All thoughts of treasures and murders slipped away, and all I could think about was how much I'd missed him.

"I'm sorry," he whispered in my ear as his lips moved from my lips to my neck.

"For what?" I whispered back. I pulled him back to my lips, but he resisted.

He let go of me and stepped back.

"Sorry," he repeated. "I hadn't meant to do that. Forget I did that."

He ran his hand through his hair and turned toward the window. The hotel room faced a wall covered with colorful advertisements for Malayalam and Tamil movies. By the look of the graphics, most of the films were tragic romances.

"You need to tell me why you're here," I said, my heart still racing from the kiss I wasn't likely to forget, "and what you meant about Naveen."

"Your colleague Naveen is on the same treasure hunt you're on," Lane said, turning back to me but keeping his distance. "He killed Steven Healy and now you're the one in danger."

"You came all the way to India because you thought I was in danger from *Naveen*? The Naveen who freaks out if he spills a drop of tea on one of his suits?"

"It's him, Jones. I couldn't reach you, so I had to come warn you."

I found myself temporarily speechless. Lane hated flying. He'd endured the slog of two long flights across the world because he believed I was in danger.

"Are you okay?" Lane asked.

"That," I said, "has got to be the most romantic thing anyone has ever done for me. Twisted and incredibly screwed up, but also horribly romantic."

Lane's lips twitched and he began to laugh. I had missed that. This time when he swept me up in his arms, he didn't kiss me. Instead, he held me in his arms so tightly that I wasn't sure he'd ever let go.

"I'm happy to see you," I said when he finally pulled away, "but there's no way Naveen killed Steven. Naveen didn't know about the map until I showed it to him. I grant you he's a devious bastard. If he's here in India, it's because he's trying to hone in on the discovery after I inadvertently handed him the information. That makes him a jerk. Not a killer."

"You're forgetting something," Lane said.

"What?"

"Somebody," Lane said, "had already translated the map."

I stared at Lane, letting the idea sink in. "You think *Naveen* was the one who translated it in the first place?"

"He's a linguistic wunderkind," Lane said. "When I looked him up I saw that he'd won some big award last year, before you two were hired as faculty."

"Don't remind me."

"He'd be the natural person for Steven to go to when he needed to translate the map."

I groaned. "I had the sense Steven was lying to me when he told me the map was already translated when he found it. That explains why Naveen was so surprised that I'd bring him the map! I thought he reacted oddly when I showed it to him. And that also explains why he was so insistent that the translations were perfect."

"I wasn't making up my suspicions about him," Lane said. "He *already knew* Steven Healy."

"Back up. Tell me why you suspect him." Something else dawned on me. "And how did you find me to warn me?"

"You registered under your own name, so it only took a few calls to figure it out."

"Guess I'd make a terrible spy."

"That's not such a bad thing, you know." A smile crept onto his face.

"And Naveen?"

"He's working with an archivist at the University of Kerala, after the same letters you are."

"You mean Naveen is the person who stole the letters?"

Lane's smile disappeared. "The letters have been stolen?"

"That's why I'm back at the hotel already. Otherwise I'd still be there looking at them."

"Damn," Lane said. "Maybe Naveen bribed the archivist."

It made sense. Bribery was common in India, and wasn't thought of in the same morally corrupt way that it was at home.

"How did Naveen know where the letters were?" I asked. "I didn't tell him."

"You clued him in that you were on to something," Lane said. "It was Naveen who I saw outside your apartment, not your friend Sanjay. I'd gone to your place to see you, to make sure you were all right. This was the day before yesterday, in the morning after Inspector Valdez contacted me, before I caught up with you at Lands End—"

"It was the morning *before* that when Sanjay was at my house," I said, thinking over the confusion when Lane first told me he saw an Indian guy outside my house. "Naveen showed up a few minutes after I'd talked to him, while I was at the library doing research. I thought it was a little weird that he came to find me to essentially tell me nothing new, but at the time I chalked it up to Naveen's big ego that he wanted to tell me again that he was right."

Lane nodded. "The strange thing about him the first time I saw him was that he was looking around like he was trying to find a way into your apartment."

"You didn't call the police?" I asked. "Never mind. I forget who I'm talking to."

"He didn't behave like a burglar, so I didn't know what was going on. Then I saw him again when I saw you later that day—"

"You were following me again?"

"You were the last person to see a man who was murdered, Jones. And don't you dare say that's romantic."

"I won't say it out loud, then," I said. It was reassuring to have Lane there, on my side. I was beginning to feel optimistic again. "I suppose I should get you up to speed."

"That's probably a good idea."

I told him what I'd learned about the treasure's historic significance to India and the pirate stories I found at the library. I ended with my discovery that the map was of Kochi, not San Francisco, so the missing treasure was somewhere in Kochi.

"Clever," Lane said. "You and that uncle of yours are both very clever. But you still don't know what the treasure is?"

"I can't figure it out," I said. "If we had those missing letters, maybe they would tell us."

"You just told me a murderer stole the letters. You can't be serious about going after them."

"You really think Naveen could have killed someone? I can't see it."

"Believing the best about people is a luxury you can't afford right now," Lane said. "Just because you know him doesn't mean he wouldn't kill someone. You need to get out of his way."

"I can't get out of the way. The only chance I've got at going back to the normal life I want is to solve this."

"Are you listening to yourself?" Lane stared at me for a moment before beginning to pace. He kept his distance from me in the small room. "You don't have to be involved."

"The police can't—"

"The police are good at doing their jobs, Jaya. You're kidding yourself if you think you'd be arrested for a murder you didn't commit, so don't use that as an excuse."

"It's not only that," I insisted. "Anand's treasure is out there—his secrets are out there. You understand what this means to me. How could I live with myself if I don't figure this out? I don't have a choice."

"No, you *do* have a choice." Lane shook his head. "The misdeeds of a long-dead ancestor of yours don't matter. Not really. If you really wanted that nice safe life you claim to want, you'd be at home rewriting your research paper and getting ready for the semester. But you're not."

"You don't know me at all," I said, feeling my voice shake as I spoke. "Not the way I thought you did."

"I'm not wrong about this," he said. "I'm not wrong about you. You're here because you like the danger and excitement."

I had been confused about Lane, then comforted by his presence, but those feelings were gone now, replaced with white-hot anger.

"I can't believe I thought you knew me," I said, "and that I thought I knew you. I never should have rescued you that night in the Scottish jail. I should have told them what you really were."

I regretted the words as soon as they came out of my mouth, but it was too late to take them back.

Lane stopped his anxious pacing. He stood still, his body rigid.

"You want to be on your own?" he said. "Fine. You're on your own."

CHAPTER 27

I wasted several hours being upset about things that had nothing to do with the reason I was in India. How could Lane think I wanted to be here? He was projecting his own desires on me. He was the one who was used to having a life full of danger and excitement. He probably missed it, now that he'd gone straight. That's why he'd jumped on a plane to India, not because he cared about me.

I took the phone off the hook in my hotel room. I told myself it was so I could focus without distractions, but in truth it was more likely I did it because I was afraid Lane would call. I didn't know what I would say to him if he did. I felt terrible about what I'd said. But he'd hurt me, too.

I tried to focus on what I should do as I sat in front of the window of my hotel room drinking too much coffee. Instead, the most productive thing I did was doodle on the complementary newspapers that had been left outside my door. At least the view from my window didn't include romantic Indian movie billboards. I had a view of a modern building that looked like a government office. A man with a bicycle cart had set himself up in front of the building. He was selling a larger variety of bananas than you'd imagine existed if you'd only seen bananas at American and European supermarkets. The fruits covered most of the spectrum of the rainbow, from dark red to muddy green to bright yellow.

I was hungry, but I didn't want to leave the hotel until I was sure I wouldn't run into Lane. He was probably already gone, but I was feeling risk-averse. And if I was avoiding him, that only proved my point. He was way off base with his assessment of me.

The good thing about wasting time being indecisive was that it allowed me to reread bits and pieces of the information about Kochi that I'd printed out at my office the night I bought my plane ticket. The more I looked at the maps of Kochi, the more I was optimistic that I would be able to find what I was after there. Even without Anand's letters, Kochi was a small enough area that my recollection of the notations on the map would be useful. Though the peninsula of Kochi has the same geographic orientation as San Francisco, it's about a seventh the size.

I put a change of clothes and sandals in my small backpack and caught a cab to the airport.

King Fisher Airlines—the same company as the beer—deposited me at the Kochi International Airport before nightfall. It was only about 125 miles from Trivandrum to Kochi, but along the roads of the west coast of India the drive would have taken a minimum of four hours—and that wasn't counting traffic or the time it would have taken to hire a driver.

The airport was twenty-five miles outside Fort Kochi. Twenty-five miles might not sound like much, but with traffic and road conditions as they were, I knew the journey wouldn't be as quick as I wanted.

The driver I hired at the airport careened around two trucks and an auto-rickshaw on the road without a single vehicle honking. I held my breath for a second or two. It would take a few days to get back in the swing of Indian traffic.

"Do you feel motion sickness, miss?" the driver shouted at me to be heard above the din of the traffic.

"Nope," I shouted back, shaking my head.

"This is good. Long drive. I will drive faster."

We made the first leg of the journey in well under an hour, but as we approached the city, rush hour made traffic come to a standstill. It was understandable why entire families of four traveled on the back of one motorcycle—it allowed them to weave through traffic when they would otherwise spend their entire day stuck on the road. Women often rode sidesaddle behind their husbands to accommodate their saris. Little children usually sat in between their parents so there would be less risk of them falling off.

On the bridge approaching the fort city from the south, we drove through pothole after pothole, with motorcycles, mopeds, bicycles, and auto-rickshaws squeezing between the cars and trucks on the narrow bridge. The roads were slick from an earlier downpour, courtesy of the monsoons. It was a perilous enough ride that I was able to focus on the road rather than Lane.

It was sunset by the time I arrived in Fort Kochi. Shops, including the craft emporium, would be closing, and soon it would be too dark to explore the northwestern coast where the X had appeared on the map. I shouldn't have wasted so much time earlier that day. Why did Lane have to throw me off balance? There was no way I'd be able to find what I needed in Kochi that night.

I had the driver drop me off along the western coastline. It took me a few minutes to convince him I'd be fine. He was skeptical that I really wanted to be dropped off alone on a stretch of the beach instead of at a hotel or restaurant. I was tempted by the offer of a restaurant, but I needed to make use of the last light of the day.

I didn't waste any time heading for the waterfront walkway. Brightly painted cartoon animal trashcans lined the way, an interesting choice for the breathtaking view out to the Arabian Sea. I was reminded of a carnival in small-town America more than an international, historic city along the coast of south India.

It might have been a pleasant evening if I had been there under different circumstances. The weather was much less oppressive than it often was in August. The monsoon rains weren't coming down, and the temperature was kept relatively in check by the clouds. The energy of the city was vibrant, too. The compact city was cosmopolitan without being as crowded as other Indian cities I'd visited. The streets were alive but had a small-town feel.

I was surprised by just how much Fort Kochi looked like the colonial city it once was. There wasn't a skyscraper in sight. I passed churches and a Dutch cemetery from the time the Dutch controlled Kochi after wresting power from the Portuguese.

I walked briskly along the sidewalk promenade of Mahatma Gandhi Beach toward the northern beach with the fishing nets. Since the rain had passed for the moment, people were out walking. Paved paths made it easy to follow the coastline. The waterfront was covered with stones and rocks, not the pristine sands of nearby tourist beaches. This was a city full of history, not a city for tourists in search of hidden beaches.

I reached the part of the waterfront where Chinese fishing nets lined the northern coast of the old fort town. The nets were mammoth contraptions, at least fifty feet across and twenty-five feet high. Wooden arms radiated from a cantilever, with large stones suspended by ropes to act as counterweights to pull in the nets. I could see the giant nets clearly as the sun set over the water, though the water itself was dark.

Based on the location of the X on the waterfront—or rather, my memory of where that X was—it would be west of the nets where I'd begun my walk, but still along the water. The X had been drawn over water. A hundred years of shallow water with rocky sand... It was too much to hope for.

A bigger problem was that I didn't know what I was looking for, and without the map, I was lost. Kochi was small, but not small enough. I'd rushed off impetuously, without thinking it through. Could Lane have been right about me? No, that wasn't it. He didn't fully understand what Anand had meant to my family—to my mom. Though I did have a choice, it wasn't the clear-cut one that Lane made it out to be.

I glanced around uneasily, feeling the darkness descend. Now that Naveen had Anand's letters, did he know more than I did?

I checked myself into a cheap hotel that had once been a royal residence. From the crumbling paint I could tell it had seen better days, so it was perfect for my budget.

* * *

In the morning, I was far from refreshed and ready for the start of a new day. The bed must have been left over from the colonial era just like the building. I woke up with a stiff neck, mad at Naveen and even madder at Lane. I hadn't brought my running shoes with me to Kochi, so I couldn't even go running to clear my head before the day heated up.

When I grabbed my backpack and unlatched the oversized wooden door of my hotel room, I realized I should have looked through the cut-out peep hole first. There was someone waiting for me in the hallway.

"Truce?" he said.

I regarded him for a moment as I caught my breath.

"I didn't mean to startle you," Lane continued. "And I didn't mean for anything that happened yesterday to happen."

"What I said..." I began, "I shouldn't have said it. I didn't mean it."

"I know," he said, but he didn't look like he believed it.

"You're not mad?"

"Let's just get you through this, okay?"

Lane had abandoned his local attire and was wearing his usual horn-rimmed glasses, tan cargo pants, and a white cotton dress shirt. Wearing a white dress and tan sandals, I matched him. We might have looked like a cute couple if we weren't the exact opposite.

I couldn't get a firm grasp on any of the conflicting emotions clouding my thoughts. It was clear Lane hadn't forgiven me, but he'd stayed when he said he wouldn't. He wasn't making things easier for either of us. I didn't know if I wanted to walk past him and go off on my own, or if I wanted to see if we could start from scratch.

"How did you find me?"

"You're still being a terrible spy," he said. "If Naveen is looking for you, it wouldn't be difficult for him to find you either."

"If you're right about him," I said, "he already has the letters, which means he doesn't need me."

"Maybe."

"You look well-rested for someone who spent the night in this hallway."

"I rented a room. But just in case I didn't catch you, I paid the front desk night clerk to wake me up if you left. The security guard, too."

I couldn't help laughing at the absurdity of the situation. As I did so, I realized for the first time that maybe Lane was right about my motives. I was scared of Naveen and confused about Lane, but that didn't stop me from being filled with excitement as I closed in on answers about Uncle Anand and his treasure. I didn't want to be anywhere but where I was.

"Does this mean you're delirious from the heat?" Lane said.

"I accept your truce," I said. "I'm looking for two locations on the map. I don't have enough information to find the X that possibly marks the treasure, but there's something significant about the *MP Craft Emporium* and *The Anchored Enchantress*. If you want to help, let's get going."

That morning, we stayed busy making inquiries about the two locations at a few of the local historical sites—to no avail. When monsoon rains broke, we took a lunch break. At a family restaurant with a large covered patio, I ordered a spicy dish of fish stewed in coconut milk. I was glad for the force of the downpour, because it made it easy to sit back and watch the rain instead of feeling like we needed to talk about anything I wasn't ready for.

Once the rains cleared, we tried a different tactic. We hired an auto-rickshaw to drive us around the small peninsula in hopes of seeing something that fit.

"We're looking for two things," I said from the narrow backseat. "The *MP Craft Emporium* and *The Anchored Enchantress*."

The driver wasn't familiar with either one, but he was happy to drive us through the narrow streets in the vicinity of the two areas where I remembered the notations on the map. The streets began to blur together. Every few blocks, he asked if he could take us to some shops. I knew he'd get a commission if he took us to the specific stores he had arrangements with.

"I take Mr. and Mrs. to great shop. You like silk? Great deal on carpets?"

"I'll give you twice your commission," Lane said, leaning forward in the rickshaw, "if you stop circling the same streets with your friends' shops."

The driver was happy to oblige.

I was hoping I'd know what I was looking for when I saw it, but the longer we circled the streets, the less sure I became. "Maybe we should try this on foot?" I suggested after we'd spent hours searching in vain. "I'm starving. Why don't we stop for dinner?"

The driver dropped us off in front of a café in the neighborhood that I thought was our best bet. Lane added a hefty tip to his payment before stepping out of the rickshaw. I climbed out after him, bumping into him where he stood frozen in place.

"We have company," Lane said, pointing across the street.

Naveen Krishnan was in Kochi.

CHAPTER 28

"What are you doing, Jones?" Lane said, trailing after me.

"What does it look like I'm doing? I'm going to talk to Naveen." I kept walking. "Naveen can't do anything to us here in the crowded street."

We dodged traffic to make our way across the dusty, crowded street. This central part of town with traders and retail shops was much busier than the coastal region I'd explored the night before and the historic areas we'd visited that morning.

Instead of looking surprised to see me, Naveen hailed me in greeting. He wore a white muslin suit and a broad-rimmed hat.

"Nice to see you keeping up," he said to me. "And you must be the art historian."

"How did—" I began.

"You think you're the only one who can do their homework?" Naveen answered.

"What are you doing here, Naveen?" I asked. Lane remained uncharacteristically mute.

"I have just as much right to be here as you do," Naveen said.

"You think you have the right to murder someone?" Lane said. He took a few steps to the side. Did he think Naveen was going to try something?

"Nice try, but I didn't kill anyone," Naveen said calmly. "Don't worry. I don't think Jaya here has the guts to kill anyone, either."

I wasn't sure if I should take that as a compliment or not.

"Steven's son is crazy," Naveen said. "I wouldn't put it past him to have killed his father. Connor doesn't care about the treasure, though. He won't bother me when I find it."

"You admit Steven came to see you to translate the map," I said.

We all dodged out of the way as a family of three on a bicycle came precariously close.

"Of course," Naveen said, dusting off his slacks. "There's no crime in that. There's also no crime in beating you to the treasure."

"What did Steven tell you about the treasure?" I asked. And why wasn't Lane questioning him along with me?

Naveen answered with a thin smile.

"He didn't tell you enough to find anything," I said. "I knew it. You didn't make the Kochi connection until I naively told you about the Chinese fishing nets. Then you bribed the archivist at the University of Kerala when you realized what I was on to."

Naveen's smile faltered at that. "I figured it out," he said, his smile returning. "I'm not saying anything else."

"I'm the one you stole the information from to get here!" I said, feeling terribly petty, but this was *Naveen Krishnan.* There was no way I was going to let him best me.

"All's fair in love and academic war." He tipped his hat and walked off.

"You were right," I said to Lane after Naveen's figure had disappeared down a narrow side street. "I wouldn't put it past him to kill for this treasure. Not for the wealth, but for the academic glory." I shivered in spite of the sticky heat.

"Hmm," Lane said.

"You could have helped me out with him," I said. "I thought that's what you were here for. Maybe he knows where the shop we're looking for is. He must have made a copy of the map."

"I was doing something more important," Lane said.

"Which is?"

Lane pointed to a faded wall a few buildings past where we stood. "I was making sure he didn't turn around and see that."

A modern sign with a new name hung above the bright blue door that was the shop's main entrance, but the weather-worn wall had once borne the words *Marikayaer Paravar Craft Emporium.*

CHAPTER 29

"That's it," I said. "The *MP Craft Emporium* on Anand's map."

Lane and I rushed to the front of the store. A man with young eyes and a wrinkled face stepped out of the shop to greet us, the sound of small bells ringing above the door as he stepped through it. He wore a white dress shirt and a long white lungi. A taqiyah cap covered the top of his head.

"May I interest the lady in some jewels?" he asked, extending his arm toward the shop.

"Perhaps in a moment," I said. "I wanted to ask a question about this shop."

"Anything for the lady," he replied.

"How long has this shop been here?" I asked.

"My great-grandfather opened it to sell his sculptures with the inlaid jewels."

"He was a sculptor?"

"Yes. Very famous sculptor in his day." I glanced at Lane.

"We have many souvenirs," the proprietor added. "Many items. You come see."

I followed him into the *Marikayaer Paravar Craft Emporium*, Lane trailing behind me.

The shop was filled with intricately carved statues, some wood and some stone. A giant stone Shiva, the destroyer god, was the centerpiece of the high-ceilinged room. Shiva had a staff in one hand and a cobra around his neck.

More my style was the wood carving of Ganesha playing the tabla. Too bad it was over six feet tall and would never fit in my suitcase, let alone my apartment door. Ganesha was the remover of obstacles. I could have used some of his powers right about then.

"Smaller items are along this wall, miss," the proprietor said, ushering me toward the items that would fit into a suitcase.

"This may sound like a strange question," I said, "but do you know anything about a man named Anand Selvam Paravar, who had something to do with this shop a hundred years ago?"

"Anand Selvam *Paravar*?" the man repeated.

"Yes," I said, "the same as one of the family names of the shop."

"Yes, yes," the man said, rocking back and forth on his feet. "I have not heard that name in many years."

"You know of him?"

"When I was a boy, I was told he had the Heart of India."

"The Heart of India?" I repeated.

"The statue my great-grandfather carved when he was involved in the Indian Nationalist movement. The elephant statue was carved in this studio by my great-grandfather, with the help of many other men. The Paravars provided their most precious pearl to be held in the trunk of the elephant. Our families worked together for many years."

Lane swore under his breath. The man glanced between us.

"Of course," Lane said. "*The pearl.*"

"What do you mean?" I asked.

"Didn't you say you were a Paravar? You're a terrible Indian, Jaya."

And thus continued the story of my life, even with Sanjay 10,000 miles away.

"The Paravars operated pearl fisheries," Lane continued. "They found pearls that became famous in Indian art. The most symbolic piece of the Heart of India was that pearl."

"I know all about the Heart of India," I said tersely. "Anand supported the Indian Nationalists who made the statue as a symbol of a unified Indian national pride. But it was lost when it was swept out to sea. That's why I didn't think of it."

"That's what the official story was," Lane said.

"What's that supposed to mean?"

"There were rumors it was stolen," Lane said. "I should have thought of it. The Heart of India disappeared at exactly the right time. It's a huge treasure—and one that your uncle was involved in. It makes sense that someone would kill over this."

"Excuse me, miss," the proprietor said. "You say you are a Paravar?"

I nodded.

"I have not thought about it in so many years," the man said, a wistful expression coming over his face. "I am Abdul."

I introduced myself and shook Abdul's hand. His skin was rough and wrinkled but his handshake was strong. I was again struck by the fact that I couldn't remotely guess his age.

"Though I have not thought of it in many years," he said again, "Now that you are here, asking about the Heart of India... Wait here one moment."

He hurried to the back of the shop, disappearing behind a curtain. I heard the sound of drawers opening and closing as Lane and I looked quizzically at each other. Abdul reappeared seconds later. He held an envelope that was worn with age.

"My great-grandfather, Faruk Marikayaer, received a letter from a member of your Paravar caste, a friend of his called Anand."

I stared at Abdul.

"Anand was my great-granduncle," I said.

Abdul smiled. "This letter is for you, then." He handed me the wrinkled envelope. "My great-grandfather told his sons to save the letter. His friend Anand wrote to him that if he failed in his quest, his brother Vishwan might need his assistance with the Heart of India. Anand asked Faruk to help Vishwan in whatever way he could."

"What happened?" I asked, my voice shaking. I had never heard any of this. Had my grandfather kept this from my mother?

"Vishwan never came to my great-grandfather," Abdul said. "Faruk did not know where to find Vishwan. He was told Vishwan would find him. My grandfather kept the letter, and asked his sons to see to it that Anand and Vishwan's family should have whatever help they needed when they did come."

Abdul bowed. "I am your humble servant. The Heart of India—the pearl of freedom, purity, and Indian identity, under the protection of the elephant—disappeared in 1906. Is it your wish that we rescue the Heart of India from the magic that has made it disappear?"

"You mean it really was stolen?" I asked. "Not swept out to sea?"

"No, miss," Abdul said. "It was not stolen. Nor was it taken by the sea. It disappeared."

"How did something so big disappear?"

"*Insha'Allah.*" The proprietor raised his hands to the sky. "Magic."

CHAPTER 30

San Francisco, 1905

"What is that thing?" Anand asked.

"I thought you'd seen one of these before," Samuel said. "It's a spirit cabinet."

"The box from which you can pretend spirits appear?"

"Precisely."

"It looks like a regular cabinet."

"Good," Samuel said. "That's very good."

"You spent months of wages on a cabinet," Anand said. "That does not sound good to me."

Samuel laughed.

"How does it work?" Anand asked.

"I'll show you."

Samuel asked Anand to bind his arms and legs with rope before leaving his bound body inside the cabinet. Anand was skeptical, but trusted Samuel knew what he was doing. Once he was satisfied Samuel was securely tied, Anand closed him into the empty cabinet.

Within the space of a minute, the sound of a ghostly fiddle could be heard.

"A trifling trick," Anand said. The sound was eerie, but he would not admit that to Samuel. "You must have hidden a knife and the fiddle inside this special cabinet."

The sound ceased. A moment later, the curtains fluttered. Anand whirled around. How had the window opened? The two men were alone. Anand pushed the curtains aside. He was alone. When he turned around, Samuel stood before him.

"As you can see," Samuel said, "this is not a regular cabinet. It's magic."

CHAPTER 31

"Wait here," Lane said to me as he ducked out of the front door of the store.

"Oh no, you don't," I said. "You're going to disappear again."

"I won't," he said before turning away from me. "Abdul, could you come with me?"

I waited inside and opened the folded letter. I skimmed Anand's short letter to his friend Faruk Marikayaer, which had been written in English.

I have the Heart of India. I have a plan, but I must not say more. If I encounter difficulties, I will give my brother Vishwan the information he needs to retrieve it from where it is kept. He may turn to you for assistance. Treat him as you would a brother.

A hand touched my elbow, startling me and nearly making me drop the letter. It was a man I hadn't seen before. Though much younger, he had the same eyes and nose as Abdul. His son?

"Madame," he said, tugging on my elbow. "Madame would like to see one more thing. Special for you. In the back of the store."

Had Lane sent him to get me? I gave a hesitant nod.

"Thank you, madame," the younger shopkeeper said. "Just this way, madame. Through this curtain."

The moment I stepped through the door, strong arms grabbed me.

"Don't scream, Jones," a familiar voice said in my ear. "I'm trying to save you. Naveen is here." Lane relaxed his grip on my arms as I stopped squirming.

"I've got us a motorcycle," he continued. "Abdul is fulfilling his duty to help you. It'll get us away from here—and back to Trivandrum before Naveen can get there. There isn't time to catch a flight tonight. But I want to talk to the archivist again in person before Naveen can."

I hesitated.

"We don't have much time," Lane said. "Do you trust Naveen?"

"No."

"And he isn't stupid. He'll realize before too long that we're out back. He's too involved to get out now. He's already killed once. Who knows what he'll do?"

Before I had time to think about what Naveen might possibly do, the bells at the front of the store jangled.

Our young helper poked his head out from behind the curtain into the front section of the store. "One moment, sir!" he called out.

Lane grabbed my hand with a firm grip and pulled me toward the back door.

"Even if you're right," I said, "we can't outrun him and make it to Trivandrum on some moped Abdul uses to get around Kochi."

"That's not what I had in mind," Lane said, pushing open the back door.

In a small alley, a bright yellow motorcycle as large as a baby elephant sat on a small strip of concrete behind the shop. This was no outdated city bike. In spite of the dirt and mud in the alley, the bike had been polished so rigorously that any bugs that landed on it must have slipped right off. And there were a lot of bugs flying around that alley. One of them flew into my mouth that was hanging ajar.

I coughed. "This isn't a moped."

"This isn't Abdul's bike. You met his son inside just now. This is *his* bike. I paid him generously for it, so he was happy to do as his father wished."

"A racing bike," I said, feeling my stomach churn—whether with excitement or fear, I wasn't sure.

"Indians do love their motorcycles." Lane picked up the helmet from the bike's storage basket and tossed it to me. It was as sleek as the bike.

Lane straddled the bike as I adjusted the helmet strap. Luckily Abdul's son was a small man, so the helmet was only a couple sizes too big for me.

"*Acha!*" A muffled voice yelled from behind the door.

More raised voices sounded inside the shop. Lane looked up sharply at me. I slid onto the leather seat behind him.

"You know how to drive this type of bike?" I asked as I wrapped my arms around him.

"Only one way to find out." He revved the engine. I held on tighter.

Abdul appeared in the back doorway. "*Assalamu alaikum,* my friends," he said.

"*Walaikum assalam,*" Lane replied.

A cloud of dust filled the alley as we sped into the streets of Kochi.

CHAPTER 32

The hazy light of dusk filled my vision beyond the motorcycle helmet's visor. I was glad for the fading light and the obscured view from my helmet. It meant I couldn't clearly see just how close we came to every object we passed, be it building, automobile, pedestrian, or animal. The Kochi streets were narrow, but Lane barely slowed as he snaked the bike through holes in traffic no wider than the scrawny men pedaling their bicycles through the same spaces.

The heat of the day had covered most of the evidence of the monsoon, drying the roads except for the potholes, numerous and deep. I knew I should have stuck with black rather than wearing white.

But being covered in mud was the least of my problems. I hung on for dear life on the back of a high-octane motorcycle, holding onto a man I couldn't figure out, running from another man who might be a murderer. Mud was the least of my problems.

As we emerged from the winding side streets and turned onto the road that ran along the waterfront, I caught a glimpse of the red sky of the sun setting on the horizon of the Arabian Sea. The sight was so beautiful that for a second, I forgot where I was. I was back in Goa as a small child, riding on the back of my father's moped along the beach, breathing the scents of fresh rain and the sea mingled together, laughing as bicycles passed our sputtering contraption. My father used to laugh back then.

The bike tilted at a precarious angle as we rounded a curve leading to the bridge that would take us out of Kochi. My memory vanished as I held on tighter to Lane.

Rush hour traffic was over, but the main road—two lanes rather than one—looked as full as ever. The difference was that when it wasn't rush hour, the cars actually moved.

Traffic came to a standstill at one of the few intersections managed by a traffic light. The scent of the ocean was replaced by dust and manure. Underneath the signal, a counter indicated the seconds before the light would turn back to green. It didn't seem to stop drivers from inching forward and circling around other vehicles to gain a better position on the road.

Lane pulled up next to a shiny red moped carrying a man in a dress shirt and slacks. Lane raised his voice above the din of the engines to ask if we were heading the right way to the highway heading south to Trivandrum. Lane spoke in English, and the man answered in kind.

"Straight," the man said, bobbing his head back and forth in that Indian way that looks neither like a shake nor a nod, and pointing straight ahead.

The light turned green. I felt Lane's muscles tense as he wove between the trucks, cars, auto-rickshaws, motorcycles, and the occasional street vendor pushing his cart. He kept up our speed wherever he could reasonably manage it, and sometimes when he shouldn't have. I understood the urgency. It wasn't possible that Naveen could be following us, but he must have known where we were headed, because I had stupidly told him I knew he'd gotten to Joseph. He could hire his own transportation and meet us there. Our only hope of getting to Joseph's office first was speed.

A swarm of shabby auto-rickshaws honked repeatedly from a few yards ahead of us, all trying to sneak into the narrow gap between two open-backed trucks full of laborers returning home. A herd of goats along the side of the road merged into traffic, much to the dismay of the boy leading them. Some of the braver drivers wove their mopeds and motorbikes between the scrawny animals.

Lane revved the engine before changing his mind and slamming on the brakes. Lane's feet touched the ground as we came to a full stop, steadying us so we wouldn't be run over by the drivers who wouldn't be deterred. My chest pressed into his back at the unexpectedly harsh stop.

I couldn't blame the drivers for their impatience and willingness to keep driving in spite of what was in front of them. A timid soul might spend the entire day on the road without ever reaching his destination. There was a time when I'd been used to it, but it took time to readjust.

When we finally emerged from the swell of traffic, the sun had finished its descent. Traffic on the dark highway was dense, but moved freely. It was here that I could feel the power of the motorcycle doing what it was made to do. For the next hour, we made good time, only slowing when traffic merged into a single lane to go around the elephant strolling down the left lane with his master and a stack of hay on his back.

When the highway diverged, Lane pulled off the road at a late-night restaurant.

At first I thought we were going to eat—which I had mixed feelings about since I knew we were in a hurry but my stomach screamed at me in hunger—but I was quickly proven wrong. Without leaving his perch on the bike, Lane pulled up alongside two men smoking in the parking lot.

"Trivandrum?" he asked.

"Straight," the men said, their heads bobbing in unison. The one with the bushier mustache pointed onward to the road from which we'd come.

Lane nodded and we headed back to the road.

The next time we stopped, Lane pulled off the road in front of an Indian Oil petrol station to put gas in the bike.

I leapt off the bike and shook out my hair. It felt like an entire dust cloud was forming between my hair and the helmet. I looked at my unruly mane in the bike's side mirror as Lane filled up the tank.

"Why doesn't Aishwarya Rai's hair look like this when she gets off the back of a motorcycle in the movies?" I said.

"I kind of like it like that," Lane said.

"You like the rat's-nest look?"

"I like any look on you, Jones."

I watched the ease of the movements of his lean body. The sides of his shirt were pressed with sweat from where I'd held onto him on the back of the motorbike. The night was hot. I breathed deeply in the humid air.

We made better time than expected, arriving in Trivandrum a little after one o'clock in the morning.

Lane dropped me off at my hotel so I could get a few hours of sleep before going to see Joseph. He said he'd do the same and come back to pick me up.

I walked up the drive of the hotel. I don't know what it is with me and hotel lobbies, but a familiar face was waiting for me when I walked through the glass doors.

A man was having an animated discussion in English with the clerk at the front desk. I knew that voice.

"Sanjay?" I said.

He turned from the clerk to face me. A travel bag sat on the floor next to his feet. He wore a jacket in spite of the warm night air. He must have just arrived on one of the flights that arrive in the middle of the night.

"You're alive," he whispered. A smile lit up his face, but it didn't hide his pallor.

Something was wrong. Not just the strain of a long flight.

Sanjay took two steps toward me before staggering. The flap of his jacket opened up. That's when I saw it. The front of his shirt was drenched with a thick, dark red liquid. He took one more step forward before his legs gave out. Sanjay collapsed at my feet in a pool of blood.

CHAPTER 33

San Francisco, 1905

The knock at the door was timid. Anand opened it to find Li's sister Mai standing there. She looked stunning in a modern crimson dress. She had become a beautiful woman in her seventeenth year.

"My brother says you have not been to The Siren's Anchor lately. Is it because of what happened to your friend Samuel?"

"I hope Li told you that Samuel is unharmed," Anand said. "It was only a trick."

"Yes," Mai said. "Li did not wish me to worry. I knew Samuel had been working as a spiritualist, but never thought it could be so dangerous."

"Samuel has gone to find his fortune in the Colorado silver mines," Anand said. He suspected his friend had departed in part because of unrequited feelings toward Mai, but he kept that to himself. "And I have been contemplating returning to India. It was not prudent for me to remain there at the time, but I have now seen much of the world. This is a strange but marvelous country, but I think it may be time for me to go home."

"You're leaving us?"

"Is there anything keeping me here?"

"I enjoyed our walk the other day." She blushed. "It is a lovely afternoon. Perhaps it would help calm your worries to walk with me? You could tell me of your home."

"You wish to hear of the Kingdom of Travancore?"

"I have never been outside of San Francisco," Mai said. "I would like that very much."

Anand took Mai's arm. She was stronger than she looked. He liked that. He liked her. Yet it was with trepidation that he took her arm. He knew how fragile life was. His own death, he could tolerate. But truly caring for another, in the way he could imagine caring for Mai? That was enough to frighten even Anand Selvam Paravar.

CHAPTER 34

Hospitals can be stressful under any circumstances, but it's especially true when it's in a foreign country. Almost everyone involved understood English, but that didn't help much since I had no idea what had happened to Sanjay.

Sanjay was still unconscious when the doctor cleaned and bandaged his wound. After clearing away the blood, they determined it was a knife wound. It wasn't deep enough to have hurt any internal organs.

Thank God. I don't know what I would have done without Sanjay. He was the most solid thing in my life.

The strange thing, they said, was the amount of blood. The knife wound didn't seem serious enough to merit that amount of blood. They asked if Sanjay was a hemophiliac, which I knew he wasn't. He'd had several injuries from his magic act, but none of them were life threatening like they would have been to a hemophiliac. *Then why was there so much blood?*

I paced the crowded hallway in a daze, waiting for him to wake up. I walked down the hall to a waiting room where a colorful musical flickered on a small television screen. Even if I'd spoken the language of the film, I doubt anything could have held my attention.

After what seemed the length of at least five Bollywood films—but was in reality somewhere around an hour—the doctor finally came to get me and led me back to Sanjay's room.

I sat at the edge of Sanjay's cot, all too aware of the cloth bandage that covered his midsection.

"You're wearing pink," was the first thing out of Sanjay's mouth as he took my hand in his.

"Your blood was all over me. In the confusion I left my backpack at the hotel. I had to buy a new blouse from one of the vendors outside. This country is worse than Telegraph Avenue in Berkeley—it's impossible to find anything without color."

"It looks good on you." Sanjay squeezed my hand and attempted a smile. His lips were dry and his thick hair was a mess. "It's been a year since I've seen you wear color, after the airline lost your luggage and you had to improvise."

"How could I forget?" I said, looking Sanjay over with relief. "Something looks different about you," I added.

"Besides the blood loss, you mean?"

"I know what it is. You don't have your hat. Did the nurses take it?"

"I didn't bring it to India. Didn't want to deal with airport security taking it apart. You know how many illusions are in that bowler hat?"

"You probably could have used it to defend yourself," I said. "What on earth happened?"

Sanjay's smile faded. "A package."

"A package?"

Sanjay let go of my hand and sat up on the cot.

"I got home to my loft, the day after you left," he said. "Outside my door, a large package was waiting for me. I didn't remember ordering anything online, but with everything going on, I thought maybe I'd forgotten something I ordered for an illusion. I didn't open it right away. I made some dinner first."

"Sanjay," I cut in.

"What? I was famished. I ate. Speaking of which, I'm pretty famished now. I haven't had a chance to eat since I arrived. I was too worried about you. Can't we get out of here and get some food?"

"The doctor is waiting for some test results," I said. "You lost a lot of blood. You're not going anywhere until then."

"It doesn't make any sense," Sanjay said. "How did I lose so much blood?"

"You're going to finish telling me what happened, so we can figure that out. But you don't have to tell me in *quite* so much detail."

"Can't you go get me some food? I don't know Trivandrum, so I don't know the best places to eat. If we were in Delhi—"

"Sanjay. Nobody tried to stab *me*, so you're the one who tells your story first. Now."

"It wasn't a person who stabbed me," Sanjay said.

"What? How did you get stabbed, if not by a person?"

"When I looked at the box," Sanjay said, "I saw that it had been hand delivered, not mailed. I was curious. I opened the top of the box and saw the lid of a serving tray. Weird, right? Turns out it was spring-loaded. That's when a knife popped out of the box and slashed my stomach."

"A booby trap?"

"Sort of," Sanjay said, shifting uncomfortably. "The weird thing, though, is that it didn't seem bad at all. I didn't think I needed to go to the doctor. It wasn't much worse than cutting a finger while cooking. And it wasn't nearly as serious as some of the injuries I've gotten when practicing a new illusion. I thought it must have been my magician friend Tempest playing a practical joke. She's got a wacky sense of humor."

"You've got some great friends, Sanjay."

Sanjay had told me something more important than he'd realized. If someone had put the box at Sanjay's door yesterday, it couldn't have been Naveen.

"I bandaged it up with a couple of Band-Aids," Sanjay said, squirming in his bed. "That was really all it needed. Only after I was on the plane did I realize something was wrong."

"Why were you getting on a plane to fly to India anyway?"

"I—"

The elderly doctor who'd attended to Sanjay stepped back into the room.

"Rat poison," the doctor said. "Your cut was full of rat poison. Helpful in killing rats, yes, but a dangerous substance. When it comes in contact with an open wound, the blood does not stop flowing as it should. A small cut creates much blood. You would not have noticed at first."

"So it's not serious?" I asked.

"Correct," the doctor said. "No reason for losing consciousness."

"There was so much blood!" Sanjay insisted.

"He fainted," the doctor said.

Sanjay never ceased to amaze me. The man could escape from the most dangerous situations he created on the stage, but he fainted because of a little blood.

"He'll be fine?" I asked.

"Very much so. Rest here one more day, you will be right as rain. In the future, you should be more careful when working with rat poison, young man."

Once the doctor was gone, I turned back to Sanjay.

"Maybe the police can get fingerprints off of it," I suggested.

"Well..."

"You didn't save the evidence? Sanjay, what were you thinking?"

"I told you I thought it was a friend playing a practical joke! Why would I leave a bloody knife in my loft? That's gross. I washed everything. Of course in hindsight now that I know it wasn't one of my friends, I would have done things differently."

"The only person I can think it might have been is here in India," I said. "So it can't have been Naveen."

"Wait," Sanjay said. "You need to tell me what's going on." He tried to cross his arms over his chest, but groaned as his forearms brushed against his abdomen. "You're the one who took off in search of a treasure without thinking of telling me until you were on the other side of the world."

"You still never told me why *you're* here in India now."

"I thought you were dead."

"Because I didn't check in with you constantly? Really—"

"Or at least that you were in trouble. You don't have your cell phone, so I left half a dozen urgent messages for you at your hotel."

"I left there."

"You didn't check out!" Sanjay said. "I asked the front desk. Repeatedly."

"I was coming back, as you can see."

"You could have *told* me. There's a murderer running around."

"Why were you trying to reach me in the first place?"

"Oh," Sanjay said, blinking in surprise. "I didn't tell you?"

"You mean before you collapsed on the hotel floor in a pool of blood and gave me a heart attack? No, you didn't."

"You were that worried about me?" he asked.

"Don't ask such a stupid question."

Sanjay smiled. "You'll never guess what I found."

"Not the location of Anand's treasure."

"That," Sanjay said, "I would have gotten out of my mouth before passing out. No. But it gets us closer to it. I was at the library—"

"*You* went to the library?"

"Somebody had to pick up the slack. And you'll be glad I did. Your librarian friend Tamarind found the next missing piece in the history. Anand's friend Samuel—Spiritualist Samuel who you discovered—went *missing* in 1905."

"What happened?"

"He was working as a spiritualist, as you know. The disappearance was written up in the papers with a story that he was leading a séance, when something went wrong."

"What went wrong?"

"He *disappeared* from his spirit cabinet."

"Isn't that what illusionists are supposed to do?"

"They're supposed to reappear, too."

"And he didn't?"

"Nope."

"The trick went wrong, then?"

"Illusion," Sanjay corrected me automatically. "That's what the papers reported at the time. Since a body can't actually disappear, they suspected foul play. There was blood found inside the empty cabinet. The press reported that he was killed and the body was hidden to cover it up."

"But you don't think that's what actually happened."

"There were gaps in the newspapers. Tamarind said pre-1906 records are spotty because the earthquake destroyed so much."

"Then it's just a hunch the initial newspaper reports were wrong?"

Sanjay smiled and shook his head. "No, I'm sure of it. Samuel didn't die."

"They found him alive?"

"No. But I know it wasn't an accident. He disappeared *on purpose*."

"How do you know?"

"I found the spirit cabinet."

CHAPTER 35

Sanjay was still talking, but I ceased listening. Through the open door, a tall man with wavy blond hair was talking with a nurse.

"I'll be right back," I said to Sanjay, my eyes never leaving the door.

Lane stood in the hallway, an agitated expression on his face. He was speaking a mix of English and Malayalam, trying to get information from the nurse. He broke off as soon as he saw me. He wrapped his arms around me in a hug that squeezed the breath out of me.

"Does this mean I'm forgiven for the awful things I said?" I whispered.

"They told me you'd been taken to the hospital," he said, pulling back.

"Who told you that?"

"When I went back to the hotel, the clerk at the desk said you'd been taken away in an ambulance. But you weren't registered here at the hospital."

"That's because it wasn't me who was hurt."

"You're all right?" He looked me up and down. "Naveen didn't try anything?"

"This has nothing to do with Naveen. It was a friend of mine admitted to the hospital. He was attacked back in San Francisco. That means Naveen *can't be* our guy. He was only trying to scoop me with a discovery."

I rubbed my hands over my face. I was so very tired. When I looked up, Lane was looking over into Sanjay's room.

"Interesting," Lane said, shaking his head. "I was so worried about you... But that means the murderer who also attacked you is still in San Francisco."

"Looks like it."

"I should go," Lane said, looking in Sanjay's direction. "I'm interrupting."

"You're not interrupting."

"Since Naveen can't be our guy, you'll be okay here. Especially now that you've got your friend with you."

He started walking down the hallway toward the exit. I jogged after him.

"You're *leaving* again?"

Lane kept walking through the doors. The motorcycle was parked on the curb right outside the doors. He slipped onto the seat.

"What about Joseph and the missing letters?"

"I suppose if I told you to forget about them, you wouldn't listen to me?"

"Why would I forget about them? They're why I came—"

"I don't want to have this fight with you again. If you're going to pursue it, that's your right. Now that I know you're not in danger from Naveen, you can handle it yourself."

"You're really leaving?"

"I shouldn't have come in the first place," he said. "Sorry I bothered you while your friend is in the hospital."

"You didn't bother me."

"No?"

Lane wrapped his fingers around mine. He pulled me forward in a smooth motion. His lips found mine before I realized what was happening. I felt myself lifted onto the seat of the motorbike. His arms wrapped around me as his warm lips explored mine. The movement was intense, almost desperate. I responded on every level. My fingers ran through his hair as his ran through mine. I couldn't tell if the intense heartbeat I felt was mine or his. I felt as if I was drowning, and I wanted more.

He pulled back slightly, leaving our noses touching. "Jaya Anand Jones," he whispered. "Victory, Happiness, America. I'm going to miss you, you know."

"That's not fair," I said, feeling the warmth of our breath entwined. "You can't decide this on your own."

He smiled that sad smile of his. "You're right. I have a feeling I won't be able to stay out of your life. But that's for another day. Go take care of your friend."

CHAPTER 36

"Who was that?" Sanjay asked when I walked back into the hospital room.

"I have no idea." I touched my fingers to my lips.

"He hugged you in the hallway like you knew him pretty well."

"It's a long story."

"There seem to be a lot of those going around right now," Sanjay said with a scowl.

Sanjay blackmailed me into getting him out of the hospital. He swore he wasn't going to say another word to me about Samuel's mysterious spirit cabinet until I sat him down at a proper restaurant and got him some clothes.

I was nothing if not resourceful. I returned within ten minutes after buying Sanjay a bright orange tunic and red lungi.

"This is a woman's shirt," Sanjay said, holding up the orange fabric lined with a design woven in red along the bottom.

"This part of town isn't exactly a tourist destination. The guy only spoke Malayalam. I didn't know how to tell him I needed a shirt for a man without making a very rude gesture."

"You really are the worst Indian ever, Jaya."

Sanjay refused the skirt-like lungi, insisting his jeans didn't have *that much* blood on them, but accepted the orange shirt instead of his blood-soaked white dress shirt that the doctors had cut off of him. At least the shirt had been cut for a large woman, so it was big enough to fit over Sanjay's broad shoulders.

We left the hospital with Sanjay looking more like a *hijra*—the Indian equivalent of transvestites—than I'd ever admit to him, with his well-cut features and large eyes that were perfect for performing on the stage. Luckily we found a restaurant quickly, before any passersby began pressing coins into Sanjay's hands, as was the custom.

"Mmmm," Sanjay said, licking the fingertips of his right hand after taking a bite of seafood biryani. "We should ask Raj to put this on the menu at the Tandoori Palace."

"I don't think he's going to expand his menu to include South Indian food."

"I wonder if I can get this back in San Francisco."

Most of the foods thought of as Indian food in America were North Indian and Pakistani cuisines. Sanjay was right that there was something about the freshly caught fish surrounded by spicy sides eaten with our hands and served on a banana leaf that made the food more flavorful. There was also the fact that I hadn't eaten in ages either.

If you're not used to eating whole meals with your hands, it might sound unsanitary, especially in a country with as many diseases as India. But eating with your hands was done for that exact reason. You could wash your hands before and after eating, eat with your right hand, and use your left hand for anything "impure."

"I promise I'll take you to a good South Indian restaurant once we're home," I said. "Now can we get back to the matter at hand? You said you found the spirit cabinet Anand's friend Samuel used during a fake séance."

"Let's order some more of this fried fish first," Sanjay said.

I flagged down a waiter and ordered more of the bright red fish.

"When I hit a dead end with Tamarind at the library," Sanjay said, "I called a guy I know who runs a magic supply store that specializes in antiques and memorabilia. I asked him about a spiritualist from the turn of the last century called Spiritualist Samuel."

"I thought you said spiritualists were nothing like magicians."

"Morally, yes. But they do use some of the same tools. Houdini did fake séances to prove how they were done."

"Really?"

"It ruined his friendship with Arthur Conan Doyle, who believed in séances."

"They let their spiritual beliefs ruin their friendship?"

"They were both strong-willed guys." He shrugged. "But that's beside the point. Back to Anand's friend's spirit cabinet. The dealer I know was able to track down Samuel's spirit cabinet. It was in Las Vegas. I lucked out—it was for sale by a dealer, not in a private collection." He paused. "I bought it."

"You have it at your loft?"

"It should arrive by the time we get back. But I had a chance to study photos of it before I bought it, so I'd know what I was getting." Sanjay paused to scoop up another piece of fish.

"And?"

"I know how he did it—and *why*. Based on what you told me about the Heart of India disappearing, this cabinet explains what happened."

"People said the Heart of India *disappeared*," I said, thinking of Abdul's certainty, "not that it was stolen. Exactly the kind of illusion a spiritualist could pull off."

Sanjay grinned. "Magic."

"Anand was in San Francisco," I said, "presumably being a pirate in the bay—while his accomplice Samuel left for India and stole the Heart of India. *Samuel* was the one who stole the Heart of India from Thoothukudi. But Anand wanted it for himself and his own family, so he stole it back."

"It looks like it," Sanjay said.

"This sucks."

"I love it when you're so eloquent. It's good to see all those years of schooling paid off."

"This *does* suck. Anand was a common thief."

"Not a common one. Pirates have a certain cachet."

"He was still a thief."

"It certainly looks like it," Sanjay said. "But you shouldn't worry about that. You never knew your great-granduncle, so you shouldn't care about what he was or wasn't."

I was no longer hungry.

"You don't understand," I said pushing aside my banana leaf. "He was a hero in my family. It's the stories about his life that are the reason my mother had the courage to make her own way in the world and marry my father. If it wasn't for Uncle Anand, I wouldn't exist."

"But you *do* exist, Jaya. You don't need to live in the past."

"If you hadn't noticed, I kind of signed up to live in the past."

"I don't mean your job—"

"It's more than a job. Aside from my dad and brother, I have no family. No one. This is my way of being connected to the world."

"You've got *me,* you know." Sanjay suddenly grew fascinated with his banana leaf and cast his eyes downward.

Sanjay's brush with death must have given him a burst of sentimentality. He didn't usually say silly things like that. I gave his forearm a little squeeze. He looked up at me.

"I used to have Anand, too," I said. "The knowledge of his life gave me some semblance of a personal history."

"You don't need anyone to make you any more than you are. You're the most—" Sanjay broke off.

"What?"

Sanjay cleared his throat. "Nothing," he said, his face turning red.

"You were going to say something."

"Nothing." He coughed. "I think I swallowed a pepper."

"You didn't even have any food in your mouth," I pointed out.

"Look, I know it's not the news you wanted to hear about Anand. But what you should care about more is that there's someone in your life right now who isn't what they seem."

"You mean the murderer," I said, giving up on getting Sanjay to tell me whatever he was starting to say. "Yeah, I know. It's kind of hard to forget."

"I have a theory." He paused. "You're not going to like it."

"Since when have you ever held out on me?"

Sanjay gave me a cocky half smile, back to his old self. "There was someone else enquiring about Samuel's spirit cabinet. Someone else is following all the leads that we are. The dealer didn't have a name—but it was *a woman.*"

"A woman?"

"It's got to be Tamarind," Sanjay said. "She hit the same dead end as me at the library. I was thinking about how strangely she acted when she found that information about Samuel disappearing. And she had the research skills to pursue it."

"You're saying all amazingly competent librarians should be murder suspects?"

"Then forget that point. There's more. She conveniently disappeared right before your mugging."

"She was *working,* Sanjay. Some of us have real jobs."

"But you can't swear it wasn't her who attacked you. She's tall enough to be a man. She could have changed clothes quickly. It would explain the face covering."

"I don't think it was her. It felt like a man."

"Even if your senses are to be believed—which I'm not sure about since it was a stressful situation—there's more. You told her about the treasure *right before* Steven was killed."

"Coincidence."

"She was *the only one* who knew."

"Anyone Steven knew could have killed him," I said.

"You said his son and daughter-in-law have alibis."

"Christine and Connor," I said. "If they were covering for each other, I wouldn't believe it, but there was a crowd at an art show."

"Tamarind—" Sanjay began.

"My colleague Naveen was working with Steven *before* that night."

"That makes my case even stronger," Sanjay said. "Tamarind is the only one who would want to kill him *that night.*"

"But why kill him at all?" I asked.

"I don't know yet. Maybe she went to see him and something went wrong. She's a strong woman. Maybe she didn't mean to kill him. There's more. Tamarind is your friend, even though she's crazy. She wanted the map from you, but she didn't want to hurt you to get it. I'll give her that much credit. The mugger didn't stab you or anything that would have gotten that bag from you much more easily. That also explains that attack on me—serious enough to look bad and to scare you off, but not serious enough to do any real damage."

I closed my eyes. I couldn't believe it. Not Anand. Not Tamarind. But who did that leave? Steven's son and daughter-in-law had alibis. Could Lane be keeping something from me about his involvement, if someone from his past had forced his hand? And did Naveen's involvement go deeper than I thought? Something wasn't right with the picture Sanjay was painting. I didn't know what it was, but I felt in my heart that something was very wrong.

"Things aren't always what they seem," I said.

"That's true when I'm on stage," Sanjay said, "but not in real life. Anand stole a treasure, and Tamarind is after it now. Like it or not, she betrayed you."

CHAPTER 37

San Francisco, 1905

"You're sure?" Anand asked.

"Samuel didn't go to Colorado like he told us," Li said. "He didn't leave to try his hand in a silver mine."

"Why would he--"

"He wanted to disappear," Li said. "He faked his disappearance with the spirit cabinet that night so he could go somewhere much further without debt collectors looking for him."

"Samuel told us that much," Anand said. "We know he faked his disappearance at the séance, leaving blood behind so his creditors would think he was dead and would not search for him."

"That's not who he was hiding from," Li said. "He was hiding from us."

"Why would he do that?"

"To journey to a land of riches that you'd told him all about."

"What are you trying to tell me?"

"I saw it with my own eyes," Li said. "Samuel is headed for India."

"There is no reason for him to go there."

"He asked you so many questions about the treasures of South India," Li said. "I heard him with my own ears."

"That does not mean he is going to India," Anand said. "We both spoke of our homelands over many evenings of whisky. I know much of Ireland, yet that does not mean--"

"He used details of India for his fake séances with Mrs. Lancaster," Li said. "She collects many treasures. How would Samuel go to India if not with her financial backing?"

"I do not believe he would betray me," Anand said. "Things are not always as they seem."

"But you know what, Anand? Sometimes they damn well are."

CHAPTER 38

Sanjay and I had been so focused on our conversation that I hadn't realized the rains had begun again. Calling the monsoon "rain" wasn't a particularly accurate description at any time, but it was especially true at that moment. The monsoon that day was a powerful force impossible to confuse with a shower of rain. It was a blanket of water that didn't seem to consist of individual drops of liquid.

As Sanjay and I exited the restaurant and stood under the awning, sheets of rain obsured our view beyond a few yards. The water splashed back up from the ground, spraying our bodies with mist. Neither of us moved back inside. It wasn't cold, and we both knew it was futile to fight it. Unless we wanted to stay inside the restaurant all day, there was no avoiding becoming soaked at some point.

I had told Sanjay about everything that had happened in India. Well, almost everything. I didn't think it would be a good idea to tell him about my last encounter with Lane. I wasn't sure why.

"Plan?" Sanjay said.

"We can go back to the hotel and see about flights."

"Go home?" Sanjay said. "You're joking. There's no way we're going home yet. Didn't you listen to yourself about Naveen and the archivist?"

"What do you mean?"

"They're withholding an important letter. We need to see it."

"How do you suppose we convince them?"

"You said the archivist who you suspect Naveen bribed is religious," Sanjay said. "I can make him think the wrath of God is upon him."

"That's cruel."

"Hey, he's the one who's holding Anand's letter captive."

It had been the middle of the day when we left the hospital, so we found Joseph still in his office. When he saw us, his reaction was not what I was expecting.

"Hindi Houdini!" Joseph said, clasping his hands together and rising to greet us. "It is truly an honor, sir. I was not to be recognizing you at first, not expecting you to be wearing..." He trailed off as his eyes stayed locked on the bright orange women's tunic I'd purchased for Sanjay.

I stared dumbfounded at Sanjay. "You're famous here?"

Sanjay shrugged.

"Indian MTV did a few shows about me a few years ago, featuring my magic tour. My agent tells me the ratings were pretty good. It was before I met you."

Joseph's face fell. "You are here with Professor Jaya?"

"I'm helping her with some research," Sanjay said. "You must be Mr. Joseph."

"Yes, yes, that is I." His head bobbled as he blinked furiously, looking torn between nervous anxiety and boyish excitement. "You wished for my assistance, Mr. Houdini?"

"Thank you, Mr. Joseph," Sanjay said, shaking his hand.

"Anything I am able to do, I will do it."

"We're looking for some letters," Sanjay said.

Joseph hesitated. "My most humble apologies," he said. "The letters for Professor Jaya are not here. Anything else you would like? We have much information. Very much information."

"You know The Hindi Houdini can read minds," I said.

I'd been skeptical of Sanjay's strategy, but now that it appeared Joseph was in awe of Sanjay, giving him the right prompting might just work.

Joseph gulped. His moustache twitched.

"Yes," Sanjay said, following along. He touched his index fingers to his temples. "I sense you are hiding something from Professor Jaya."

"I did not know Professor Naveen was involved in murder!" Joseph said.

"So he did bribe you for the letters," I said.

"He called me," Joseph said, sinking into his chair, "speaking Malayalam. He told me I could not trust Professor Jaya. He mentioned he would be so very grateful if I would help him with his important research. He made a donation... But he said nothing of a man being murdered in America because of the letters! I do not want anything to do with that."

"We know you did not think you were doing anything wrong," Sanjay said. "Paying you to borrow the letters—"

"No, no," Joseph said. "He did not take them."

"He didn't?" I asked.

"What do you think of me?" Joseph sniffed indignantly and adjusted his glasses. "The archives must not leave the property. No, the letters are here. Professor Naveen's donation was made so he could *read* the letters with an understanding that no other scholars would be granted access."

"The letters are here?" Sanjay said.

Joseph hesitated again.

"Naveen lied to you about not being able to trust Jaya," Sanjay said. "He tricked you so he could make a discovery first. Remember," he added, "Jaya is the one who told you the truth about a murder. Naveen only told you what you wanted to hear."

"Yes," Joseph said, "he lied to me. He should not receive his donation back."

"We don't care about that," Sanjay said. "We only care about being able to see the letters. You'll take us to them now?"

"Are you feeling up for this?" I asked Sanjay. "There are a lot of letters to go through."

"Not necessarily," Joseph said.

"What do you mean?" Sanjay asked.

"I watched Professor Naveen as he read the letters," Joseph said. "There was one letter he was most interested in. One letter that made him smile and say Professor Jaya was looking in the wrong place."

CHAPTER 39

Joseph made a photocopy of the relevant letter for us, which he tucked into an envelope and handed to Sanjay. Before we left, he got Sanjay's autograph and invited him back any time. Sanjay was much more gracious than I was while we said our goodbyes. I was anxious to read the letter. After extricating ourselves from Joseph's repeated handshakes, the sun had returned so we found a shady spot under a cluster of coconut trees and opened the envelope.

April 2, 1906

Thambi Vishwan,

I may not be able to write for some time, but do not worry. I have seen the world and I do not fear anything in it.

If anything should happen to me, I will write to you with information about something important for you to find in San Francisco. Follow the paths on the map. Ask my friend Faruk Marikayaer, in Kochi, for assistance. He knows to expect you. You will do me proud.

Anand

"Something important for him to find on a path in San Francisco," I repeated, looking up at the coconut tree leaves swaying above me. "The letter takes on a whole new meaning once we know that there's a treasure map. He wasn't asking his brother to come visit him. He was telling Vishwan that he needed to find the Heart of India in San Francisco!"

"Wait," Sanjay said. "I thought the map was of Kochi?"

"It's *both* cities," I said. "Naveen was right about the translation of *My Cities*—it was plural. The map served the purpose of telling two stories. Where the treasure was lost, from its origins in Kochi, and found, where it ended up in San Francisco."

"Why didn't your grandfather ever receive the map?"

"It sounds like Mai was supposed to send it to Vishwan if anything happened to Anand. But for some reason she didn't."

"Who's Mai?" Sanjay asked.

"She's the woman who wrote to my family telling them that Anand had been killed in the earthquake trying to save her brother, Li."

"But Steven Healy told you Anand was murdered. How does that fit?"

"I feel like I'm so close to understanding what's going on, but I can't quite grasp it. If only I still had that map..." I closed my eyes and tried to think. A hot breeze blew over me. I could feel the approaching rain in the air, but I couldn't recreate the map in my mind.

"I don't remember the details either," Sanjay said. "Only those fishing nets Nadia made such a big deal about."

"It's no use," I said, opening my eyes and standing up. "I don't remember enough."

"Why is this letter so vague, anyway? This would be so much easier if Anand hadn't been so cryptic."

"It makes perfect sense that Anand didn't want to write openly to Vishwan about the Heart of India. You never knew who would read your mail, and the Heart of India was controversial. Revolutionary. Anand had been involved in the movement for Indian independence. It wasn't a good idea for him to write openly about anything concerning the Indian National Congress."

"Which included the Heart of India that its supporters created," Sanjay said.

"Exactly. So Anand broke up the information into different letters. He wrote to his friend Faruk about the Heart of India, and to his brother Vishwan about the hidden location of the treasure."

"I get it," Sanjay said. "He expected them to find each other if necessary."

"Kochi held the clue to the treasure," I said, "but the treasure is in San Francisco." I groaned.

"What's wrong?"

"Naveen already knows all of this. That's why he looked so self-satisfied in Kochi. I was wrong about him coming back to Trivandrum. He's probably already back in San Francisco, figuring out where the treasure is."

"What do you say we get going, then?" Sanjay said.

I kicked off my shoes and stretched out my legs on the reclining seat in the First Class section of our flight home to San Francisco via Dubai. Sanjay had bought the tickets. After learning he was more successful and famous than I'd realized, I didn't put up a fight about being treated to the seat.

"Why aren't you worried about Naveen?" I asked as I ate a warm cookie the flight attendant had given out. The food in First Class was even better than the luxurious seat.

"We know he didn't kill anyone," Sanjay said. "You figured that out." He sat with his seat reclined, a pillow under his neck and a beer in his hand.

"I know I said that. But he could have been working with whoever left the package at your door."

"You're grasping at straws," Sanjay said. "We need to focus on devising a plan to get the treasure map back from Tamarind."

"Tamarind wouldn't kill anyone," I said.

"What if they're working together?" Sanjay said. "You just said so yourself."

"That's a ridiculous idea."

"Remember, Tamarind is the only one besides us who knew about the map *that night*," Sanjay said. "The only one with a reason to act that night."

"But—"

"You're saying you don't want that map back?" Sanjay said. "Did you suddenly remember the rest of what's on the map? Do you have any better ideas?"

I grumbled.

"What was that?" Sanjay asked.

"No, I don't. You saw the map, too. Is your memory any better than mine?"

"If I'd known it would be stolen," Sanjay said, "I would have paid more attention—"

"You have any suggestions?"

"I do," he said. "A séance."

I shifted in the soft seat to face Sanjay. I could really get used to flying First Class. "Are you still drugged up from the hospital?"

"I'm serious," Sanjay said.

"You're serious?"

"I've got Samuel's spirit cabinet."

"I know you *can* perform a fake séance with it," I said. "But why?"

"Tamarind is superstitious."

"True. But remember, if you're right that she stole the map, then she doesn't actually believe it was Samuel who came back from the grave to steal the map from me."

"Doesn't matter," Sanjay said. "She's superstitious, so if she stole it she'll be even more freaked out when Samuel appears. If she's working with Naveen, I bet she'll reveal that, too."

"You're going to make Samuel appear," I repeated skeptically.

"Jaya, when are you going to learn to trust in my abilities? With me in control, the séance will look real. If you can get people together for a séance, I can make Tamarind confess."

CHAPTER 40

San Francisco, 1906

The Heart of India -- the pearl with its elephant protector -- was gone from the town of Thoothukudi in the British territory.

Anand learned of the theft from Vishwan, although Vishwan didn't call it a "theft." Vishwan wrote to his brother to tell him about the strange storm that had made the statue and its pearl disappear into the sea.

Since Thoothukudi had a viable harbor with frequent arrivals and departures of merchant ships, Anand knew Samuel could have taken a ship from there to China, where he could return to San Francisco.

Anand had not thought Samuel audacious enough to steal the Heart of India. But when he heard the news, he knew it was true. Samuel had taken his illusions a step further, stealing the statue and pearl for Mrs. Lancaster. She was as eccentric as she was rich, and Anand had seen how fascinated she was with antiquities from China and India.

Samuel had perfected his skill with his spirit cabinet, and taken the principles of illusion to a grand stage. The Heart of India was no small trinket! But Anand should have known. His friend who had become like a brother was too smart to fail.

Anand was too late to stop the theft, but through his connections to many boat builders, he was able to find out which departing ships could be transporting the statue.

There was no possibility of going to the police. Anand had experienced their methods firsthand. They would never believe him over Samuel. He had to get to the Heart of India first.

PART III

THE BARBARY COAST

CHAPTER 41

San Francisco's neighborhoods had changed since the days in which Anand lived here, but they had maintained unique personalities. Sanjay lived in a 2,000-square-foot loft in SOMA, the South of Market neighborhood of San Francisco. Previously a less desirable part of town, the original dot-com boom led to lots of development in the area. Overpaid young men became the largest segment of the new population. Sanjay fit in wonderfully.

Sanjay and I caught a cab from SFO to his loft. I told him I was eager to see the spirit cabinet. The truth was I didn't want to be alone. I had no idea what was happening around me, or who I could trust. Sanjay was one person I knew I could count on.

A slip of paper was taped to Sanjay's door. I cringed as he pulled it off, thinking of the booby trap. But this note was what it appeared to be. A shipping slip, notifying him that his delivery had been dropped off in the basement of the building. Paying thousands of dollars a month in rent does buy many perks—such as a secured delivery location for all of Sanjay's illusions, and a freight elevator to easily move things into his loft.

I rooted through Sanjay's fridge while waiting for him and the building's super to retrieve the crate. The interior of his fridge was the opposite of mine. A selection of cheeses and fruits, two loaves of bread, several half-eaten packages of takeout. A full shelf was packed with artisan beers and champagne. The door was stuffed with condiments, but none of them were the least bit spicy. I grabbed the bag of rye bread and a wedge of strong cheese, and made do with a honey-mustard spread since there was nothing with more zing. The cheese was flavorful enough to make up for it. I'd been on far too many international flights lately, so before tucking into my sandwich I fixed myself a cup of strong coffee with Sanjay's espresso maker.

There was plenty to distract me while I waited for Sanjay to return from the basement. The loft was effectively two stories—one sweeping first floor and a second floor covering half of the giant loft. There was a railing but no wall so you could see down to the first floor from the second.

The main first floor consisted of an open kitchen that overlooked the open dining and living rooms, and one wall that divided the space for a studio/workroom and another bathroom. The entire north wall was made of windows that provided a view of both downtown and the bay.

Along the wall that divided the first floor, a series of posters of famous magicians from the 1800s and early 1900s hung in faux-vintage frames. Though the frames were replicas, the posters themselves were originals of some of the greats: Kellar, Thurston, Robert-Houdin. Brightly colored red devils whispered in the ears of the magicians, and white ghostly figures swirled around the edges of bold black backgrounds. Matching the macabre style of the posters, two plaster gargoyles clung high on the wall above.

I brought my sandwich and coffee to the secretary desk in the entryway and used Sanjay's computer to email Tamarind, Naveen, and Nadia to invite them to the séance, as Sanjay had requested.

The double doors of the entryway swung open. An eight-foot-tall crate stood in the hallway. With a wheeled rack underneath, it came within a few inches of the top of the doorway.

"You were right," Sanjay said. "It'll fit."

The two men pushed the crate into the loft and slipped it off of the wheels. Sanjay thanked the building super, then disappeared into his studio. He emerged less than a minute later with a crowbar. He grinned at me as he pried open the wooden crate. I polished off my food and joined him to view the contents.

Modern workmanship wasn't what it used to be. The furniture in my apartment was mostly from Ikea, with a few items that were hand-me-downs from my brother. But the construction of this cabinet was truly something from another time. The wood was more solid than any piece of furniture I'd ever owned. Beyond its solid stature, the thick dark redwood was hand-carved with intricate swirls of fire. The fire design began in large sweeps on the bottom of the cabinet, getting smaller with the tendrils of smoke and fire winding around each other toward the top.

I shivered at the sight.

"Exactly," Sanjay said, standing back and crossing his arms. "It does create its intended effect."

"I don't like it."

"Check it out," Sanjay said with a grin, popping open a tiny hidden slot inside. "Just like the store said."

"What *is* that?" I asked.

"Just one of many secrets. This one is the slot that held dried animal blood, released with a string, to make it look like something had happened to the person inside. You can still see the residue."

"That's gross," I said, stifling a yawn.

"Go home, Jaya. Get some rest."

"You're kicking me out?"

"I should get to work on the cabinet. I need to be ready for tomorrow night." Sanjay put his hands on my shoulders. "I know you don't believe me about Tamarind, but please trust me on this. Don't take any chances being alone with her right now. And don't open any strange packages."

"But—"

"Out."

I went home, but only for as long as it took me to change into running clothes. Even though I was tired, I had enough adrenaline pumping through my veins that I knew I would never get to sleep that night without drastic measures. I hoped a five-mile run would be enough. There was only one problem: music. The thief had stolen my iPod. Without the music pushing me onward, I'd give up within ten minutes.

All I had was an old handheld CD player with its ear-muff-sized headphones. Better than nothing.

I found batteries and blew the dust off a CD sticking out from between the pages of a journal on my bookshelf. But how to carry the CD player? It was the size of the flowerpot and dead flowers in my kitchen window. I flung shoes out of the back of my closet until I found an old fanny pack. My transformation to the 1990s was now complete.

Downstairs, I knocked on the front door of the house. Nadia wasn't in. She didn't check email regularly, so I knew I should invite her to Sanjay's séance in person. I'd try her again on the way back from my run. I turned up the volume and blasted a bhangra mix from years ago in college as I ran toward Golden Gate Park.

Running usually helped me focus my mind, but today it refused to do so. My thoughts flitted from Lane's kiss to Sanjay's creepy cabinet to Anand and Samuel's theft of the Heart of India—back to Lane's kiss—to Naveen's deception—back to Lane's kiss—and finally to Steven's murder and Tamarind's possible betrayal that I was loath to believe.

I knew the evidence indicated it was possible it was her. But by that logic, it was possible for it to have been *me* who killed Steven. I knew the police were doing their jobs. Inspector Valdez seemed like a good guy. But I couldn't sit around doing nothing. The police hadn't seen the treasure map. They didn't understand what was going on.

I was so distracted by my thoughts that I barely felt the fanny back carrying the gargantuan CD player bouncing against my hip—nor did I realize the time. I was deep in the park when I noticed how dark it was. I didn't have my phone or my iPod to tell me what time it was, but the sun was setting. I could take care of myself, but it wasn't a good idea to go running by myself in the park after nightfall. I turned around and headed home.

I kept up my pace to the beat of the bhangra on my headphones until I was out of the park. A group of homeless teenagers with a pit bull played an out-of-tune guitar at the edge of the park on Stanyan and Haight Street. I pulled off my headphones and slowed to a slow jog as I made my way to Oak Street—Haight Street is too crowded with tourists to walk at a faster pace than a stroll.

Outside of the park and without the music, I felt the effects of the run in my legs and chest. Cold sweat chilled my torso. I put the helmet-like headphones back on to drown out the world. The cold was again undetectable, as was the thudding of my heart.

I caught my breath and stretched outside the front of the house for a few moments, letting the headphones dangle around my neck, before knocking on Nadia's door. I swear Nadia had a sixth sense. I'd never known it to take her longer than two seconds to open her door for me.

"I thought you were dead."

Nadia was never one to mince words. She stood in her doorway in a black wrap dress and black high-heeled ankle boots, a cocktail glass of clear liquid in her hand and fur stole resting on her shoulders, looking like she was on her way to a 1930s opera.

"I emailed you that I was out of town for a few days. I didn't think you'd worry."

"Come," she said, ushering me inside with the hand holding the glass. She didn't spill a drop. "That magician of yours has been calling nonstop for days, worried about you. Until two days ago. Then I think he is dead, too."

"Sorry, Nadia. You know how Sanjay overreacts. There's nothing to worry about."

Nadia frowned and nodded. "I thought so. I would have known for sure if I had not been worried after your mugging the other day. I do not like how you get mixed up in the affairs of others. Like you did earlier this summer. It is not safe, Jaya. Neither is running after dark. Yes, yes, I know you can take care of yourself." She swatted away the protest forming on my lips. "But it is still not good.

Especially when you look so tired. You work too hard. I do not think I have seen you go on a single date since you moved in a year ago."

Was Nadia, who broke up with her on-again/off-again boyfriend Jack every other month, giving me advice about my love life?

"Since when have either of us needed a man?" I said.

"True. Yet sometimes they are quite nice to have around." Nadia gave me a mischievous smile.

"I'll keep that in mind."

"You have come for mail, yes? You are too sweaty to sit on my furniture."

"Looks like you're on your way out anyway."

She pressed her lips together. "Perhaps."

I knew better than to ask if she was getting back together with Jack tonight.

"I'm not actually here for mail," I said. "I wanted to invite you to—"

"The séance," she said, holding up a shiny new smart phone. "I have entered the twenty-first century. I received your intriguing email."

"I know it sounds strange."

"I would not," she said, "miss it for the world."

Nadia retreated to her kitchen. She emerged a minute later without her cocktail and with a small stack of mail. The top piece of mail caught my eye. It was a flat package with a red DO NOT BEND stamp across it. The return address was from Steven's daughter-in-law Christine. I opened it with Nadia looking over my shoulder.

It was a note from Christine.

I found this among my father-in-law's belongings. Thought it would be of interest to you. We want nothing to do with it, and I feel terrible about Connor's appalling behavior. I hope it will be useful to you.

It was a copy of Anand's treasure map.

CHAPTER 42

I stood in Nadia's living room clenching Anand's map that I never thought I'd see again. As I'd expected, Steven Healy had made a copy before loaning it to me.

The landmarks, the markings, the notations I'd tried to recreate in my mind—they were all here right in front of me. It wasn't the original, but I was betting Anand hadn't written anything in invisible ink. I had everything I needed right there in my hands. The landmarks Anand had selected for a reason were all right there. The exact locations of the buildings and paths were there. The exact location of the X was there.

"Oh my God," I whispered.

"Is it important?"

"Yes," I said, "it certainly is."

I went directly to a twenty-four-hour copy center to make a copy of the map. I wasn't going to repeat my earlier mistake. I wasn't going to let it get away from me again. After taking care of that, I grabbed a gooey ham and cheese biscuit from a late-night café down the street

I made sure the photocopy of the map was far from my oozing biscuit as I sat at my stubby kitchen table. The map already had stains on it—it didn't need oily cheese drops as well.

The Anchored Enchantress was the one location featured prominently that I hadn't yet been able to figure out. I recognized the area of the old Barbary Coast, the famous seedy part of town that had grown up in the 1850s during the California Gold Rush. Men flocking to San Francisco as a stop on their way to the gold fields made big business out of drinking, gambling, and prostitution. What was *The Anchored Enchantress*? Why could I find no record of it in either Kochi or San Francisco? Would it be possible to figure it out so many years later?

Usually I'm a sound sleeper, but that night my mind wouldn't shut down. I was so close to figuring out what was going on that my mind wanted to keep working. *What was I missing?*

In the morning, a knock on the door woke me up from a restless sleep. At least I was asleep in my bed this time. And this time, I asked who it was.

Tamarind's hair and lips were both a bright blue today. Her hair was tied into tiny Princess Leah pigtails.

"I'm on my way to work," she said. "Your email said you might not be back on email before tonight. You still didn't have a phone so I came in person. Mind if I come in?"

I couldn't believe that Tamarind would hurt me. Even if she was a killer after the treasure—and I wasn't admitting it was the case—she hadn't actually tried to kill *me*. I didn't believe Tamarind was involved. Still... I decided not to mention that I happened to have another copy of the map.

I held the door open wide to let her inside. Her bright blue lips smiled at me as her large frame walked through the door. A black T-shirt with purposeful rips hung on her broad shoulders.

"It's a great shirt, isn't it?" Tamarind said, following my gaze. "I love Siouxsie Sioux. I know some say she's goth, but really she's true punk. But enough about my shirt—what the hell is going on?"

Where to begin... "Coffee?"

"If it means I get to know what's going on, of course. I can be late to work. Can I smoke in here? No? Okay, better hurry on that coffee then. Are those Batman pajamas you're wearing?"

I'd forgotten I was still in my night clothes. "Kid-size pajamas don't get tangled when I sleep."

"But Batman?"

"All the petite women's ones were pink."

"I hear ya."

"Let me go change." I avoided the folded map as I scooped a mound of ground coffee beans into the coffee maker. "Pour yourself some coffee when it's done."

I emerged from the bathroom a couple minutes later in much more appropriate jeans and black sweater. Tamarind was in the process of pouring coffee.

"Nice Pirates of the Caribbean mug," she said. "Better to hear your stories of pirate treasure."

"I forgot I had that thing." My brother had gotten it for me at Disneyland years ago.

Tamarind handed me a British Library mug, keeping the pirate one for herself, and leaned against the kitchen counter. "You're not still working on this treasure hunt, are you?"

Sanjay had to be wrong about Tamarind. She was a good friend. And she was incredibly smart. She could help me. I wasn't accusing her of anything, so I couldn't think of a downside. I only hesitated briefly before getting her up to speed. I told her what I'd learned in India—leaving out the parts about Sanjay collapsing in a pool of blood and Lane's kiss.

Ten minutes later, my coffee mug was empty and I was done retelling the story.

"Shut. Up." Tamarind whispered. "This calls for something stronger than coffee. Too bad it's only nine in the morning. But I *told you* it was Anand trying to communicate with you."

"Yeah...about that. You're going to come to the séance tonight?"

"That hottie Sanjay is going to communicate with Anand and Samuel, isn't he? I knew you two were up to something."

"Something like that." I hated lying to Tamarind, but it had to be done.

"I wish we had that map! Do you think Anand could make it materialize for us? I should bring my camera, in case it just materializes as plasma and we have to photograph it before it disappears."

"I don't think that's how it works."

"No? Hmm. I've never been to a séance before. This is going to be *awesome*. Oh, I could use the camera on my phone." She pulled her phone out of her bag and swore. "I was here for too long. I'm totally late!"

She grabbed my empty mug from me and rinsed out our mugs in the sink. "What should I wear? What are you going to wear?"

I glanced down at my bare feet. "Probably this but with shoes."

Tamarind turned off the sink and turned around to face me. "Really?"

"What's the matter with it?"

"Nothing. I just figured a séance required dressing up like a flapper or something."

"Wrong decade."

"You're right," Tamarind said. "I'll figure something else out. See you tonight!"

As she headed out the door, I nearly called her back. I stopped myself. I hated the deception, but whatever good was going to come out of tonight's events, it was necessary.

I found myself yawning in spite of the large cup of coffee. I knew I should go get a new phone, but it wouldn't hurt to take a quick nap...

It was Sanjay pounding at my door that woke me up from a groggy haze.

"Are you ready?" he asked.

"I wasn't going to come over until this afternoon."

"It *is* afternoon."

"What are you talking about?" I yawned. "Tamarind was here just a few minutes ago."

"*Tamarind* was here?" Sanjay's nostrils flared.

"Yeah, we just had coffee—"

"And she apparently drugged your coffee while she was at it." He shook his head so furiously that a rose petal escaped from his bowler hat and fluttered to the floor. "Why didn't you listen to me about Tamarind? She's probably off in search of the treasure as we speak."

I gaped at Sanjay. "You can't be serious."

"How else do you explain the fact that you didn't realize it was late afternoon already?"

"Jet lag," I said. It had to be jet lag. "I couldn't sleep at all last night."

"I don't buy it," he said. "I don't buy it at all. Now get your things. You're following me to my place. I'm not letting you out of my sight before the séance."

CHAPTER 43

Lightning struck as I stood in front of the wall of glass windows in Sanjay's loft waiting for the guests to arrive. A storm was brewing in the East Bay, but hadn't yet reached San Francisco.

"The storm will be great for the atmosphere at the séance," Sanjay said, standing in front of the expansive window with me. We watched the dark clouds roll closer from the east as the sunlight faded over the San Francisco skyline before us.

Sanjay had changed into a tuxedo after lighting a series of candles he'd placed around the loft. He placed his bowler hat on his head and stood in the dim light of the window with his hands clasped behind his back, making me forget for a time what century I was in.

"I feel like I'm losing my mind," I said. "I don't understand what's going on around us."

Sanjay reached out and squeezed my hand. "I hope to get you some answers tonight."

Tamarind was the first to arrive. I wouldn't have believed it if I hadn't seen it with my own eyes. She wore a burgundy bustled dress straight out of the Victorian era that pulled in her thick, boyish waist. Her hair was now black. It was pulled back and supplemented with a matching black bunch of fake curls that ran down her back. On her lips she wore a deep burgundy lipstick that matched her dress.

"M'lady," Sanjay said, kissing her hand. Tamarind giggled.

Nadia arrived next, wearing the fox stole I'd seen her in the night before, but her dress tonight, like Tamarind's, was from another time. A silver evening gown sparkled down to her toes with pointed silver tips poking out from beneath the dress.

Was I the only one who hadn't thought of dressing up?

Sanjay handed cordial glasses of dark liquid to the two women.

Naveen arrived a few minutes before sunset. I introduced him to Sanjay, who he hadn't previously met. He was dressed in a formal suit as usual, but nothing extra like Tamarind and Nadia.

"You look like hell, Jaya," Naveen said. "Jet lag got to you? And what's with the costumes?"

"I told you we're having a séance."

"I wonder what the dean will think of your *interesting* research methods, Jaya. Hardly the type of scholarly pursuit he'd approve of, I'm sure."

I told myself to breathe. Naveen wasn't here so I could impress him. I needed to learn more about what he knew, and Sanjay thought his presence tonight would help. "The dean likes results, doesn't he?" I said.

Naveen handed Sanjay a box containing an eight-ball that predicts the future. "I brought this," he said with a laugh.

"Is this going to work with an unbeliever?" Tamarind whispered to me.

Nadia remained uncharacteristically silent. Her eyes twinkled as she watched us spar. This show probably rivaled the performance she saw the previous night, at least in terms of drama. She swallowed the entirety of her small drink.

"The electricity in the air from the spirit world runs high at this time of day," Sanjay said. "Don't worry yourselves with these petty thoughts. They'll soon pass."

Sanjay was good. Even without the help of a stage and spotlight, he was a master performer.

"Introductions are in order," Sanjay went on. "May I present a librarian of the first class, Tamarind Ortega, and the most fetching landlady this side of St. Petersburg, Nadia Lubov. Professor Naveen Krishnan, whom I had not had the pleasure of meeting until tonight. And you all know esteemed historian Jaya Jones, whose great-granduncle is the reason we're all here tonight. We will be attempting to contact him and his associate, Spiritualist Samuel, who once owned an object that has recently come into my possession."

A clap of thunder sounded. Tamarind jumped. The rest of us turned our heads toward the windows. The storm was approaching as quickly as the sun was fading.

"People assume that midnight is the best time to conduct a séance," Sanjay said, his face dead serious, "because of the myth of it as 'the witching hour.' In truth it's the turning points of the day— sunrise and sunset—when the forces are strongest. We must hurry."

"No time for a second aperitif?" Nadia asked. "That would put us all more in the mood."

Sanjay shot her a sharp look. "We need to be holding hands when the sun sets," he said. "If you'll follow me. Leave your bags and cell phones in the main room. You will not need them where we are going."

He pushed open the sliding metal doors leading to the section of the loft that served as his practice studio. The doors formed one wall of the room, the glass wall of windows another, and two brick walls provided atmosphere along the other two sides. At least three-dozen candles flickered around the edges of the room.

In the center, two objects had been placed: Samuel's spirit cabinet, and a simple round wooden table just big enough for four people to sit around. A single candle glowed in the center of the table.

Tamarind stopped short when she saw the setup. Her lips trembled. She must have been even more superstitious than I'd realized.

"The four of you," Sanjay said, "will sit around the table and complete the circle." He pushed shut the sliding door behind us, trapping us inside the candle-lit room.

"What about you?" Nadia asked.

"I must take another journey," Sanjay said. "I will be inside the cabinet of fire."

CHAPTER 44

Nadia frowned at Sanjay. "Is that safe? The solid wood does not seem to give air flow."

"Thank you for your concern, madame," Sanjay said. "I assure you I will be perfectly safe. This cabinet once belonged to the great Spiritualist Samuel, a man who did what I am about to do, one hundred years before me. You can all feel that it holds power, can you not?"

Tamarind elbowed me. "Does he always talk like that?" she whispered.

I'd seen Sanjay perform enough times that I knew he'd stay in character regardless of what happened. His stage voice carried more of a suggestion of British pronunciation than Indian, like the Cary Grant era of movies where the actors enunciated in that style.

"Miss Ortega," Sanjay said, "will you do me the honor of binding my arms and ankles?"

The look on Tamarind's face told me she thought she'd died and gone to heaven. She took the rope he handed to her. After he stepped into the cabinet, she wound the rope around his wrists.

"Tighter," he said. "And quickly. We only have a few minutes before sunset is fully upon us."

Tamarind grinned as she squatted in her bustle dress and bound Sanjay's ankles.

"Madame Lubov," Sanjay said, squirming in his seat in the cabinet, "will you will check the knots?"

Nadia stepped up to examine the knots. She nodded. "What is the purpose?"

"I must bind myself to this world," Sanjay replied. "For my own safety, you understand. We wouldn't want the spirits to carry me away with them. I can already feel that there are forces connected to this cabinet trying to break through."

Tamarind stumbled backwards in her voluminous dress. I can't say I blamed her.

"Now, Naveen," Sanjay continued, "please close the door of this cabinet and wrap this chain here tightly around the top and bottom of the cabinet."

"I don't like this," Tamarind whispered as Naveen worked. "This isn't right."

"The time has come!" A voice echoed throughout the room. This time we all jumped. "Seat yourselves around the table and clasp hands. Whatever happens, do not break your bond."

"His voice echoes from within the cabinet," Nadia said. She was the first to move. We followed her lead, sitting down around the table. I sat between Nadia and Tamarind, with Naveen opposite me.

"It is done," the booming voice said. "The sun has slipped from our world. I can feel the power flowing."

The hairs on the back of my neck stood up. Not because of Sanjay's words, but because of what I felt. Cold wind blew over me. It was so cold I could have sworn I felt icy tendrils touching my neck. I wasn't the only one who felt it. Tamarind gasped. I glanced around the room. The only light came from the candles along the edges of the room and the solitary candle in the middle of the table. I couldn't see well enough to tell where the breeze was coming from. Sanjay must have hidden a fan somewhere. He must have.

"Samuel!" The voice was simultaneously a whisper and a shout. How had he done that? "You are here with us. It is your presence I feel, is it not?"

The cold wind picked up. The candles flickered violently.

"No? I am mistaken. Is it Anand who is here with us tonight?"

The wind swept around us, extinguishing the candles along the sides of the room. Only the light from the candle on the table remained. But not for long. I felt myself shiver as another light appeared.

A ghostly glow materialized above the cabinet. A strangled scream escaped from Tamarind's lips.

"The air is cold," the voice said. "So cold in this place. Not like the sandy beaches of Cape Comorin where Vishwan and I played as children."

The sound of rain striking against the windows shifted my attention. The storm was now right above us.

"I know," that strange loud whisper continued. "I know who has killed."

I knew it must have been Sanjay speaking. It had to have been. But it certainly didn't sound like him. He spoke with only a hint of an Indian accent—probably because he didn't know how to do a South Indian accent, only a North Indian one, which is quite different. Not that Tamarind would have noticed. But when Sanjay performed, he did it right. Was he using a distorted amplifier to deepen and disguise the voice?

The glow that had appeared above the cabinet continued to hover there like an oversized lightning bug. The glowing circle didn't exactly move, but it wasn't completely still either, its energy pulsing. It didn't take shape. Of course it couldn't. Because it wasn't really Anand. But what on earth *was it*?

"What the hell?" Naveen said.

I felt Nadia's body jerk. "Do not break the circle," she whispered tersely to Naveen. Air swirled around us. I swallowed hard, reminding myself this was only a trick. It was only a trick.

"Tamarind Ortega," the disembodied voice whispered.

A burst of frigid air blew against my ear as the words were spoken. Tamarind screamed, but she didn't move from the circle.

"What do you want from me?" Tamarind cried out, clasping my hand tightly.

"Murderer," the voice whispered. "Thief!" Cold air whipped around us. The candle on the table blew out. The glow above the cabinet was the only light left in the room. "Tell what you know!"

Tamarind screamed.

"Stop!" Tamarind shouted. "You win! I promise I'll tell them everything! Just go away! Go away!"

A popping sounded. Along with the noise, the glow disappeared. But the room did not fall silent. A low rumbling began. It was a voice, but unlike the disembodied voice echoing through the room before, this one was clearly coming from the cabinet. It grew louder into a piercing deep scream. It was so loud, we let go of each other's hands to cover our ears. The horrid sound chilled me to the bone.

The scream stopped. Its echo reverberated.

Nadia was the first to lift her hands from her ears as she ran toward the cabinet. "Do not just stand there," she cried. "Help me get this chain off."

"Where's the key?" I asked. I couldn't look at Tamarind. Sanjay was more important right now. "Sanjay?"

There was no response.

"That wasn't at all like I thought it would be," Tamarind said, her voice dead of emotion.

"We have to get him out of there," Nadia said.

Naveen rushed to help her, and Nadia stepped away from the cabinet.

I thought of what Sanjay told me of Samuel's faked death. What if he was wrong? What if Samuel really *had* died in this cabinet? What if there wasn't enough air inside, like Nadia had thought? Was that why Sanjay had screamed so horribly?

Nadia gently pushed Naveen aside. "I have found the solution," she said. In her hands, she held a large set of wire cutters. "These were in the closet."

With a snap, the front section of chain fell to the ground.

Naveen pulled the chain from around the cabinet, not worrying about scraping the intricate fire carvings. As the last strand of chain hit the floor, he yanked open the door of the cabinet. The rope that had bound Sanjay's hands and feet lay at the bottom of the wooden cabinet, along with Sanjay's black bowler hat. But there was no sign of Sanjay.

The cabinet was empty.

CHAPTER 45

San Francisco, 1906

Anand was nervous about meeting Li at the Siren's Anchor that night. He was sure that Li would see from his face that he had been courting his sister Mai. But Li's note had been insistent.

When Anand entered the saloon, Li was standing at the bar with a young Chinese man, at the age between a boy and a man. There was something familiar about him...

The young man smiled at Anand and extended his hand for Anand to shake. A scar ran from the man's hand up the side of his arm.

"Recognize your friend?" Li asked. "This is Eddie. This is the boy whose life you saved three years ago. He's here to return the favor."

The three sat at a table together and leaned in close.

"Eddie is from a family of sailors," Li explained.

"I owe you a great debt," Eddie said.

"It was nothing more than any man would have done," Anand replied, remembering that dark night when he, Li, and Samuel had rescued Eddie from the gang of men beating him. There was never any question that he would help the boy.

"You are too humble," Eddie said. "My brothers agree we are in your debt. We want to repay you."

"No payment is required, my friend," Anand said.

"Wait until you hear what he has to say," Li said.

Eddie grinned. "We're going to help you intercept the ship you're after," he said. "The ship that holds the treasure you seek."

CHAPTER 46

"Oh my God!" Tamarind screamed, pulling at the sides of her hair. "Where did he go? Something went wrong! Anand's ghost took him!"

Though I didn't agree with her assessment, I didn't like this one bit. Where could Sanjay have gone? The wind had distracted us in the near darkness, which would have allowed for his escape, but I didn't see where he could be hiding. I found my way to the wall in the semidarkness and fumbled for a light switch. The lights came on, but didn't do much to illuminate the situation. I still didn't see where Sanjay could be.

I knew why I was so uneasy. I couldn't think of any reason why Sanjay would be hiding.

"There is no such thing as ghosts," Nadia said. "You have all been deceived. Am I correct that this was for the benefit of Tamarind?"

"We have to find Sanjay," I said.

"He will reveal himself in good time," Nadia said.

"Tamarind," I said, squinting in the new light, "what were you talking about back there?" I wasn't sure I wanted to hear her confession, but it's what we'd set out to do, and I knew I needed to hear it. I still couldn't quite believe Sanjay had been right about her all along.

Tamarind lifted the bustles of her dress and walked over to the window. She looked out over the rain falling between us and the sparkling lights of the city before turning back to face me.

"I never wanted you to get hurt," she said. "That's why I did it."

"What did you do, Tamarind?"

"I did it to protect you."

"What did you *do*?"

The metal sliding door to the room groaned as it slid open. We all gave a start, but we must have been all screamed out, because nobody screamed.

Sanjay stepped into the room. He looked no worse for wear except that his bow tie was askew and his thick black hair was running a bit wild without his hat.

"Tamarind didn't do it," he said. A stack of papers was clenched in his hand.

"Hey," said Tamarind. "Those papers are from my bag."

"I know. You were trying to protect Jaya. Not to hurt her or anyone else."

"Would someone," I said, "please tell me what's going on."

"I was trying to protect you from the truth about your uncle," Tamarind said. "I know how important he was to your family. I didn't want you to know the truth, or get yourself killed in the process."

"You didn't kill Steven?"

"What are you talking about?" Tamarind gaped at me.

"She didn't do it," Sanjay said. "Tamarind has been lying, but about something else. She was lying about the documents she found, not about what she'd done."

"Wait," Tamarind said. "Anand yelled both thief *and* *murderer*. He thought I killed someone? Anand's spirit wasn't talking about himself?"

"Tamarind," Sanjay said. "I'm really sorry, but that was me. Not Anand."

"Shut. Up. You're lying. That was totally Anand. How could you fake that?"

"It was an illusion. That's what I do."

"You're trying to do a cover-up?" Tamarind crossed her arms and shook her head firmly. "After what I just saw, I don't think so."

Sanjay set down the papers in his hand so he could remove his bow tie and unbutton the top buttons of the dress shirt of his tuxedo. After reaching the third button, I caught a glimpse of a shiny object under his shirt. He pulled the shirt open wider, revealing electronic equipment duct taped to his chest.

"You're sworn to secrecy," he said. "If any of you ever reveal this—"

"We have no idea how those wires did anything we saw tonight," I said. "Your secrets are safe. Now will someone *please* explain what you two are talking about?"

"You're all crazy," Naveen said. "All of you."

Tamarind walked up to Sanjay and ran her fingers over the duct tape, frowning. Sanjay didn't seem to mind.

Nadia cleared her throat.

"Right," Sanjay said, buttoning up his shirt. "I knew Tamarind was lying about something. I thought she had murdered Steven, but what's really going on is that she withheld information she found in her research so that you wouldn't get hurt, either emotionally or physically, by learning the truth."

"I'm sorry, Jaya," Tamarind said. "Anand wasn't who you thought he was. But that's pretty awesome that you thought I could kill someone to watch out for you. I guess I've got some street cred left after all."

Sanjay and I looked at each other. Neither of us had the heart to tell her that's not why Sanjay thought she killed someone.

"These papers," Sanjay said, "contain information Tamarind found in her research that she kept from both of us. This information suggests that Anand was a murderer."

"You think Anand was a murderer?" I said. Maybe Tamarind was right that I didn't want to know. "How did you find out?"

"After you found those first references," Tamarind said, "it wasn't hard to find. But you were so distracted after you were mugged and left the country that you didn't follow up at the library. I kept looking. Sanjay came over to look as well. But I didn't like the last part of what I found, so I kept it to myself."

"What did you find?"

Tamarind hesitated.

"Anand killed his friend. It was never proven, but it's pretty clear."

"You got it wrong," Sanjay said. "Anand didn't kill Samuel."

"He did it using that *thing*," Tamarind said, gesturing toward the spirit cabinet. "It was reported in the papers. That's why I freaked out when I saw it here. And why I really thought Sanjay was able to communicate with Anand, who murdered someone inside it. That's what I was keeping from you, Jaya."

"That's why you lied to Sanjay about those particular newspaper records being missing," I said.

"The newspapers were wrong," Sanjay said. "Samuel didn't die."

"But I have the reports," Tamarind said, pointing at the stack of photocopies Sanjay had found in her bag.

"I figured it out when I bought the cabinet," Sanjay said. "Didn't you wonder how I got out? It has a hidden escape hatch. An ingenious one. I could have been halfway to Mexico by now without any of you knowing that I'd left."

"Well," Naveen said, "this certainly has been enlightening. I've learned a lot about Jaya's research methods."

"Hold on, Naveen," Sanjay said, holding up a cell phone.

"Hey," Naveen said. "That's my phone."

"You should have a more creative password if you don't want people to read your mail."

"Give that back," Naveen said, running up to Sanjay to grab the phone. Sanjay handed it back to him.

That's why Sanjay had wanted Naveen at the séance. He'd planned to do these searches all along.

"He's innocent, too," Sanjay said, looking at me.

"Reading other people's email is illegal," Naveen said. He tucked the phone into an inside pocket of his suit and glared at Sanjay.

"If you really want me to tell everyone about—"

"I can overlook it in this case," Naveen said hastily. "Even though you're all crazy, so nobody should believe anything you say."

"Naveen has been trying to track down the Heart of India," Sanjay said to me, ignoring Naveen. "But nothing more."

"I already told you that," Naveen said. "I learned about it first. It's my discovery."

"It's nobody's discovery," I said. "If anyone could claim credit, it would have been Steven Healy, but even he had the information handed to him, just like you did."

Naveen glowered at me as the faint sound of birds chirping filled the cavernous room.

"That would be my phone," Nadia said. "You have searched it, too?"

Sanjay shook his head. "I wouldn't dream of touching your bag, Nadia."

She hurried from the room to grab her bag, returning a few moments later with her cell phone at her ear and a grave expression on her face.

"Why did you—" she said. "Yes, I know, but— Why did you not call? Messages? I have been occupied. No, it is fine. You did the right thing. I do not want you to lie to the police." She hung up the phone and swore in Russian.

"Jaya, you must leave. That was Carol from next door. Why could she not lie to the police?" Nadia threw her hands up in frustration. "The police were at our house, looking for you. If you do not wish to go to jail, I expect you will leave here. Carol told the police I had gone to your magician friend's house. I do not think it will take the police too long to figure out where you are."

"The police?" I said. "What do they want with me?"

"They mentioned the murdered man to her. It does not sound good."

My heart sank.

They couldn't possibly think I murdered Steven Healy. Could they?

A different phone rang. Sanjay picked up a subtle phone built into the wall next to the light switch. He mumbled something and hung up.

"Too late," he said. "That was the doorman. The police are on their way up. They're taking the elevators. You guys take the stairs. *Hurry*. Everybody *out*!"

CHAPTER 47

San Francisco, 1906

Because of the size of the Heart of India statue, Anand knew Samuel would have no choice but to take the whole journey by boat, rather than taking a ship bound for New York and switching to a train. The journey by ship would take weeks.

Anand would be ready.

Eddie proved to be the most dedicated of men, doing much more than was necessary to repay his debt to Anand. He secured a ship, enlisted a dozen men from his extended family who were skilled at sea, and swore the men to secrecy.

Eddie's men listened attentively to Anand's plan, interrupting to make suggestions but never doubting their involvement.

They were honorable men, Anand hated that they must risk becoming outlaws. Pirates.

Anand knew what he must do to minimize their risk. If anything were to go wrong, he would take the blame himself. Anand was a Pirate now. If he and his men were caught, he would claim he commanded the crew against their will.

He had the perfect name for himself. A name that signified restoring order and balance.

He would be Pirate Vishnu.

The plans of the honorable pirates were coming together perfectly--until they attacked the wrong ship.

The mistake wasn't the crew's fault. Anand and Li had pieced together the information as best they could, but it was uncertain what day Samuel's ship would arrive and similar vessels approached on the same sea route.

Pirate Vishnu and his crew made sure they did not harm any of the men on the ship they attacked. The pirates were seen by the ship's crew, but escaped without capture. They retreated into the fog and waited.

A few days later, when the ship they sought rolled into the Golden Gate, they were ready.

Chapter 48

"You can't go home or go to the university," Sanjay whispered in my ear, pulling me aside while the others rushed out of the loft and down the stairs. "They'll look for you there."

"You want me to *run*?" I asked.

"Do you want to be arrested," Sanjay hissed, "or do you want to be free to figure this out? The police are only going to get in the way right now."

"I don't know..."

"Technically you don't *know* they want to arrest you," Sanjay said. "So it's not really like you're evading them. They just happened to miss you."

He had a point.

"Where am I supposed to go?" I asked. "The police could pull any credit card transactions."

Sanjay pulled out his wallet and frowned. "I've only got fifty dollars on me. Doesn't your father live around here? There are enough people named *Jones* that they shouldn't find you there right away."

"You've met my father. You can't think he's the best—"

"You don't have a lot of options, Jaya. Unless you want to go to jail or hide in the spirit cabinet, I suggest you take the other stairs—"

"There's another set of stairs?"

"Of course. I wouldn't have told everyone to take the stairs if there wasn't. I'm sure any second now Naveen will be telling the police where to find you. "There's no way you should go down the same set of stairs as him. You'll be taking the service stairs."

"Naveen," I muttered in anger before another thought occurred to me. "What was it you found on his phone that he didn't want anyone to know about?"

"You need to go, Jaya." Sanjay pulled me into the hallway and led me to a discreet door I never would have noticed, even if I'd been thinking straight.

Right before closing the door behind me, he popped his head into the stairwell and grinned.

"Nothing," he said.

"What?"

"It was a bluff. I didn't have time to find anything embarrassing on Naveen's phone. But everyone has *something* to hide."

The problem with my father was you never knew what to expect. Richard Jones was a selfless parent, but in his own way. He didn't live on the same planet as most of us. I knew he would do anything to protect me, but what he thought was good for me might be even more questionable than Tamarind and Sanjay's "help."

It had come to this. Running to a home where I'd never felt very much at home. Sanjay was right that it was the best alternative I had. I needed time to regroup and figure out my next steps.

My father lived in Berkeley, just ten miles away over the Bay Bridge from San Francisco, in a small Craftsman house in what was considered a bad neighborhood. The income of a sitar teacher wasn't very much, but it was enough to clothe my brother and me in second-hand tie dye clothing, furnish a modest home with bean bags as couches, use incense to cover the smells of what my father and his friends were smoking, and feed us meatless meals. The experience taught me that color is overrated, intoxicants should be imbibed rather than smoked, and meat is the most exquisite food on earth.

When I reached the bottom of the stairs in Sanjay's building, I saw something that made my heart sink even lower than I thought possible. I didn't see any police, but my car was being towed. My parking karma had run its course—I had parked too close to a fire hydrant.

I took a deep breath. I didn't have a car, but I could catch a BART train to Berkeley. The closest stop would drop me off within less than a mile of my dad's house.

I didn't have my headphones to listen to music on the ten minute run to the BART station. I had nothing to distract me from thoughts about what I was missing from Uncle Anand's treasure map, Lane Peters, who flashed in and out of my life, or this trip to see my father. It was probably for the best to be in silence anyway, so I could be on the lookout for the police. How had this become my life?

I was slightly winded as I slid my ticket through the stall at the station. I'd never thought about closed-circuit video cameras before, but now I noticed them everywhere. I wished I'd thought to take a hat from Sanjay's place. I wrapped my arms around myself and sunk down into a seat in the train headed to Berkeley.

I closed my eyes and wondered if I was doing the right thing. My dad might be stoned out of his mind, blocking out thoughts of my mother and her untimely death, but he'd do what he could to help me. When I stopped growing just under five feet tall, he drove me around in his VW van to every self-defense class in the Berkeley area to make sure I found a way to protect myself. When I graduated early from high school at sixteen, he supported my decision not to go straight to college. He also didn't pressure me when I turned eighteen, which led to me not starting college until I was in my twenties.

My father's house sat at the corner of two residential streets. As I approached the house from the smaller side street, I saw a movement through the window. It was my father walking through the room, his gray-blond hair long in a ponytail resting on his back over a white linen shirt. I took a deep breath and knocked.

"Hi Richard," I said as he opened the door.

My father blinked at me in astonishment. He looked much the same as the last time I'd seen him six months ago. I think he was wearing the same flowing white shirt over white linen trousers with orange Birkenstocks on his feet.

"Did you tell me you were coming?" He blinked again. I detected a faint whiff of sweet smoke coming from inside the house. Now that I looked more carefully, I saw that his eyes were mildly bloodshot.

"Can I come in?" I asked. "I'm sorry to interrupt, but it's kind of important."

"Of course! Would you like an acai smoothie?" My father put his arm around me and pulled me into the living room where bean bags lined two walls. It was forever 1969 in that house, even though we hadn't moved there until the 1980s. Two large framed photographs of me and my brother were center stage on the mantle above the unused fireplace.

"No, I'm fine," I said. "I mean, I'm not fine, but I don't need a smoothie."

"What's happened?" Richard eyes grew wide with alarm. "It's not your brother—"

"Mahilan is fine. At least as far as I know. I'm here because of something that's happened to me." I paused and concentrated on forming words that were difficult to say out loud, especially to my father. "I'm in trouble. Can I stay here for a few days?"

"Are you hiding from the police?"

My father was definitely smarter than he sometimes seemed.

"It was a misunderstanding," I said, averting my eyes.

Richard put his hands to his temples. "Didn't I always teach you and your brother the dangers of getting mixed up in drugs that aren't marijuana?"

I looked up at him, dumbfounded. "You think I'm on *drugs*?"

"Why else would the police be after you? They don't care about pot. No, no, it's all right. I won't judge you. Just be honest with me about how serious it is. Is it cocaine? Please tell me it's not heroin."

"Richard—"

"Do you need to go into rehab? At a first offense, they usually give you that option. I know some good places."

"Richard! I am *not* on drugs."

A knock on the door sounded. "Richard Jones?"

"I know that knock," my father whispered to me, his eyes darting around the room.

"Berkeley Police," the voice continued.

I closed my eyes as the full weight of my actions sank in. Why had I listened to Sanjay and thought they wouldn't find me here? Of course the police would have other means of finding my relatives besides looking in the Yellow Pages. I groaned. Everything was happening so quickly that I didn't have time to think.

"Use the back door," my father whispered in my ear. "There's a hole in the fence that leads to the back alley. Mick used it when they came for him. If the cop's partner is out front, they won't see you go out that way."

My stoned father gave me a bear hug, then pushed me out the back door.

CHAPTER 49

San Francisco, April 10, 1906

A storm came out of nowhere, and water from the
sky and the sea drenched them, but the storm also
provided the extra cover they needed. Anand and
the crew succeeded in capturing the ship with the
Heart of India.

But the challenge was not yet over. He knew he
could not go to the police. Even with his debts,
Samuel had a higher social standing than himself,
and would be believed. Anand would hide the
treasure until he was able to get the Indian
authorities to come to his assistance. He had a
plan. All his years building and fixing boats had
taught him how to alter the appearance of a ship.
He could hide the treasure in plain sight.

With a little paint and a new figurehead on
the front of the captured boat, the vessel would
not be recognized. The crew helped him accomplish
the disguise within a day. The riskier part of
the plan was where he would need to leave the
ship. The safe ports would need to make note of
it, and Anand could not take the risk. He left

the boat anchored near the rocky cliffs of the northwest coast of San Francisco. It was not ideal, but he would not need to leave it for long.

Samuel met Anand at The Siren's Anchor the day following Anand's recapture of the stolen treasure.

Samuel's beard was unshaven, his hair wild. His body, once muscular, was now gaunt. He looked as if he had not slept.

"You have ruined me, Anand."

"You have ruined yourself."

"Mrs. Lancaster invested in the expedition to win her prize. She expects a return on her investment. I must have that statue back."

"She cannot possibly think she can display it."

"Not publicly."

"Then what is the point?"

"You think you are worldly, but you have much to learn about people."

"That statue belongs in India," Anand said.

Samuel pulled two whiskys toward them that Faye had set down on the bar.

"It is only a piece of carved rock and a pearl, Anand. You and I know it holds no mystical significance."

"It is meaningful to people, which makes it significant. It brought together men across caste and geography. We are fighting for independence from the British and from unjust maharajas. As you well know from what I have confided in you, the Heart of India pearl is a symbol of freedom, purity, and identity. And the elephant is its protector. Though it is not mystical, it has more meaning than you realize."

Samuel shook his head. "You will not reconsider?"

"And let a selfish woman with money she never earned herself keep a toy she does not understand?"

"If that is your decision," Samuel said, "let us forget about our current troubles, at least for one last night."

"I will drink with you one last time."

"To old times," Samuel said. They raised their glasses and drank.

"I wish it did not have to end like this," Anand said.

"So do I," Samuel said. His eyes filled with tears. "I have poisoned your drink."

CHAPTER 50

I woke up with a stomach ache. It probably wasn't the best idea to eat the last tacos at a taco truck right before it shut down for the night.

I had slept at a hotel, hoping the police weren't desperate enough to find me to pull my credit card transaction records.

Taking a look at myself in the bad light of the hotel bathroom mirror, I hardly recognized myself. Why had I let Sanjay convince me to run from the police? He was the one who'd had the oh-so-brilliant idea that Tamarind was a killer who had mugged and drugged me, when in reality all Tamarind had done was be a good research librarian and friend, and all that had happened after coffee with her was that my travel exhaustion had kicked in. Though Sanjay was unquestionably a skilled illusionist and performer, his deductive skills left much to be desired.

What was I doing? Did I really think I could solve the mystery and clear my name before they found me?

As soon as the university library opened, I slipped into a study carrel. Tamarind hadn't yet arrived for her shift at the research help desk. At ten a.m. I peeked into the main section and saw Tamarind. She spotted me as I walked up to her.

"This time," she said, her purple-eye-shadowed eyes growing wide, "I'm *getting* someone to cover for me."

She whisked me away to a back room in the library away from prying eyes, the metal hoops on her black cargo pants clanging into each other as we walked hastily through the library.

"I need you to help me look some things up," I said as she plopped me down on a backroom couch.

"Pigs still after you?" Tamarind asked.

"Probably."

"You're on the lam?"

"Hopefully not for long," I said. "I'm trying to figure out who's after the treasure and is framing me."

"Nobody is framing you," a deep voice said from behind us.

I turned and saw Inspector Valdez. They say palms sweat when you're nervous. At that moment, *all* of me started to sweat.

"You continue to be a difficult woman to find."

"Were you looking for me?" I asked. My voice may have come out in a squeak.

The inspector held up a familiar bag in his hand. "I thought you might want this."

I was still sweating, but now a little less. *That's* why he'd been looking for me? I could have killed Sanjay and Nadia. It was their overactive imaginations that had convinced me Inspector Valdez wanted to arrest me.

"You found Jaya's bag!" Tamarind said.

"And," Valdez said, "we arrested the person who stole it."

"Shut. Up." Tamarind stared at the inspector.

He gave her a funny look.

"This is Tamarind," I told him. "She's a librarian here. An enthusiastic librarian."

He gave her a brief nod before turning back to me and handing me my messenger bag. I took it and found my laptop inside.

I was beyond happy to have my laptop back. There weren't many things I could be happy about right then, so I'd take what I could find. Naveen Krishnan wouldn't be the only one with an impressive academic publication coming out soon.

"Who stole it?" I asked.

"Connor Healy."

"Steven's *son?*"

"He hasn't confessed yet, but we've arrested him."

"For his father's murder as well?"

"I was trying to find you last night to tell you," he said. "But we kept missing you. You should really get a new phone."

"Guess you don't have to solve the crime to keep the police from arresting you," Tamarind said once the inspector had left.

"It's strange that it's Connor," I said. "It makes sense, but it feels... odd somehow."

"Probably nerves," Tamarind said. "You've been on the run."

"Inspector Valdez told me Connor had an alibi."

"He probably got someone else's opinion," Tamarind said. "Aren't eyewitness accounts unreliable?"

That was it. I knew what I was missing. I knew what we were *all* missing.

Naveen had done *both* of the translations. That meant I hadn't gotten an objective second opinion about the translations.

Since the writing on the map was in Tamil script, I couldn't easily use an online translator. However, there was a different angle I hadn't thought to pursue. I could look for alternative meanings of the already-translated English words. I opened my laptop and searched for several meanings of *The Anchored Enchantress* before I found what I was after.

The literal translation of the Tamil could have been the Anchor of Mohini, a female incarnation of the Hindu god Vishnu—often thought of as a femme fatale. An enchantress. *A Siren.*

The great Naveen Krishnan had gotten the translation wrong.

The Anchored Enchantress was supposed to be *The Siren's Anchor.*

I had seen that name before, when looking at a map of San Francisco from a century ago. *The Siren's Anchor* was a saloon from the days of the Barbary Coast.

CHAPTER 51

"I can't believe you didn't tell me you had a copy of the map!" Tamarind said.

"Steven's daughter-in-law Christine found a copy in his possessions. She thought I'd want it so she gave it to me."

"Shut. Up. And you just cracked it."

I spread out the map. "The X is where the treasure should be found, so what's the significance of this saloon in the Barbary Coast?"

"Don't you know your San Francisco history?" Tamarind asked. "Much of the coastline was filled in with landfill."

"I do know something about San Francisco history, you know," I said. "But why would that matter to Anand's map? The land was *already* filled in when he got here."

"It matters because of the name of the saloon you mentioned," Tamarind said. "Most of the Financial District is built on top of land that's mixed up with sunken ships that sailed into the bay during the Gold Rush and never left. But there are a few buildings still made out of the tops of some of those ships. There's at least one of those old ship saloons that survived the earthquake and that still exists."

"Really?"

"*The Old Ship Saloon* is the favorite pub of one of my ex-boyfriends." Tamarind paused and rolled her eyes. "He thinks he's so edgy, but really you're more likely to find a banker hanging out there than a beat poet. I'd bet you a round of drinks that *The Siren's Anchor* was a ship before it was a saloon."

"A ship…"

"Yeah, that's what I said. Are you all right, Jaya?"

I smoothed out the wrinkled copy of the map. "The X," I said, feeling my body begin to buzz with excitement. "The X is at the edge of the water. What if it didn't mean something was buried on land? What if it meant something actually in the water? *What if it meant the location of a ship?*"

"Are you sure you can tell where the X is meant to point to?" Tamarind asked, picking up the map and squinting at it. "This is a pretty faded photocopy."

I snatched the wrinkled paper back from her. The map was still quite visible through my folds and the photocopied coffee stain. The stain…

"Oh no…" I said. My throat tightened. How had I not made the connection before?

"I knew it," Tamarind said. "You folded it beyond recognition. You should really be more careful—"

"Not that. *The coffee stain.* This stain was from when Sanjay put his coffee mug down on the original map at my apartment."

"It's still legible," Tamarind said. "I was just giving you a hard time."

"That's not it," I said. "The stain *wasn't there* when Steven showed it to me. That means he couldn't have made a copy of the map with the stain on it. This *isn't* one of his original copies, like Christine said it was. She lied to me. She's been lying to me this whole time. It wasn't Connor. It's his wife *Christine.*"

CHAPTER 52

San Francisco, April 10, 1906

"You poisoned me?" Anand staggered back from the bar, knocking over his bar stool.

"I have the antidote," Samuel said. "But you must tell me where you have hidden the Heart of India. The poison takes several hours to kill. You can take me to the treasure and save yourself."

Anand laughed. "You do not know me as well as I thought. You have killed me, my brother." He stood up to leave the saloon.

Samuel grabbed Anand by his shirt collar.

"Don't you dare walk away from me to be a damn martyr," Samuel said.

Anand stared Samuel down for several seconds.

"I wasted six months of my life to get Mrs. Lancaster her treasure," Samuel said. "I was ill for months with malaria and dysentery. You're not taking this away from me! I earned it."

"What's going on?" Faye called out from behind the bar. "You know the rules. If you're going to be rough, take it outside."

In the time Samuel took to glance at Faye, Anand had his chance. He pulled out of Samuel's grasp and swung at his old friend. The punch hit Samuel firmly in the jaw.

"Anand!" Faye yelled over the rising din of the saloon's customers.

Samuel swung back. Anand ducked, and Samuel's punch landed on the ship's wheel mounted on the wall. He cried out in pain and gripped his broken hand. Anand ran at Samuel. The Irishman dropped his hand and spun Anand around as the two men collided. With a shove, he sent Anand toward the wall -- and right into the fishing spear.

The men of the saloon who'd been cheering fell silent.

The spear poked out through where it had pierced Anand's white shirt. Blood spread across his stomach.

"No!" Samuel cried out as Faye began to shriek.

Samuel stood stock-still in shock. Three men rushed to Anand. They lifted him gingerly off of the mounted spear. Anand stumbled as he winced in pain, but did not fall.

"Run and get a doctor," Faye said to one of the men, an urgency in her voice that Anand had never before heard.

"Do not bother, Faye," Anand said. "This is not a wound a man can recover from."

CHAPTER 53

Tamarind wasn't happy that she had to stay at work while I left to figure out what I was going to do with the two realizations I'd made. Christine had lied about the map, and the Heart of India might be in a ship once docked along the treacherous coast of San Francisco. *What had happened to that ship?*

"I have an idea," Sanjay said. Though he usually hated to be distracted while working on a new illusion, he seemed glad to see me when I showed up.

"You going to share?"

"You're not going to like it." Sanjay twirled his hat in his hands.

"I don't like much of anything right now."

"I know a magician—he's not a *friend*, exactly. I don't like his methods. He is a crap mentalist, so he uses this drug, kind of like a truth serum, to control people on stage."

"Does it work?"

"It does put people into a suggestible state, and they don't remember what happened afterward either. It's an aid to hypnosis."

"You think it'll work?"

"This is me you're talking to, Jaya. But what I don't have figured out is how we'll get Christine in a position where we can get her to meet with us so I can give it to her."

"I can answer that," I said. "She wants the Heart of India—andI have a suspicion where the treasure is now."

* * *

Christine jumped at the chance to meet us at Lands End the following morning. I didn't tell her we'd figured out she was the bad guy. I told her the map had led me to the treasure, and that since she'd given it to me I wanted her to be there.

Sanjay had met with his friend and gotten some of the drug the night before, along with champagne and plastic champagne glasses for our excursion. The plan was for Sanjay to pour champagne for us to toast the discovery. With Sanjay's sleight of hand, he'd get the drug into Christine's drink.

He picked me up that morning. He was dressed strangely, in a trench coat rather than one of his usual stylish jackets. I supposed he was playing the role of detective or P.I. today. His bowler hat looked appropriate with the 1930s coat.

The fog rolled in across the water as we waited for Christine at the plaque with the information about the ships that had sunk in the rocky waters off the coast. When I had first visited Lands End, I'd noticed the commemorative plaque listing of sunken ships— including one ship that had never been identified. If I was right, this would explain *why*.

Christine arrived wearing a thick, white wrap in lieu of a coat. She wore matching white shoes that didn't seem to have accumulated any dust on them in the half-mile walk from the car.

"I was so sorry to hear the police mistakenly thought you had anything to do with my father-in-law's death," she said. "I can't believe I was so wrong about Connor... But it's best to honor his father's legacy by finding his treasure."

"Hear, hear," said Sanjay, popping the cork on the bottle. The sound of fog horns drowned out the sound of the pop. He set the glasses down on a concrete bench at the overlook, pouring the bubbly liquid halfway. I didn't notice him put anything into any of the glasses before he scooted one toward Christine. She swung her wrap over her shoulders against the wind, then picked up the glass.

"I'm so glad the map came in handy," she said, raising her glass and taking a sip. "Where is the treasure?"

"I should back up a little bit first," I said. "I'm not sure how much you know about the treasure map of your father-in-law's."

"Not much," Christine said. "I knew he was behaving strangely, obsessed with something, but I didn't know much about it. Only Connor did."

"Steven came to see me because my Uncle Anand was the one who drew the treasure map that ended up in Steven's grandmother's possessions," I said. "He knew I was a historian and that I might know where the letters Anand wrote to my grandfather were kept. He hadn't been able to decipher the map, so he thought there must have been a clue."

"How interesting," Christine said. "*Was there* a clue?"

"There was. But the biggest clue wasn't in the letters themselves." I glanced at Sanjay. The plan was for me to keep Christine talking until the drug took over.

"The letters did say what to look for on the map," I continued, "but the biggest clue was that the map itself wasn't what it seemed."

"It wasn't?"

"I don't know how closely you studied it," I said, "but it looks like a map of San Francisco."

"Isn't it?"

"Yes and no. The city of Kochi, in India, was a major trading center for centuries. It has a nearly identical orientation to San Francisco. Anand worked there as a boat builder before living in San Francisco. Are you feeling all right?"

"Oh yes, just a bit cold." Christine wrapped her shawl more tightly around her.

"Certain locations drawn on the map were meant to be the Kochi that Anand knew, and certain locations were meant to be San Francisco. Anand's accomplice stole a treasure in India that was crafted at a location marked on the map with the notation "lost," and Anand had hidden the treasure in San Francisco where he marked "found" on the map.

"Buried here at Lands End?" Christine asked.

"Not exactly buried," I said. "*Sunken.*"

I pointed to the plaque commemorating the ships that had sunk off the coast. My research had confirmed that *The Siren's Anchor* was an older ship that had been buried along the eastern coast of San Francisco during the Gold Rush and been turned into a saloon. And as I had seen on my earlier walk at Lands End, there was an unidentified ship of unknown origins that sank the day of the Great Earthquake.

"The treasure was never found," I said, "because it sank along with the ship it was hidden within on April 18, 1906."

"The Heart of India is right here?" Christine ran to the edge of the lookout.

"You know what the treasure is?"

"What?" Christine turned. "Oh, you said... No, Connor's father must have said."

"Lands End." Sanjay giggled, pointing at Christine. "The end of the land. Bye, bye land." He swayed back and forth, putting his face in his hands.

*Oh no...*This wasn't happening.

Sanjay had drunk from the wrong glass. He was the one who was drugged. Not Christine.

"Sanjay," I said sharply, taking his trench coat by the lapels and shaking him. "You're in control."

Sanjay opened his fingers and peeked through his hands.

"I'm in control?" he said.

"Yes. You—"

Sanjay dropped his hands and wrapped them around me. He lifted me off the ground and brought his mouth down on mine. His arms were strong from the strength training he did for his more complex illusions. He held me in place without effort. I was so surprised that I didn't resist. His lips caressed mine in a rhythmic motion that was much more skilled than his sitar playing.

And damn if Tamarind wasn't right—my thighs did feel like they were on fire.

CHAPTER 54

San Francisco, April 10, 1906

Mai kissed Anand and held him tight. They were in Anand's boarding house room. He'd sent a local boy to find her.

"You must let me fetch a doctor," she begged. She had already wrapped his wound, but she was not a nurse. She didn't know what else she could do.

"It is no use," Anand said. "I have already lived ten more years than I should have. I lived long enough to meet you."

"But--"

"That is enough." He wiped away a tear from Mai's cheek.

"I'm with child," Mai said, pausing for a moment to give herself the strength to carry on. "Your child, Anand."

Anand's sharp intake of breath pained him physically, but the psychological blow was greater.

Anand looked at his beautiful Mai. Brave, happy Mai, who now looked so sad.

"That changes things," he said.

"You'll let me get a doctor?"

Anand shook his head sadly. "There is no use. But now, I know I cannot risk Li going to jail for me. I was going to ask him to retrieve the Heart of India from where it is hidden, to return it." He broke off in pain, taking a moment to compose himself. "Li's involvement in stealing the ship already puts him in danger of being arrested. He cannot take the added risk. He must be here to help you raise the child."

"Is there nothing that can be done?" She squeezed Anand's so hard that the pain made him smile. He knew it was no act she was putting on. She loved him as much as he loved her.

"There is something else you can do for me."

"Anything, Anand."

"Fetch me a pen."

"After that, I will also fetch a doctor--"

"I know what it feels like to die," Anand said. "It is what gave me so much life these past years. It is also why I know with certainty that death has hold of me."

Mai held Anand close, not caring that blood soaked her dress.

"Please hurry," Anand said. He coughed, and blood trickled from his mouth.

Mai fetched a pen, and Anand began to draw a map on a page of the diary he kept with him. She watched, rushing to his side to bring water to his lips when he faltered. Anand's hand shook as he wrote a few words in Tamil on the sketch. He usually wrote to his brother in English, but he needed to make sure this map would not be understood by anyone before it reached India.

Before his strength left him, he wrote a short letter for Vishwan, explaining the map. He then wrote a page in his diary, completing the story of his life that he had been keeping during his travels.

Anand tore out two pages from the diary and handed them to Mai.

"You must mail this map and letter to my brother, Vishwan," Anand said. "Mail them separately. Li need not be involved. Vishwan will take care of the Heart of India."

Mai took the letters, then kissed Anand. She tasted blood, but she did not care. Anand rested his head on her shoulder and willed himself one last burst of strength. There was one last thing for him to do.

CHAPTER 55

Sanjay held me so tightly that I could barely breathe. I had a vague recollection that Christine had swept her large wrap around her right before picking up a glass, masking our vision to see which glass she picked up. That was how Sanjay must have mistakenly gotten the glass with the drug in the champagne. But at that moment, with Sanjay's lips on mine, I didn't seem to care.

I had to focus. Really. Truly. I was going to focus. Any second now. A gust of cold wind swept around us. I pulled away. Our lips broke apart, but Sanjay still held me off the ground.

"I'm in charge now," I said, catching my breath. "Put me down, Sanjay."

He dumped me unceremoniously onto the ground. I fell to my knees. Not my most graceful moment. I stood up and brushed the dirt off the knees of my jeans. When I looked up, I couldn't believe what I was seeing.

Sanjay pulled a gun from the pocket of his trench coat. *Where the hell had he gotten a gun?*

Christine screamed. I might have done so, as well.

"Why did you do it?" Sanjay asked, waving the gun at Christine.

"Sanjay," I said, trying to keep my voice level. "You don't want to do this. This isn't you. You're drugged. You drank from the wrong glass."

Sanjay ignored me, his attention fixed on Christine.

"It was all Steven's idea," Christine said, staring at the gun. "He's the one who came to me."

"Why would he come to you?" Sanjay asked, the gun flailing precariously in his hand.

It was a good question. Maybe Sanjay was more lucid than he appeared. I hoped he was, considering how much the gun swung in his hand.

"Last year," she said, answering him quickly, transfixed on the gun. "When he was moving into a bigger house, before he got disbarred. He found a box from his grandmother, Maybelle. He found this map, and a letter from his grandmother explaining how this treasure, the Heart of India, was stolen and hidden. Your great-granduncle had fathered a child with Maybelle—"

"Wait—what?"

"Her maiden name was Mai Fong," Christine said. "She explained everything in the letter she left for Steven. Your great-great uncle died before the child was born, and she later married Steven's grandfather. He was a spiritualist, which is how he knew my family."

"Spiritualist Samuel," I said.

Christine nodded. "Real name Samuel Healy."

"He knew your family?"

"The treasure was meant for the Lancaster family," Christine said. "*My* family."

"You're a Lancaster?" I said.

I hadn't looked into any family connections because I thought Steven Healy had lied to me about this being a family treasure. But he *hadn't* lied. He hadn't told me everything, but in a way, it was truly a family treasure. And not just a family treasure for Steven Healy, but for me too, in more ways than I ever imagined. If Christine was telling the truth, that meant I was related to Steven and his son Connor.

"That's why Steven thought I might know something more about where the treasure was hidden," Christine said, pulling her eyes away from Sanjay's gun and looking at me. "He was desperate to restore his reputation after he was disbarred. He wanted to find the treasure to redeem himself."

"Your marriage to Connor was about the treasure?" I asked.

Sanjay looked from Christine to me. His eyes were glazed, but he looked like he was following the conversation. He wouldn't shoot anyone, would he? Even when under the influence of a persuasive drug, someone wouldn't do anything that wasn't in them, would they?

"Steven introduced me to his son," Christine said. "Connor was working at his father's law firm at the time. Connor and I fell in love. Or at least, I thought we did... He and I are very different people. He didn't care about the treasure, even from the start. It was left to me and Steven."

"You had Naveen translate the map."

"Steven read about him," Christine said. "We knew he was the best person to ask."

"But Naveen didn't do a good translation. He did a *literal* translation, but that wasn't right."

Christine nodded. "It didn't get us any closer to finding the Heart of India. But then Steven read about you this summer, and made the connection. He thought you'd provide the missing piece to help us find the treasure."

"Why did you want an old treasure, anyway?" Sanjay asked.

Christine laughed a bitter laugh. "Steven wanted accolades, but I wanted something more practical. Money."

"A reward?" I asked.

Christine looked at me with cold eyes. "I told him he could return the symbolic statue and we could keep the pearl."

"But you have money," I said.

She laughed again, stopping herself as Sanjay waved the gun. "We *used to* have money. My great-grandmother wasted a good bit of the family fortune financing this stupid expedition, then the Great Earthquake's aftermath ate up most of the rest. My father tried to turn things around, but we've been living on credit for years. And after Steven's law firm went under, Connor decided he didn't care about money. Said he wanted to follow his childhood dream and be an artist." She laughed spitefully. "An *artist*! Is there any profession that makes *less* money? But Connor didn't care about that."

"It was you who killed your father-in-law," I said, "not Connor."

Christine gasped. "What are you talking about? I didn't kill anyone. Neither did Connor. We were together that night."

"But—"

"Wasn't it *you*?" she asked me, her eyes narrowing. "Isn't that why you tried to drug me? I was suspicious when you asked me here, but I couldn't resist the temptation of finding the treasure after all this time... I thought you might try something, so I took a different glass than the one you offered me."

"You really thought I killed your father-in-law?" I asked.

"I brought mace in my purse, but I didn't expect that." She looked from me to Sanjay's gun and gave a nervous laugh. "Silly me, bringing mace to a gun fight."

"I met Steven for the first time that night," I said, more confused than ever. "Why would I kill him? You and Connor were the ones after the treasure with him. He didn't even tell me this was about the Heart of India."

"Yes, I was trying to find the treasure," Christine said. "I went back to Naveen for more help, but he was useless. He had the technical skills to help us translate the map, and to work with anything handed to him, but he couldn't come up with any ideas on his own. That's why he followed your leads."

I would have felt a lot more self-satisfied that I'd been right about Naveen's shortcomings if I wasn't being told about them under these circumstances, standing at blustery Lands End with Sanjay out of his mind and waving a gun.

"That's why I wanted your help," Christine continued. "Why do you think I was so shocked when I first met you and you told me about the map being stolen? I came to see you because I wanted to feel you out." She took a deep breath.

"Connor was devastated by his father's death, and I was telling you the truth that he believed you might have had something to do with it. I thought so myself. Who else could it have been? Though Connor didn't care about the treasure, he didn't want you to have it because he thought you killed his father. That's why he stole the map from you. Naveen doesn't have it in him to kill anyone."

Christine looked me in the eye.

"But you're tougher than him. Tougher than both of them. I could tell when I met you. When I learned from Naveen that you were on to something, I wanted you to have the map back. Regardless of what you'd done, I wanted you to lead me to the treasure. It belongs to my family. They were the ones who financed the expedition to procure the Heart of India. I deserve it."

"So *neither of you* killed your father-in-law?" I said.

"No," Christine said. "But you don't have to take my word for it. Our alibis are airtight." She glanced nervously at Sanjay, who was beginning to sway back and forth.

"I don't feel well," Sanjay said. "Take this," he said, and thrust the gun into my hand.

The gun felt light in my hand. Too light.

It was a plastic prop from the theater.

Sanjay left the plastic gun in my hands and proceeded to faint.

CHAPTER 56

San Francisco, April 10, 1906

When Li returned to his rooms from his night working in Chinatown, he found Mai waiting for him, crying. But Li did not notice her tears at first. Though Mai had washed her hands, blood covered her neck and the front of her dress. Li rushed to her, sure she had been assaulted.

"I'm not hurt," she said between sobs. "It's Anand." Mai told Li what had happened.

"I'm going to kill Samuel," Li said. "And I don't care if I'm arrested. I'll see through returning the Heart of India."

"You can't," Mai said. And she told him why.

"A child?" Li said after she'd told her story. "Anand's child? Why didn't you tell me?"

"I'm telling you now. Please do not do anything else to risk yourself, brother. I need you. The child needs you."

Anand did not wish for Mai to see him die. After he kissed her goodbye one last time, he took his bound diary with him. He was headed to the ship he had disguised with the name of the saloon ship that had been the center of his life in San Francisco: The Siren's Anchor.

He was weak with blood loss, but he no longer felt any pain. He walked with purpose. With his last breaths he was setting the stage for the return of a meaningful treasure. Though he would not live to see a unified India free of British rule that the Heart of India's creators hoped for, he felt blessed with the meaningful life he'd been given.

The ship was in rocky waters, but it would hold until Vishwan came. He had hoped it would not have come to this, but he knew what he needed to do. He wrapped his diary tightly in a leather satchel and left it inside a trunk in the hull of the ship with the Heart of India.

As he climbed to the bow, he felt his body grow numb as it shut down. Anand smiled. He did not fear death. He had been given ten years longer than his due. He had cheated death once, and it had allowed him to travel the world and to find Mai. Though he would never see his brother Vishwan again and would miss meeting his child, it had been more than he had dreamed possible when he lay dying of typhoid ten years before.

He took one last look at the world before jumping into the freezing waters below.

CHAPTER 57

"You don't remember *anything*?" I asked Sanjay.

"Nothing. Did I really faint?"

"For the second time this week."

Sanjay groaned. He lay back on the modern black couch in the main room of his apartment and covered his face with his bowler hat.

"But it was after you heroically captured one of the bad guys at gun point," I said. "Even if it was plastic gun point."

"I didn't do anything too stupid, did I?"

"That's not the word I would use." I felt my cheeks flush as I remembered Sanjay's kiss. It was so intense that it surprised me he'd forgotten it, regardless of the drug. It must have been, because he thought nothing of it. It was nothing of consequence to him, only something he'd done because he was drugged. Otherwise he would never have dreamed of kissing me.

I, on the other hand, found myself wondering what it would feel like if he kissed me again... I pulled my thoughts back to the present. It was the day after our adventure at Lands End, and Sanjay had slept off the remaining effects of his accidental drugging.

I went over what we'd learned from Christine, spelling it out for Sanjay since he said he didn't remember anything. How Christine had confessed to plotting to find the Heart of India and steal the valuable pearl before returning the statue, and how she told us that Connor had stolen the treasure map because he didn't want the person who killed his father to get the treasure.

But neither one of them was Steven's killer. *So who was?*

Christine was right that I didn't have to take her word for it. Before coming over to Sanjay's loft I'd gone to see Inspector Valdez, who had triple-checked Christine and Connor's alibi, confirming that they were at an art show the whole night Steven was killed. They were telling the truth that neither of them had killed Steven.

"It wasn't Tamarind, either," Sanjay said, shaking his head.

"I don't think I've ever heard you admit to being wrong before," I said.

"I wasn't completely wrong about her, you know. She *was* keeping something from you."

I picked up a fluffy rabbit stuffed animal sitting on the end table and threw it at Sanjay. It knocked off his bowler hat.

"Hey! What was that for?" Sanjay bent down to pick up the rabbit and the hat. A few rose petals fluttered out of the hat as it hit the floor.

It was definitely easier to stop having ridiculous romantic feelings about Sanjay now that he was acting like an eight-year-old again.

"I tend to agree with Christine that Naveen doesn't have it in him to kill anyone," I said. "Plus we know he couldn't have been the person who left the booby trap at your door to scare you off. Who does that leave?"

"I'm sure that detective is on it," Sanjay said.

"Instead of following up on finding the Heart of India," I grumbled. "Even after I gave him all the information!"

"If you're right about where it is," Sanjay said, "it's been safe for over a hundred years. Another couple of days won't hurt."

"It'll only hurt my sanity."

"Ever wonder if you've got the wrong temperament for a historian?"

"Do you want to go get some food? I'm starving."

"You're always starving, Jaya."

"Are you coming out to eat with me or not?"

"I can't. Grace is coming over with takeout. When I told her what had happened, she was worried and didn't want me to have to drive anywhere."

"That's nice of her."

"I feel bad," Sanjay said. "She still seems really shaken up about that death in her family."

The buzzer alerted us that Grace had arrived at the front door of the building. A minute later, she came into the loft with a large enough bag of Thai takeout to feed at least half a dozen people.

"Hi, Jaya," she said, smiling shyly at both of us. "I thought you might be here, so I got some extra food. This restaurant makes curry almost as good as my mom's."

"You are a doll, Grace," Sanjay said. "I don't know what I'd do without you."

Grace blushed and took the food to the island in the kitchen.

"Sanjay told me you found the treasure," she said to me. She unpacked the large paper bag, not looking at me as she spoke. The scent of Thai curry and peanut sauce wafted out.

"They haven't unearthed the sunken ship yet," I said. "So I can't be sure that I'm right."

"I should have known if anyone could do it," Grace said, "it would be you."

Sanjay took plates and small clay bowls out of a kitchen cabinet. "Jaya was telling me how the police still don't know who killed the guy who brought Jaya the map."

One of the take-out containers slipped out of Grace's hands. A splash of coconut milk soup spilled onto the marble counter.

"Don't worry about it," Sanjay said, wiping it up with a kitchen rag that appeared out of thin air.

"Why do you care about that?" Grace asked. "Isn't it dangerous? Didn't the threat against your life convince you not to worry about that?"

Sanjay stopped mopping up the counter. "I thought I didn't tell you about that," he said.

"Sure you did," Grace whispered.

"I didn't want you to worry," Sanjay said, "so I thought I was careful not to tell you."

I stared at Grace. Sanjay had been convinced Tamarind was the culprit because she was the only one who could have known about the treasure that night and wanted to act on it then. But *Grace* had been at the restaurant the evening I met Steven Healy. I replayed the night in my mind, feeling my pulse quicken as the pieces fell into place. We'd seen Grace not long after I texted Tamarind. As usual, she had been so quiet that we had no idea how long she'd been standing there...

Sanjay shrugged. "Guess I was wrong." He tossed the kitchen rag aside and began to fill the bowls with soup. "I'm not at my best today."

I thought through the timing. Grace had showed up to talk to Sanjay in the early part of the evening, and Steven's body wasn't discovered until hours later.

Grace saw me staring at her. Her expression changed in reaction to mine. Her eyes were pleading.

"Why did you do it?" I asked.

"You don't know what it's like," she whispered. "Being invisible."

Sanjay stopped dishing up food. "What are you two talking about?"

"I think Grace has something to tell us," I said.

Sanjay looked back and forth between us. "About what? Did you need more time off, Grace?"

"I knew you were as smart as I thought, Jaya," Grace said. "I should have known—" She broke off and ran away from us.

She didn't go for the door, but instead ran to the section of Sanjay's loft that served as his practice magic studio. The large sliding door that separated it from the rest of the loft was already open. She fiddled with a switch on the wall, and a light that mimicked a spotlight shone from the high ceiling onto the loft's stage. She stepped into the spotlight.

When she turned to face us, shy Grace was gone. She held herself with the confidence she used on stage.

"I didn't mean to do it," she said, her strong voice projecting through the loft. "You have to understand that. I only wanted to be more like Jaya."

"You overheard me talking to Sanjay that night at the restaurant," I said. "When I was telling him about the treasure map Steven Healy had given me."

"You two didn't see me," she said. "I was invisible. I tried to interrupt, but you two were so caught up in your conversation that it took you forever to notice me."

"What does this have to do with anything?" Sanjay asked.

"As smart as you are, Sanjay," Grace said, "you haven't got a clue sometimes."

Sanjay frowned and walked closer to Grace. I followed.

"You dismissed me so quickly that night," Grace said to Sanjay. "I thought you needed me. You're always telling me how you can't do your magic shows without me, but you didn't care that I had to miss the show! You said Jaya could replace me."

"I didn't mean it like that," Sanjay said, the look of confusion still on his face. "Jaya can't do most of your acts. We had to modify—"

"You don't get it! I see the way you look at Jaya. I could never compete with her when it comes to how smart she is... But I thought at least she could never take my place as your assistant. You showed me I was wrong. But at the same time, I knew something you two didn't know. You were talking about Steven Healy like you didn't know who he was. *But I did.* I followed the scandal on TV last year. The TV news loves to cover people falling from grace. They camped outside his house."

"That's how you knew where he lived," I said.

Grace nodded. "I knew more about him than you did. I thought if I could talk to him, I'd find out more about the treasure than he'd told you. I could be as smart as you. Even smarter. Then Sanjay would notice me. He wouldn't think I was stupid."

"Grace?" Sanjay said, staring wide-eyed. "I've never thought you were stupid—"

"I was that night," she said. "I pretended I was on stage. I told myself I was playing a role. I thought he would listen to me... But instead, he got angry. So angry! I knew from the scandal last year that he had a temper, but I thought that was only because it was so important for him to give a bad man what he deserved. I didn't think he would do anything to me—but he grabbed me so hard." She rolled up her sleeve. A large bruise was visible on her toned upper arm.

"It was self-defense?" I said.

"You mean—" Sanjay began, finally catching on. "You mean *Grace* killed Steven Healy?"

"I didn't mean to! He was so angry, I got scared. When he grabbed me, I picked up something heavy from his desk, just to get him to stop... Only after I hit him, he didn't move. I was so scared."

"That's why you wanted to get us to stop looking for Steven's killer," I said. "You sent Sanjay a harmless booby trap to scare him off."

Grace nodded. "I couldn't read the instructions on the rat poison. I must have used too much."

"Grace?" Sanjay said.

"I never meant to hurt you, Sanjay," she said. "I never meant to hurt either of you."

Sanjay swore. "It was self-defense. The police will see that. This was all a big mistake."

"Will they believe me?" Grace asked.

Sanjay and I looked at each other, unsure of what to say.

"I taped it," Grace added.

"You *what*?" Sanjay and I said at the same time.

"With my phone," Grace said. "You know I can't write very well. I wanted to be sure to remember what he told me, so I turned on the tape recorder on my phone before I knocked on his door. You can hear him grab me, and me scream before I found something to hit him. Do you think that will help?"

CHAPTER 58

San Francisco, 1906 and beyond

The earthquake on the eighteenth of April wasn't the worst part of the disaster.

It was the fire that followed.

Flames ripped through large swaths of the city, especially destructive to buildings that were too close together -- which included most of Chinatown.

The water supply failed, leaving nothing to stop the flames.

Mai had been living with her parents in a section of Chinatown that had enough warning for them to escape. Li, however, lived in an unsafe building on the edge of the neighborhood.

Two days after the earthquake, Mai was camping at Golden Gate Park when she heard the news. Her brother Li was dead.

She had escaped with one bag, which included Anand's map and letter. She and Li had been arguing about whether Li should risk jail by returning the stolen treasure he and Anand had stolen back. Mai needed him, but Li felt honor-bound. They were at a stalemate. Neither had taken any action that week since Anand's death.

And now the earthquake. Mai had lost both Anand and her brother. What could she do?

Mai would have mailed the letters and map then, if not for the chaos of the city following the earthquake and fire. So she waited for the postal service to return to normal. Days seemed surreal.

She didn't know how he did it, but Samuel found her. He cried in her arms like a babe as he spoke of his regrets. He wished he could take back his actions. Mai knew he was a good man, deep down. That's why, when he told her he would take care of her and her child, she gave him a chance to prove himself. She didn't have any options. Anand was dead. Her brother was dead. Her parents wouldn't support her having Anand's child. What else could she do?

Samuel took a job at the shipyard where Anand had worked. He gave up his fantasies about striking it rich, instead working hard each day to support Mai and her child. He did not ask anything of her in return. He came to love the child as his own. That was when Mai forgave him.

Mai put the treasure behind her. It had caused too much heartbreak already. Samuel was a good man, but she did not want to tempt him with the treasure and upset the balance in their lives. She never told him that Anand had left her with a map she was supposed to send to Anand's brother. Instead, she wrote to Anand's brother Vishwan, telling him that his brother died a heroic death in the earthquake. It was true enough. Her beloved Anand had died heroically. There was no need to upset Vishwan. People were more important than treasures. She wouldn't ruin her and her son's life by involving them in returning the Heart of India. Instead, she would leave the map and letter to her grown descendants when she died.

As her son grew up, Mai saw so much of Anand in him. His sense of adventure, his curiosity, his loyalty. As Anand had often told Mai, life does not follow the course we expect. But looking at their beautiful son, she knew he was right that it was enough.

CHAPTER 59

Grace turned herself in to the police. Inspector Valdez listened to the tape and told her it sounded like she had a good case for self-defense. It wasn't up to him, he said. The DA would decide what to do. He asked her why she didn't turn herself in in the first place. Her only encounter with the police had been before she came to the United States as a child. Back in Thailand, two of her relatives had been railroaded into false convictions by the police. It was one of the main reasons her family wanted to come to the U.S.

Connor was out on bail. He was charged with assaulting me and stealing my bag. He truly believed I'd killed his father, so when he didn't think the police were taking his concerns seriously, he took matters into his own hands. It was true he didn't care about the treasure his wife and father cared about. But he didn't want the person he believed killed his father to have it either. He knew from his father that we were distantly related. That was what he had tried to tell me the night of the magic show before Christine stopped him.

Divers found the unnamed sunken ship off the coast of Lands End. Hidden inside the cargo was the Heart of India. Aside from being a little worse for wear due to barnacles, the elephant statue and massive pearl were intact. Even with evidence of its sojourn in the ocean, it was an impressive sight when it was hauled up. The statue representing a free and unified India that Anand had given his life to protect was more powerful than I'd imagined it could be.

It made me smile that the stone-carver had the skill to give the elephant a personality—the creature was fierce, as was common in Indian art, but at the same time had the hint of a smile.

Along with the Heart of India, the divers found a diary that had been securely wrapped. The leather-bound journal was water-damaged but intact. It was Anand's diary. Between the letter that Steven Healy's grandmother had left him and Anand's diary, we had the rest of the missing pieces of Anand's story.

As Christine had said, Anand's friend Spritualist Samuel was Samuel Healy. Samuel had betrayed him, looking for fast wealth through stealing the Heart of India for an eccentric patron, Mrs. Lancaster of the prominent San Francisco Lancaster family. Anand and Samuel were friends with a third man, Li Fong, the brother of Mai Fong. Samuel called Mai by the nickname Maybelle, and it stuck.

Mai was pregnant with Anand's child when Anand died in what Mai described as a tragic accident. She wrote that Samuel had made the mistake of letting greed overtake him. He stole the Heart of India, and Anand went to great lengths to steal it back, to return it where it rightly belonged. Samuel and Anand fought, and Anand received a mortal wound. The Great Earthquake struck the week following Anand's death, killing Mai's brother Li. Mai was all alone, and Samuel wanted to make amends. It was many years before Mai would forgive Samuel, and they bore no children together, but she did accept his offer to take care of her and her son.

Samuel was a good husband, raising Anand's son as his own, but Mai did not trust him when it came to the treasure. She never showed him the treasure map Anand had drawn and asked her to mail to his brother. She put that part of her life behind her, never sending it to Vishwan. She did write to Vishwan so that he would know his brother was dead, but she did not want him to grieve more than was necessary. She wrote an account that was as close to the truth as she dared come: that Anand had died trying to save his best friend, her brother Li, in the earthquake, when the truth was that he had died to save something greater than both of them.

Though she did not send the map, she could not bring herself to destroy it. She left it for her grandson in her will—a grandson and great-grandson who I now knew I was related to.

Connor showed up at the expedition to unearth the treasure. He wasn't after the treasure, but he was there because he wanted to apologize for the grief he'd caused me.

He'd sobered up and seemed like a decent guy who'd made a bad choice in who he married. He told me what I expected, that he'd realized Christine only wanted him for his wealth. He'd made a lot of money when he worked for his father's firm, and until they lost it, he hadn't realized he didn't care about money. He wanted to live a fulfilling life. Part of that, he said, was making amends with me. He hoped that once he'd had a little bit more time to come to terms with his father's death and finalize a divorce from Christine, he and I could meet over coffee to get to know each other. After all, we were distant cousins. I told him I'd like that.

After I'd seen the contents of the ship safely removed and saw Anand's diary, I sent off my completed paper for publication. I was in my office when a familiar face poked his head in my door.

"I thought you were off treasure hunting," Naveen said.

"You mean the Heart of India?" I said. "The divers already located it where I thought it would be, if you hadn't heard."

"I've been too busy working on my book to keep up with trivial things," Naveen said. "You might not know how that is."

"Actually," I said. "I've just sent off an article."

Naveen frowned as I showed him my computer screen with the name of the journal.

"Knock knock," said a voice from behind Naveen, and the dean stepped in. "Jaya! I was hoping I'd find you here. Bang-up job with the Heart of India. I'm told that no other historians suspected it wasn't swept out to sea and that it was waiting to be rescued right here in San Francisco. Keep up the good work."

Naveen's mouth hung open as he watched the dean leave.

"Sorry I don't have time to stay and chat, Naveen. There's somewhere I need to be."

CHAPTER 60

Nadia poured me a glass of gin, getting a vodka for herself.

"Why don't you tell me about him," she said.

"Uncle Anand?"

Nadia snorted. "You've already told me about him. No, I mean you should tell me about the man who is confusing you so."

"Is it that obvious?"

"You have a look about you."

"It's complicated." I took a large swig of the gin.

"Life is always complicated, Jaya. If you wait for it to be simple, your whole life will pass you by."

"Why did you leave Russia?" I had never asked Nadia the question before, though I had often wondered. She spoke so little of her life before she came to San Francisco.

"That was another lifetime ago." She paused and twirled her drink in her hand, a mischievous smile forming on her lips. "It is the future we should think of. This man in your life—is it the art historian you met earlier this summer?"

"Maybe."

"How can the answer be *maybe*? If you do not wish to tell me, you can say so."

"But that's not what I mean. I *do* mean maybe. He and I shared something—and still do—but then..." I thought of Sanjay's kiss. "Then things got complicated."

Nadia nodded and topped off my gin.

* * *

Sanjay was waiting for me outside my door when I got upstairs from Nadia's house. He sat on the top step doing card tricks, his bowler hat resting askew on his head.

"I'm surprised you didn't let yourself in," I said.

"You asked me not to."

"Come on in," I said, smiling to myself as I read a piece of mail Nadia had just handed to me.

"There's one thing I'm still not clear on," Sanjay said. "What ever happened to that guy I saw at the hospital in Trivandrum?"

"It's a long story," I said.

"But who *is* he?"

"He left me a note," I said, holding up the slip of paper that had been left with my mail in a sealed envelope bearing only my name.

"A handwritten note? Can't he email or use the phone like a normal person?"

"You want to take me to get a new phone today? My car is still impounded."

"Fair enough," Sanjay said, deftly plucking the note from my hand and reading it aloud.

Jones,

I need to lie low for a while, but I don't expect you'll let me stay away.

I should have seen the truth about your uncle as soon as you told me he called himself Pirate Vishnu. Vishnu restores order, which is exactly what Anand was trying to do. His legacy is safe.

L

"Damn," said Sanjay. "Whoever he is, he's a better Indian than either of us."

Author's Note

Pirate Vishnu is a work of fiction. Though both the treasure and characters came from my imagination, the story is based on a real historical backdrop.

I was inspired to write this book after hearing a family legend about one of the first members of the Indian side of my family to come to the United States. He was said to have died in the Spanish Influenza Pandemic of 1918 in Pennsylvania. Not everyone in the family thought that was what really happened to him. What if they were right?

Several years ago, when I was traveling through the state of Kerala, India, I discovered an interesting—and very true—parallel between San Francisco and Kochi (Cochin), which is the connection Jaya makes in *Pirate Vishnu*. That's where I got my initial idea for this book.

Over the centuries, the trading port of Kochi was home to many artisans who created artifacts and traded in wood and stone-carvings. Historically, India's southwest coast was a cosmopolitan area in general. Various religious and ethnic groups traded in spices, textiles, and other commodities, and there were many Arab and Christian settlements. Young men like Anand Paravar came under the influence of egalitarian and nationalistic ideas in the late 19th and early 20th centuries, but the authorities did not always tolerate the involvement of workers in nationalistic activities. It was not uncommon for young men to seek work on ships or in regions of India under the political control of the French or the British.

In the 1800s, a spiritualism craze swept through Europe and the United States, inspiring spirit cabinet performances and more intimate séances. Sherlock Holmes author Sir Arthur Conan Doyle was one of the people who became a believer and magician Harry Houdini was one of the people who worked to debunk spiritualists.

The Great San Francisco Earthquake of 1906 caused the loss of many city records as well as the deaths of an unknown number of people and the displacement of thousands more. The history of San Francisco's Barbary Coast area recounted in *Pirate Vishnu* is true, including the use of ships abandoned during the Gold Rush, but the saloon Anand frequented is a fictional composite of similar existing establishments.

READER DISCUSSION GUIDE

1. Chapters set in the past are interspersed with the present-day main storyline. How do details of the people and events in the past enhance the story?

2. The idea for *Pirate Vishnu* was based on family lore. Do you have any family history you think would make a good mystery?

3. *Pirate Vishnu* begins shortly after *Artifact* ends. Jaya's relationships are developing with old friends and new. Did you have a favorite character? Why?

4. What surprised you about the history of India and San Francisco?

5. Academia is competitive, especially as scholars begin their careers. Do you think Jaya is handling the pressure better than her colleague Naveen?

6. Jaya's love life takes an unexpected turn she didn't see coming. What do you think will happen in the future with the men in her life?

GIGI PANDIAN

Gigi Pandian is the child of cultural anthropologists from New Mexico and the southern tip of India. After being dragged around the world during her childhood, she tried to escape her fate when she left a PhD program for art school. But adventurous academic characters wouldn't stay out of her head. Thus was born the Jaya Jones Treasure Hunt Mystery Series. The first book in the series, *Artifact*, was awarded a Malice Domestic Grant. Learn more at www.gigipandian.com.

Be sure to check out Jaya's prequel novella
FOOL'S GOLD featured in

OTHER PEOPLE'S BAGGAGE

Kendel Lynn, Gigi Pandian, Diane Vallere

Baggage claim can be terminal. These are the stories of what happened after three women with a knack for solving mysteries each grabbed the wrong bag.

MIDNIGHT ICE by Diane Vallere: When interior decorator Madison Night crosses the country to distance herself from a recent breakup, she learns it's harder to escape her past than she thought, and diamonds are rarely a girl's best friend.

SWITCH BACK by Kendel Lynn: Ballantyne Foundation director Elliott Lisbon travels to Texas after inheriting an entire town, but when she learns the benefactor was murdered, she must unlock the small town's big secrets or she'll never get out alive.

FOOL'S GOLD by Gigi Pandian: When a world-famous chess set is stolen from a locked room during the Edinburgh Fringe Festival, historian Jaya Jones and her magician best friend must outwit actresses and alchemists to solve the baffling crime.

Available at booksellers nationwide and online

Visit www.henerypress.com for details

Henery Press Mystery Books

And finally, before you go...
Here are a few other mysteries
you might enjoy:

LOWCOUNTRY BOIL

Susan M. Boyer

A Liz Talbot Mystery (#1)

Private Investigator Liz Talbot is a modern Southern belle: she blesses hearts and takes names. She carries her Sig 9 in her Kate Spade handbag, and her golden retriever, Rhett, rides shotgun in her hybrid Escape. When her grandmother is murdered, Liz hightails it back to her South Carolina island home to find the killer.

She's fit to be tied when her police-chief brother shuts her out of the investigation, so she opens her own. Then her long-dead best friend pops in and things really get complicated. When more folks start turning up dead in this small seaside town, Liz must use more than just her wits and charm to keep her family safe, chase down clues from the hereafter, and catch a psychopath before he catches her.

Available at booksellers nationwide and online

Visit www.henerypress.com for details

DOUBLE WHAMMY
Gretchen Archer

A Davis Way Crime Caper (#1)

Davis Way thinks she's hit the jackpot when she lands a job as the fifth wheel on an elite security team at the fabulous Bellissimo Resort and Casino in Biloxi, Mississippi. But once there, she runs straight into her ex-ex husband, a rigged slot machine, her evil twin, and a trail of dead bodies. Davis learns the truth and it does not set her free—in fact, it lands her in the pokey.

Buried under a mistaken identity, unable to seek help from her family, her hot streak runs cold until her landlord Bradley Cole steps in. Make that her landlord, lawyer, and love interest. With his help, Davis must win this high stakes game before her luck runs out.

Available at booksellers nationwide and online

Visit www.henerypress.com for details

BOARD STIFF

Kendel Lynn

An Elliott Lisbon Mystery (#1)

As director of the Ballantyne Foundation on Sea Pine Island, SC, Elliott Lisbon scratches her detective itch by performing discreet inquiries for Foundation donors. Usually nothing more serious than retrieving a pilfered Pomeranian. Until Jane Hatting, Ballantyne board chair, is accused of murder. The Ballantyne's reputation tanks, Jane's headed to a jail cell, and Elliott's sexy ex is the new lieutenant in town.

Armed with moxie and her Mini Coop, Elliott uncovers a trail of blackmail schemes, gambling debts, illicit affairs, and investment scams. But the deeper she digs to clear Jane's name, the guiltier Jane looks. The closer she gets to the truth, the more treacherous her investigation becomes. With victims piling up faster than shells at a clambake, Elliott realizes she's next on the killer's list.

Available at booksellers nationwide and online

Visit www.henerypress.com for details

DINERS, DIVES & DEAD ENDS
Terri L. Austin

A Rose Strickland Mystery (#1)

As a struggling waitress and part-time college student, Rose Strickland's life is stalled in the slow lane. But when her close friend, Axton, disappears, Rose suddenly finds herself serving up more than hot coffee and flapjacks. Now she's hashing it out with sexy bad guys and scrambling to find clues in a race to save Axton before his time runs out.

With her anime-loving bestie, her septuagenarian boss, and a pair of IT wise men along for the ride, Rose discovers political corruption, illegal gambling, and shady corporations. She's gone from zero to sixty and quickly learns when you're speeding down the fast lane, it's easy to crash and burn.

Available at booksellers nationwide and online

Visit www.henerypress.com for details

THE AMBITIOUS CARD
John Gaspard

An Eli Marks Mystery (#1)

The life of a magician isn't all kiddie shows and card tricks. Sometimes it's murder. Especially when magician Eli Marks very publicly debunks a famed psychic, and said psychic ends up dead. The evidence, including a bloody King of Diamonds playing card (one from Eli's own Ambitious Card routine), directs the police right to Eli.

As more psychics are slain, and more King cards rise to the top, Eli can't escape suspicion. Things get really complicated when romance blooms with a beautiful psychic, and Eli discovers she's the next target for murder, and he's scheduled to die with her. Now Eli must use every trick he knows to keep them both alive and reveal the true killer.

Available at booksellers nationwide and online

Visit www.henerypress.com for details

PORTRAIT OF A DEAD GUY

Larissa Reinhart

A Cherry Tucker Mystery (#1)

In Halo, Georgia, folks know Cherry Tucker as big in mouth, small in stature, and able to sketch a portrait faster than buck-shot rips from a ten gauge -- but commissions are scarce. So when the well-heeled Branson family wants to memorialize their murdered son in a coffin portrait, Cherry scrambles to win their patronage from her small town rival.

As the clock ticks toward the deadline, Cherry faces more trouble than just a controversial subject. Between ex-boyfriends, her flaky family, an illegal gambling ring, and outwitting a killer on a spree, Cherry finds herself painted into a corner she'll be lucky to survive.

Available at booksellers nationwide and online

Visit www.henerypress.com for details

FRONT PAGE FATALITY

LynDee Walker

A Headlines in High Heels Mystery (#1)

Crime reporter Nichelle Clarke's days can flip from macabre to comical with a beep of her police scanner. Then an ordinary accident story turns extraordinary when evidence goes missing, a prosecutor vanishes, and a sexy Mafia boss shows up with the headline tip of a lifetime.

As Nichelle gets closer to the truth, her story gets more dangerous. Armed with a notebook, a hunch, and her favorite stilettos, Nichelle races to splash these shady dealings across the front page before this deadline becomes her last.

Available at booksellers nationwide and online

Visit www.henerypress.com for details

Quechee Library
PO Box 384
Quechee, VT 05059

Made in the USA
Middletown, DE
06 November 2015